John M. F. Ludlow

Woman's Work in the Church

historical notes on deaconesses and sisterhoods

John M. F. Ludlow

Woman's Work in the Church
historical notes on deaconesses and sisterhoods

ISBN/EAN: 9783337369361

Printed in Europe, USA, Canada, Australia, Japan

Cover: Foto ©Andreas Hilbeck / pixelio.de

More available books at **www.hansebooks.com**

WOMAN'S WORK IN THE CHURCH

Historical Notes on Deaconesses and Sisterhoods

BY

JOHN MALCOLM LUDLOW

ALEXANDER STRAHAN, PUBLISHER
148 STRAND, LONDON
1865

EDINBURGH:
PRINTED BY BALLANTYNE AND COMPANY,
PAUL'S WORK.

EDINBURGH:
PRINTED BY BALLANTYNE AND COMPANY,
PAUL'S WORK.

To

The Reverend

the

Free Church Presbytery of Strathbogie, N.B.,

who

" Overtured"

the General Assembly

of the

Free Church of Scotland

concerning the Romanising tendencies of
Two Articles in Good Words,
extracted from the present Work,

I dedicate

the Work itself

for their better information.

PREFACE.

THE following work, although but a portion of it has appeared in print already, is not a new one. Some explanation is perhaps due of its publication, after various other works bearing more or less on the same subject, and in particular after Dr Howson's " Deaconesses" (London, 1862).

In the year 1847, having been led to the subject through personal acquaintance with the Paris Deaconesses' Institute and personal friendship with its late worthy founder, I wrote for the *Edinburgh Review*, under the title, " Deaconesses or Protestant Sisterhoods," an article which was published in May 1848, and of which Dr Howson (who admits himself to have been unaware of, or to have forgotten it till recently), has said that it " anticipated much which is now accepted by public opinion."*

* See a reprint of this paper in Appendix G, p. 248.

The article attracted some attention amongst clergymen and others. In the latter part of the year 1851, having been pressed by a friend to lecture at a Mechanics' Institute in Berkshire, I mentioned the subject as one which I should be glad to have an occasion of working up more thoroughly, and eventually agreed with him to deliver a course of three lectures upon it. The present work substantially represents the lectures in question, as prepared in the course of 1852.

Shortly, however, before the time fixed for delivering the lectures above mentioned, my friend wrote to me to say that, through the influence of a clergyman, who afterwards became a dignitary of the Church, the subject had been tabooed by the Committee. An attempt to secure a hearing for me in the lecture hall of another Mechanics' Institute was equally defeated by clerical influence.

The subject having, however, somewhat taken hold of my mind, I worked it up still further, and in the course of the year 1853 offered to a publisher the result of my labours in a volume under its present title of " Woman's Work in the Church." It was declined, on the ground that whilst the work would be valuable to those who were already interested in the question, the public at large were not likely to share any such interest.

Perhaps the Crimean War, and the successive publications in reference to the subject which followed it, such as Miss Stanley's " Hospitals and Sisterhoods" (1854); Mrs Jameson's " Sisterhoods of Charity Abroad and at Home," and her " Communion of Labour" (1855 and 1859), shewed that the signs of the times had been misunderstood. Occupied, however, by other matters, I made no fresh attempt to bring the work before the public, simply lending the MS. from time to time to two or three private readers.

Latterly, however, the subject being one which appeared fit to be brought before the readers of *Good Words*, I was led to epitomize my collected matter in two articles, which appeared in that periodical in the months of February and July 1863, under the respective titles of " The Female Diaconate in the Early Church," and " Sisterhoods."

These papers, however, having fallen under the ban of the no doubt very well-meaning and estimable gentlemen to whom I have ventured to dedicate this work, it appeared to me that the best answer to their strictures would be the publication of the text from which the articles in question were extracted.

Hence the present work, which, it will be seen from what precedes, is in the main not less than twelve years old. I can truly say that the lapse of that period has not induced me to alter in it a single conclusion, or scarcely to modify a statement.

I have, indeed, in consequence of the abundant mass of detail now before the public in reference to contemporary efforts in the direction of female diaconal labour, both abroad and at home, especially in Dr Howson's work, suppressed nearly the whole of what I had originally written on that branch of the subject. A preliminary chapter, containing some general considerations on the work of women, has been probably rendered needless by Mrs Jameson's lecture on the " Communion of Labour."* Some concluding hints as to the possible developments of the principle of Sisterhoods have also been omitted, as well as some controversial matter which the greater maturity of the subject

* I may indeed add, that the MS. of this portion has itself disappeared in the hands of a borrower, and that I have not felt disposed to re-write it from some " heads" which alone remain.

seemed to me to have rendered superfluous. Some slight amount of additional matter, the result of further research and information, has on the other side been introduced.

I will now say that I felt much gratified, on looking into Dr Howson's work, to see how nearly his conclusions approached on all points to my own, after we had laboured completely apart from each other. I owe to him the reference to Baronius for a mention of the female diaconate in the tenth century, and have also borrowed from him (with acknowledgment) a few statements in the last chapter. Beyond this, the perusal of his work has suggested neither addition to nor alteration of what I had written long before, so that, wherever we agree, the testimony of each must be considered as a wholly independent one.

I must add, that if, in the present text, I have not referred to modern German writers on the subject, it is not for want of having consulted several of them, but because, with the exception of Neander, I have literally found nothing in them hitherto on the subject but theories rough-riding the facts— sometimes with a glaring perversion of references— or in the absence of such, a mass of learned inconclusiveness. The older work of Caspar Ziegler, on the other hand, quoted by Dr Howson at the head of his *Quarterly Review* article, (*de diaconis et diaconissis veteris ecclesiæ*, 1678), has not fallen into my hands. A dislike to quote or discuss opinions where facts are needed has equally led me to strike out references to the views of the " Critici Sacri," and other more modern commentators.

I cannot help, lastly, referring here to Mr Maurice's article " On Sisterhoods," which appeared in the *Victoria Magazine* for August 1863. Sharply as it criticises the " separate Sisterhoods " which it refers to as now growing up in England, I do not know that it enunciates one single view which clashes with my own. " I do not dispute," says Mr Maurice, " the benefit of organization in this or any work, I dispute only the benefit of organizing bodies of women on the principle that separation from men makes them more capable of work." Not only do I adopt every word of the passage to the uttermost, but the following pages will probably shew that what he " disputes," I deny. The present work will have been written in vain if it fails to impress my conviction that the collective diaconate of the Sisterhood rests upon that of the individual woman, man's foreordained helpmeet in the Church as in the world, and is mainly valuable so far as it re-evolves the latter. Every Sisterhood, to be really useful, to be really harmless, must, in my opinion, have at its head not only a man, but a married man.

Lincoln's Inn, *December* 1864.

ERRATUM.

At page 164, line 8 from top, for "lately improved away," read, "about to be improved away."

CONTENTS.

CHAPTER I.

THE DEACONESSES OF THE EARLY CHURCH.

PAGE

§ 1. The Female Diaconate in Apostolic Times . 1

§ 2. The Church-Widows, Church-Virgins, and Συνείσακτοι 7

§ 3. The Female Diaconate in the "Apostolical Constitutions" 14

§ 4. Early Notices of the Female Diaconate in the Greek and Latin Churches till the Days of Chrysostom 23

§ 5. Chrysostom and his Deaconess Friends . . 32

§ 6. The Greek Female Diaconate in the Fifth Century 46

§ 7. The Greek Female Diaconate in the Codes and later Councils, till its disappearance . . 51

§ 8. Latest Notices of the Female Diaconate in the Western Church 63

§ 9. Conclusion: Lessons of the Historical Female Diaconate 72

CHAPTER II.

EARLY FEMALE MONACHISM AND THE BÉGUINES.

PAGE

§ 1. Church-Virginship, and the Doctrine of the Spiritual Marriage of the Individual with Christ 77

§ 2. Early Female Monachism as Compared with Church-Virginship 85

§ 3. The Social Principle, the Mainstay of Monachism 93

§ 4. Sketch of the History of Monachism till the Eleventh Century 96

§ 5. Female Monachism till the Eleventh Century . 106

§ 6. The Béguines 114

CHAPTER III.

THE SISTERHOODS OF THE CHURCH OF ROME.

§ 1. Early Romish Charitable Fellowships—Mendicants and their Tertiarians 124

§ 2. Struggle between the Free and the Monastic Charitable Fellowships 134

§ 3. The Tertiarian Nuns—Hospitallers—Alexians 141

§ 4. Early Educational Fellowships—the Gerardins 147

§ 5. The Jesuits and Female Educational Orders, Ursulines, &c. 151

§ 6. The later Charitable Sisterhoods and Reformatory Orders—Sisters of Charity, &c. . . 161

§ 7. Persistency of Romish Diaconal Sisterhoods . 181

CHAPTER IV.

DEACONESSES AND SISTERHOODS IN REFERENCE TO THE REFORMED CHURCHES.

PAGE

§ 1. Deaconesses and Female Monachism among the Reformed Churches in the Sixteenth and Seventeenth Centuries 193

§ 2. Deaconesses' Institutes and Protestant Sisterhoods in the Nineteenth Century . . 200

§ 3. Special Characteristics of the Protestant Deaconesses' Institute 207

§ 4. Conclusion 214

APPENDIX.

A.—The Coptic Apostolical Constitutions . . 219

B.—The Canons of the Councils of Nicæa, Laodicea, and Carthage 223

C.—The Marriage of the Soul with Christ, a Doctrine not countenanced by St Paul . . 227

D.—The Church-Virgins, and the Transition of the Institution into Monachism 234

E.—The Hospitallers of St Martha in Burgundy . 240

F.—Translation of one of the later Béguine Rules 242

G.—" Deaconesses or Protestant Sisterhoods" . 248

H.—Miss Sellon's Sisterhood of Mercy . . . 293

CHAPTER I.

---

§ 1. *The Female Diaconate in Apostolic Times.*

"I COMMEND unto you Phœbe our sister, which is a servant of the church which is at Cenchrea," (Rom. xvi. 1.) If the Greek word (διάκονον) here translated "servant" had been rendered as in the 6th chapter of Acts, the 3d of the First Epistle to Timothy, and in many other passages of the apostolic writings, the verse would have run thus: "I commend unto you Phœbe our sister, which is a *deacon* of the church which is at Cenchrea," and the name at least of a female diaconate would have remained familiar to us. It is one

A

of those too frequent instances in our translation of the same word being differently rendered, which often give a wholly different complexion to passages closely akin in the original,—as the 13th chapter of the First Epistle to Corinthians, where St Paul's glorious eulogy of "charity" loses, so to speak, its brotherhood with St John's oft-repeated lessons on "love," the Greek word (ἀγαπή) being the same in the teachings of both apostles; discrepancies which for some—I may speak at least for myself—render a revision of the authorised version a matter of deep and serious interest.   Reserving therefore all questions as respects the functions of the persons whom the word designates, but adhering to the form which is nearest to the Greek, we may say that undeniably there is mention of female deacons, or deaconesses, as I shall mostly henceforth call them (Greek, ἡ διάκονος, διακόνισσα—Latin, *diaconissa, diacona,*) in the New Testament.   The deacon Phœbe must, moreover, have been a person of some consideration.   St Paul begins with her name the list of his personal recommendations or salutations to the Roman Church, and recommends her at greater length than any other person : "That ye receive her in the Lord, as becometh saints, and that ye assist her in whatsoever business she hath need of you : for she hath been a succourer of many, and of myself also." Evidently this "servant of the church," this "succourer" of apostles, couid have been no mere pew-opener, no filler of a purely menial office.

Turn now to the 3d chapter of St Paul's First Epistle to Timothy, where the apostle gives successively those noble pictures of the Christian bishop, of the Christian deacon. "A bishop," he says, "must be blameless, the husband of one wife, vigilant, sober, of good behaviour, given to hospitality, apt to teach ; not given to wine, no striker, not greedy of filthy lucre ; . . . one that ruleth well his own house, having his children in subjection with all gravity." Proceeding next to the deacons : " Likewise must the deacons be grave, not double-tongued, not given to much wine, not greedy of filthy lucre. . . . . Even so must *their wives*" (γυναῖκας ὡσαύτως)—so says our translation—" be grave, not slanderers, sober, faithful in all things. Let the deacons be the husbands of one wife, ruling their children and their own house."

Many, no doubt, will have been struck by the circumstance, that whilst the deacons' wives are mentioned in the above passage, there is no parallel injunction as to the wives of bishops, although the former are treated obviously as married men and fathers of families, in precisely similar terms ;

whereas if the example of a deacon's wife be of sufficient moment to deserve a special apostolic exhortation, that of a bishop's wife must need it far more. Accordingly, Calvin and some others have held that the word rendered "their wives" means the wives of the bishops as well as of the deacons,—an interpretation which would itself do violence to our text, and which certainly accuses St Paul of hasty and slovenly writing. For, if he had meant this, surely he would more naturally have inserted the verse at the end of the whole exhortation, after the present ver. 13, than have "thrown in"—to use an expression of Chrysostom's in a comment to be presently referred to— something about bishops' as well as deacons' wives at once in a passage referring to deacons, both before and after. This interpretation, at all events, seems to have been entirely foreign to the early Church. Two meanings only appear to have been put upon the passage till the Reformation: one which referred it to women generally; the other, which referred it to the female diaconate.

Both these senses rest indeed upon the literal text. It will be observed that the word "their," in ver. 11, is printed in italics, indicating insertion at the hands of our translators. The Greek word, on the other hand, translated "wives," signifies primarily "women." Literally, therefore, the verse might run thus : " Even so must *women* be grave, not slanderers, sober, faithful in all things." Accordingly, the Latin Vulgate translates by the equivalent for "women," (*mulieres*) not for "wives;" our own Wycliffe following in its wake, and writing, "also it bihoveth *wymmen* to be chast," &c. Upon this construction Chrysostom, in his homilies on this epistle, (the 11th,) observes as follows :— " Some say that this is spoken of women generally; but it is not so. For why should he have thrown in something about women amongst the things which he has been saying? But he speaks of those that have the dignity of the diaconate." If, therefore, " *women-(deacons)*" are meant, the sense is plain. Just as the men-deacons must be grave, not double-tongued, &c., even so must the women-deacons be grave, not slanderous, &c. Thus, to sum up the argument, if the wives of the deacons be intended, the omission of all mention of bishops' wives seems unaccountable; if the wives of bishops and deacons alike are meant, the reference to the former is strangely thrown in amidst injunctions specially referring to the diaconal office ; if women generally, the injunction is thrown in still more strangely ; but if " women-deacons " be really meant, instead of either an unaccountable omission or an illogical insertion, we have a command strictly sufficient, strictly logical, and in strict accordance, as I shall presently shew, with the facts of Church history.*

Let me observe here at once, that whatever may appear hereafter to have been the functions of the deaconess in the ministrations of charity, they had in them nothing exclusive of the active development of every Christian grace in other female disciples, to whom the title is not attributed. Side by side with Phœbe, we find mention of "Mary, who bestowed much labour on us," "Tryphena and Tryphosa, who labour in the Lord," "the beloved Persis, which laboured much in the Lord" (Rom. xvi. 6, 12); whilst in another epistle the same apostle speaks again of "those women which laboured with me in the gospel" (Phil. iv. 3). Thus is continued that bright chain of female excellence, beginning with those holy women who, with the apostles, followed the Saviour in all His journeyings, and ministered to Him of their sub-

---

* Several modern critics, especially German, infer from Tit. ii. 3. the existence of a class of female presbyters, invested with a sort of magisterial functions,—a class of persons of which some traces, indeed, are to be found later in schismatical bodies, but never in the Church (at least till a much later period). I cannot say how strongly I feel that our translators are upon this point entirely in the right, and that the apostle has simply in view a contrast of age between "aged men" and "aged women" on the one hand, and "young men" and "young women" on the other. Female bishops there were avowedly none.

stance, the Marys, and Joannas, and Susannas (Luke viii. 2, 3), and which then links itself on to the above-mentioned names through Dorcas, "full of good works and alms-deeds" (Acts ix. 36); and above all, through that remarkable personage of the apostolic age, Priscilla, the wife of Aquila, the Jew of Pontus, whom the Acts shew us with him, expounding the way of God more perfectly to Apollos (Acts xviii. 26); the husband and wife, both "helpers" of Paul "in Christ Jesus," who had for his life "laid down their necks; unto whom not only" he gave "thanks, but also all the churches of the Gentiles" (Rom. xvi. 3, 4). The female diaconate must therefore have been, from the first, like every other office in the Christian Church, only the full developed type, and not the exceptional monopoly of a woman's function and work.

§ 2. *The Church-Widows, Church-Virgins, and* Συνείσακτοι.

One great cause of the obscurity in which the history of the female diaconate has been involved has been the existence in the early Church, from the apostolic age, of another class of women in later times frequently confounded with female deacons, and who indeed seems eventually in the West to have merged into one body with them.

" Honour widows that are widows indeed," says St Paul (1 Tim. v. 3, *et seq.*) ; " but if any widow have children or nephews, let them learn first to shew piety at home, and to requite their parents, for that is good and acceptable before God. Now she that is a widow indeed, and desolate, trusteth in God, and continueth in supplications and prayers night and day. . . . Let not a widow be taken into the number under threescore years old, having been the wife of one man, well reported of for good works ; if she have brought up children, if she have lodged strangers, if she have washed the saints' feet, if she have relieved the afflicted, if she have diligently followed every good work. . . . If any man or woman that believeth hath widows, let them relieve them, and let not the church be charged, that it may relieve them that are widows indeed."

What does the picture here given amount to ? Surely it is that of the *almswomen* of the primitive Church ; persons free from all family ties (" if any widow have children or nephews "), and at the same time destitute of all family support (" she that is a widow indeed, and desolate," . . . " if any man or woman that believeth hath widows, let them relieve them "), who, after a life of Christian usefulness (" well reported of for good works," &c.), were thought worthy of being provided for by the Church ("let not the church be charged, that it may relieve them that are widows indeed ") in their old age ("let not a widow be taken into the number under threescore years"), being released from all duties of active benevolence (" she that is a widow indeed . . . continueth in supplications and prayers night and day"). Now, the details of this picture are very much the reverse of what is implied in the word deacon, *i.e.*, man or maid-servant, (glorious humility of the Christian Church, which knows no higher titles than these of " servant," " elderly man," " overlooker !"). As the primary function of the deacon was one of a purely ministerial nature, to "serve tables"—and let it be remembered that the very necessity for the office arose from the neglect of the Greek " widows" in the " daily ministration" (the original Greek word is " diaconate," διαχονίᾳ)—so we may at once assume that the female deacon's duties must have been active ones. We can hardly suppose, for instance, that a widow of sixty, such as St Paul describes, would, like the deacon Phœbe, have undertaken a long journey under all the difficulties of ancient navigation, charged, if a tradition accepted by our translators speaks true, with the care of the epistle in which she is mentioned. And shall we be far from the truth if, judging from St Paul's commendation of Phœbe, we conjecture that the female deacon was what the widow had been, a bringer-up of children, a lodger of strangers, a reliever of the afflicted, a diligent follower of every good work? If so, it would easily follow that aged female deacons would be adopted into the class of widows; that women who had actively ministered to the Church during the working time of their lives should in turn be ministered to by the Church in their old days, and allowed to devote themselves to prayer and contemplation. And thus the two ideas might in time run into one.

Two classes of women, then, appear from the apostolic writings to have formed part of the earliest order of the Church,—the one ministering, the other ministered to,—the one fulfilling an office of active duty, the other rewarded for their past services by the privilege of an honourable provision in their old age. But there is also another class of females, who, although the canonical writings certainly do not exhibit them as forming part of the order of the Church, yet seem treated of with peculiar minuteness by St Paul. We remember his judgment concerning virgins, as to whom he had "no commandment of the Lord" (1 Cor. vii. 25); how he told the Corinthians that "he that standeth steadfast in his heart, having no necessity, but hath power over his own will, and hath so decreed in his heart that he will keep his virgin, doeth well; so then, he that giveth her in marriage doeth well, but he that giveth her not in marriage doeth better" (1 Cor. vii. 37, 38*). It might naturally be expected, after such an intimation of the great apostle's private opinion—not to speak of a passage in the First Gospel (Matt. xix. 12),—that virginity would be had in favour in the early Church, particularly having reference, as the apostle him-

---

* To avoid unnecessary controversy on a point not directly concerning my subject, I adopt the common interpretation, which applies the whole passage to virgins generally, and to those who have parental or quasi-parental authority over them. At the same time, a view of it is entertained by a very dear and respected friend of mine, the Rev. F. D. Maurice,—my obligations to whom for the light which he has thrown upon many of the truths I have contended for in this work it were idle to number,—which places the passage in an altogether new aspect. He looks upon it, from v. 25 to v. 38 of 1 Cor. vii., as being the answer to a particular case put to the apostle by the Corinthians, as to the duties of a guardian towards his female ward. Not only is the absence of all mention of parental authority very remarkable in the passage, as well as the continuous reference to the marriage of men in a passage "concerning virgins," but it certainly contains a verse which it is most difficult to explain on any other view: "But if any man think that he behaveth himself uncomely toward his virgin, if she pass the flower of her age, and need so require, let him do what he will, he sinneth not: *let them marry.*" A plural pronoun very strange and unexpected, if the girl's marriage alone is referred to, or if her husband be some undefined person,—but perfectly consistent with the text, if the marriage spoken of is that of two definite individuals placed in a special relation towards each other.

self points out, to the "present distress" (1 Cor.
vii. 26), to the perplexities and persecutions which
lasted, let us never forget it,—with intervals it is
true, but yet so as never to lose the character of
a "present distress"—for at least nine consecutive
generations of human beings.· But although St
Paul clearly speaks only of virgins who are in the
power of their parents or guardians,—what would
become of females thus devoted to celibacy, as age
wore on, as family ties were snapped asunder? If
deprived of their parents, would they not be about
equally helpless and "desolate" with the widows
themselves? Would it not become equally incumbent on the Church to take them wholly or partly
in its charge, by allowing them, for instance, like
the widows, to continue "in supplications and
prayers night and day,"—or again, by assigning
to them active duties to fulfil in the Church?
We may thus imagine how easy would be the
growth of a distinct class of church-virgins—in
effect prominent in later Church history—analogous to that of church-widows in some respects,
to the deaconesses in others, and liable to be confounded alternately with both.

But again, there is another class of women
whom we must be prepared to see grow up in
Church records out of a mistaken interpretation of
that passage of St Paul, in which, by our transla-

tion, he is made to ask, " Have we not power to lead about *a sister, a wife*, as well as other apostles ?" (1 Cor. ix. 5), but which in the original may equally bear the sense of " Have we not power to lead about a *sister-woman*, as well as other apostles ?" These "sister-women,"—συνείσακτοι, as the Greeks most usually term them ; *subintroductæ*, as the Latins translate the term—became in corrupt times, and with the growth of the *idea* of celibacy, persons answering to priests' " housekeepers," &c., in many Roman Catholic countries, —too often, in plain words, the mistresses of the clergy; or if grosser sin was avoided, yet still the occasion of extreme scandal and wilful temptation. The decrees of councils, the works of the fathers, are full of denunciations of these private adoptive fraternities between male members of the clergy and persons of the other sex.

All the four classes of women I have mentioned, — the Deaconesses and Widows, both belonging to the apostolic days,—the Virgins, dating from a scarcely later period, the συνείσακτοι for sister-women, a mere corruption of later days, —as well as the female elders or presbyters of some schismatical churches,—have more or less been confounded together at some time or other by the views or practice of particular churches, and the so-called labours of commen-

tators ; and the history of the true female diaconate has to be disentangled from a mass of mis-
conceptions and misapplications of texts, wilful,
stupid, or ignorant, filling the pages of the best
books of reference, repeated without inquiry from
author to author; till they seem to borrow something of the weight of each, almost incredible to
any one who has not traced passage after passage
to its source. For myself, I have invariably referred to the original text, whenever it was accessible to me ; and I give fair notice that no array of
modern names with or without Latin endings to
them, against any of the distinctions of classes
which I have laid down, will have any weight with
me against these distinctions, when supported by
one text of Scripture or of an early authority.

§ 3. *The Female Diaconate in the " Apostolical Constitutions."*

Let us now turn to a work of which many varying judgments have been held by men of learning
and weight—for some a clumsy forgery, for others
a precious and genuine relic—the so-called " Apostolical Constitutions." Observe that, if they be
forgeries, they are forgeries of an early age, and as
such, possessed of real historical value. For every
literary forgery must bear the impress of the time

at which it was got up; it must look backward always, never forward; some vestiges of past reality must linger in it, and by those vestiges we may often complete a subsisting fragment of reality itself; somewhat as, by the footprints of some long-perished creature, left on the soft sand or clay, which the lapse of ages has turned into stone, the naturalist may piece out some fragment of its fossil skeleton, itself insufficient to reveal to us the entire creature.

Now, in the " Apostolical Constitutions," the female Deacon or Deaconess, the Widow, the Virgin, all come before us as distinct types; the first as invested with an office; the second as the object of affectionate regard and support; the third of religious commendation. Of the Deaconess (as I shall call her henceforth) it is provided (Bk. vi. c. 17), that she shall be " a pure virgin," or otherwise " a widow once married, faithful and worthy;" a very natural provision, since the cares of a family would prevent a married woman from concentrating her whole energies on her diaconal functions. She was wanted, says an early constitution, for many purposes (Bk. iii. c. 15). At service, whilst the " door-keeper" was to stand and watch at the men's entrance to the church, the deaconess was in like manner to stand (Bk. ii. c. 57) at the women's entrance (a function which indeed, in a constitution of the eighth and latest book, is ascribed to the sub-deacon), and was, moreover, to act in the same manner as the male deacon with respect to placing females in the congregation, whether poor or rich (Bk. ii. c. 58). She was also to fulfil the duties of a male deacon in those cases where " a man-deacon cannot be sent to some houses towards women on account of unbelievers" (Bk. iii. c. 15), *i.e.*, to prevent scandal. Lastly, her most important offices were those relating to the baptizing of women (Bk. iii. cc. 15, 16), the necessity for which has been obviated in later times by the discontinuance of the practice of baptism by immersion, or the practice of immersion under a form which the early Church would not have recognised as valid. It is even provided that " no woman shall approach the deacon or the bishop without the deaconess" (Bk. ii. c. 26). And it said generally, in a constitution concerning the deacons, that "the woman" (an expression strongly recalling 1 Tim. iii. 11, and affording additional ground for construing it as relating to the deaconesses) " should be zealous to serve women ;" whilst " to both pertain messages, journeys to foreign parts, ministrations, services" (Bk. iii. c. 19). The traditional journey of Phœbe to Rome with St Paul's Epistle would thus be strictly within the limits of her functions.

Towards fulfilling these duties, the deaconess is represented as receiving an ordination from the bishop, under a simple and beautiful form of service attributed to the Apostle Bartholomew (Bk. viii., cc. 19, 20) :—

" Touching the deaconess, I Bartholomew do thus ordain : O bishop, thou shalt lay on her thy hands, in the presence of the presbytery, of the deacons, and of the deaconesses, and thou shalt say :—

" O everlasting God, Father of our Lord Jesus Christ, Creator of man and woman, who didst fill with Thy Spirit Mary and Deborah, and Hannah and Hulda : who didst not disdain to cause Thine only-begotten Son to be born of a woman ; who didst admit into the tabernacle of the testimony and into the temple the women guardians of Thy holy gates : Thyself look down even now upon Thy servant now admitted into the diaconate, and give to her Thy Holy Spirit, and cleanse her from all pollution of thy flesh and spirit, that she may worthily fulfil Thy work thus intrusted to her, to Thy glory, and to thy praise of Thy Christ, with whom to Thee be glory and worship, and to the Holy Spirit, for ever and ever.   Amen."*

---

* Two other forms of service for the ordination of deaconesses (besides a Nestorian one), I believe, exist—one in the " Liturgy of Basil and Chrysostom," the other in the " Ordo Romanus."

Some may feel shocked at the idea of the ordination of a woman, of the Holy Ghost being invoked upon her. A distinction has even been made by some Protestant, as well as Romish writers, between the imposition of hands as a ceremonial benediction and a real ordination. The original word certainly affords not the slightest ground for such a distinction, which other writers, like Bingham, wholly repudiate. But it seems to me that the laying on of hands upon a deaconess was eminently characteristic of the faith of early times.   It was because men felt still that the Holy Ghost alone could give power to do any work to God's glory, that they deemed themselves constrained to ask such power of Him, in setting a woman to do church work. Nor did such ordination in the least interfere with any needful distinctions of office.   " The deaconess," it is said, " does not give the blessing, nor does she fulfil any of the functions of the presbyters or of the deacons, beyond the guarding of doors, and the supplying the place of the presbyters in the baptizing of women" (Bk. viii., c. 28).   In other words, she was ordained not to preach, not to bless, exactly as others were ordained to preach and to bless. From other provisions, it may be seen that the deaconess ranked after the presbyter and deacon, and at least on a par with, if not before, the sub-deacon (Bk. viii. *pas-*

sim). Her position indeed is, in the earlier part of the work, set forth in language absolutely blasphemous to our ears, the bishop being likened to God the Father, the deacon to Christ, the deaconess to the Holy Ghost, as " doing naught nor saying without the deacon, even as the Comforter speaketh nor doeth aught of Himself, but glorifieth Christ, and attendeth to His will" (Bk. ii., c. 26).

Very different is the language of these Constitutions respecting widows. The eight first chapters of the third book treat of these, and breathe entirely the spirit of the Pastoral Epistle, though eked out and diluted, as it seems to me, into intolerable verbiage. They are represented as provided for by the Church, with no other duty than that of prayer, as well for their benefactors as for the whole Church. Mention is made of some who "ask without shame, and take without stint, and have already made the many lukewarm to give." Elsewhere it is said expressly, " The widows should be grave, obedient to the bishops, and to the priests, and to the deacons, and also to the deaconesses" (Bk. iii., c. 7). And it is specifically stated that " the widow is not ordained " (Bk. viii., c. 25).

On the subject of virgins, the Constitutions only exhibit this departure from the language of St Paul, that they treat the virgin as having dedicated *herself* to Christ, not as having been dedicated by others. It is specifically stated of her, as of the widow, that she is " not ordained " (see Bk. viii., c. 24). The virgins are not yet represented as forming a distinct class, nor are even spoken of with widows as persons to be relieved, although " orphans " are in one or two places.

The contrast between the ordained deaconess and the non-ordained widow or virgin illustrates well the typical, universal character which belongs to the offices of the Christian Church. Deaconesses were ordained, because the Diaconate was the type of that universal duty of serving one another, which our Lord so specially inculcated in the washing of His disciples' feet. Widows were not ordained, because widowhood and virginity are not offices, but mere conditions of life ; because they have nothing of a universal character, but are merely exceptional in their nature. So with, as it seems to me, perfect consistency, are sub-deacons and readers included in the ordained clergy, whilst confessors and exorcists are excluded (Bk. viii. *passim*).

Let us pause for a moment over the evidence of the " Apostolical Constitutions." Grant that they are not apostolical. Grant even that they do not represent the actual discipline of the Church at any period of her existence. Still they prove to us beyond a doubt that there was a time in the history of the Church when a clear idea was held by some writer of the office of the female deacon, as essential to that discipline, and as being wholly distinct from the position of the widow,—the alms-woman, as I have already called her, of the Church. If, therefore, at any future period of our inquiries, we should find the two ideas growing together in any portion of the Church, we shall, at least, be able to say that the Constitutions represent an older view of the church system. But the teach-ings of the "Apostolical Constitutions" on this sub-ject, I must say, appear to me quite in accordance with the view now perhaps most generally enter-tained, that they represent the condition of the Greek Church at some period of the second cen-tury.*

* I should be the last, indeed, to deny that the Constitu-tions appear to be of very unequal antiquity. As respects the particular subject in question, I think the earlier consti-tutions are indicated by the use of the older form ἡ διάκονος (Bk. ii., cc. 25, 26, 57, 58; Bk. iii., cc. 7, 15, 16, 19), the later by that of the form διακόνισσα, unknown to the New Testament, (Bk. iii., c. 11; Bk. vi., c. 17; Bk. viii., cc. 13, 19, 28, 31). There is a complete opposition of tone between ch. 15 of Bk. iii., which says that " we need a woman-dea-con for many purposes," and ch. 28 of Bk. viii., which re-duces her functions to door-keeping and ministering at female baptisms; between ch. 26 of Bk. ii., which compares her to the third person of the Trinity, and ch. 31 of Bk. viii., which gives her, out of eight parts in the eulogies or

We possess, indeed, other collections of the Apostolical Constitutions, to one of which the late Baron Bunsen, in his " Hippolytus," has ascribed a higher authority than to the Greek—the Coptic, edited and translated a few years since by Archdeacon Tattam. My own opinion, I must say, is that the Coptic collection, in its present shape, whatever early fragments may be imbedded in it, is, on the contrary, later than the Greek.* The

consecrated bread, only one in common with sub-deacons, readers, and singers. Evidently, in the older Constitutions, the deaconess's office is far more real and more honourable.

* Without pretending to any Coptic scholarship, I cannot but observe that the Coptic collection introduces, without a single exception, I believe, not by way of translation, but as imported forms, all the terms of Greek Church language,— *episcopos, presbuteros, diaconus, ecclesia,* and even to *anagnostes* for reader, and *chera* for widow. This is surely, to begin with, a token that it belongs to a period when, amongst the Greeks, all these simple words of overlooker, elder, servant, assembly, reader, widow, had, in church-language, already slid away from their usual significance in daily life, and had become " words of art," as our old jurists would have said, to express the special Church functions which they represent. Next, it seems to me but fair to infer that this period is one later than that of the fixing of the Latin Church language, when, although the words *episcopus, presbyter, diaconus, ecclesia,* were embodied as they are into it, yet the names of lower offices or conditions in the Church—those of the reader, the singer, the widow, were simply translated. Lastly, many of the passages of the Greek collection,—some even naming the deaconesses,—are repeated in the Coptic, and in particular it contains, almost unchanged, the eighth

passages in it relating to our subject, are, at any rate, confused and discrepant, and do little more than shew that the Coptic Church, like the Greek, deemed the appointment of ministering women an essential feature in the organisation of the Church.*

§ 4. *Early Notices of the Female Diaconate in the Greek and Latin Churches till the days of Chrysostom.*

Except in the "Apostolical Constitutions," up to the latter end of the fourth century, there is little of real moment, less of real interest, to be found in Eastern Church writers respecting our subject, although Hermas, as once mentioned by Principal Tulloch in *Good Words*, indicates the existence of women who seem to have had authority over the widows and orphans. The epistles falsely attributed to Ignatius, whilst referring to the deaconesses as "keepers of the holy gates," bear witness of their later date, by the far greater prominence they give to virgins,—treating them as "priestesses of Christ,"—holding them up to veneration,—and confounding them, according to one text at least, with the widows. Not to speak of a doubtful pas-

and avowedly latest book of the latter, attributed to Hippolytus.
* See Appendix A.

sage in Clement of Alexandria (150-220),—generally interpreted of the deaconesses, but by some
of the deacons' wives—Origen, an Egyptian writer
of slightly later date (184-253), in commenting on
Phœbe and her mission, speaks of the ministry of
women in the Church as both existing and necessary.

If we turn now to the Western Church,—a remarkable passage from the letters of the Younger
Pliny (Bk. x., ch. 97), writing for advice to Trajan,
how to deal with the Christians, shews that it was
upon two deaconesses* that the elegant letter-
writer—the Chesterfield of antiquity—sought to
prove by torture the truth of those strange confes-
sions of the Christians, " that they were wont on a
stated day to meet before dawn, and repeat among
themselves in alternate measure a song addressed
to Christ, as to a god ; and by their vow to bind
themselves, not to the committing of any crime,
but against theft, and robbery, and adultery, and
breach of faith, and denial of trust, after which it
was their custom to depart, and again to meet for
the purpose of taking food."   In the Latin Church,
however, the distinction between the deaconess

* Ex duabus ancillis, *quæ ministræ dicebantur.*   The word
"ministra" is the term applied to Phœbe, both in the old
Italic version and in the Vulgate.   Hence, probably, the use
of the word " servant," rather than "deacon," by our own
translators.

and the Church-widow, and between the latter and the Church-virgin, appears to have become early obliterated. Neander, indeed, shews well that the more stringent separation of the sexes in the Eastern Church created a more permanent necessity there for the peculiar services of the deaconess, whilst more exalted notions of priestly privileges tended in the West to impart a something offensive to her position as a recognised member of the ordained clergy. Tertullian (150-226, or thereabout) supplies us with the first Western instance of growing confusions; inveighing indeed (De Virg. vel. c. 9) against that between the widow and the virgin, but in terms which indicate the presence in his mind of a feeling that the widow, whilst receiving maintenance from the Church, is one engaged in the active duties of religion, and holding a place of actual honour. Another passage of his, however, which has been relied on as a staple authority for the identity of the two characters of deaconess and widow, if interpreted by earlier records, will be found, I think, on the contrary, to bear an exactly opposite construction.*

---

* As an argument against second marriage, he urges that "the apostolical injunctions forbid the twice married to be bishops, nor suffer a widow to be received to (or selected for) ordination—*allegi in ordinationem*—except she has been the wife of one husband only; for the altar of God must be exhibited without spot " (Ad Ux., Bk. i., c. 7). The

A century later, a canon of the Nicene Council (326) bears witness to the existence of an ordained female diaconate amongst the Paulianist heretics, and by implication also in the Church itself, although it has been strangely interpreted to forbid altogether the ordination of deaconesses.   A canon of the Council of Laodicea (360 to 370) has been still more strangely pressed into this service, although it only forbids the appointment of female elders in the Church.   In the Fourth Synod or Council of Carthage (398),—whose canons have been considered to be, in fact, a collection of those of many African Councils—we find, again, passages which have been used, without the slightest testing of their weight, as authorities in treating of the female diaconate, whilst in fact they only shew us widows and consecrated virgins invested with some of the functions of the deaconess.*   The students

above passage *may*, of course, refer only to 1 Tim. iii. 2, and v. 9 ; but the singularity of the expressions " allegi in ordinationem," as applied to the latter verse, entirely disappears if we refer it to chap. 17 of the 6th book of the " Apostolical Constitutions," which embraces both injunctions, requiring, as before mentioned, the deaconess to be " a widow once married,"—the " ordination" in question being, as I view it, simply that of the widow as deaconess.

We shall not, of course, attribute any weight to a supposed decree of Pope Soter, quoted by Baronius in his annals for the year 179, bearing " that no deaconess is to touch the consecrated pall, or place incense in the Holy Church."

* See Appendix B.

of Church history will recollect that we have now attained to the days of female monachism, 'one of the earliest records of which is a well-known letter from Augustine to the nuns of Carthage, only a few years later than this period. Tertullian and Cyprian, two African fathers, had written successively in enthusiastic praise of female virginity. It was but natural that we should find their exhortations bearing fruit on the African soil, and the "religious virgins" (sanctimoniales—the *moniales* or nuns of later times) thus invested by the African Church, along with widows, with diaconal functions, and the ascetic spirit already embodied in a system of religious communities, composed of women who had professed celibacy.*

The latter half of the fourth, and former half of the fifth centuries form, however, the period during

---

* I cannot help pointing out that as, in the Greek, the female deacons may often be spoken of together with the male under the epicene term διάκονοι, so they may be also in Latin under the curious form *diacones*, which I believe occurs in some of the oldest Latin MSS. of the New Testament, and which is especially frequent in Cyprian (martyred 258). I believe, indeed, that in the former case it is sometimes used where none but male deacons can be meant; in Cyprian on the other hand, so far as I have observed, never but where the context might include both sexes. The introduction of this barbarous-looking epicene form in place of the more natural, but specially masculine *diaconi*, certainly might seem to have been prompted by the very purpose of including both.

which the female diaconate of the East appears to have attained its highest importance. All the leading Greek fathers and Church writers of the age—Basil* (326-379), Gregory of Nyssa (died 396), Epiphanius (died 403), Chrysostom (344-407), Theodoret (393-457), Sozomen (fifth century) refer to it, and notices of individual deaconesses become frequent in Church annals, whilst everywhere the female diaconate is spoken of as an honourable office, and one filled by persons of rank, talent, and fortune. Thus Sozomen, in his Ecclesiastical History (Bk. iv., ch. 24), relates how the Synod of Rimini (latter half of the fourth century) deposed a certain Elpidius for having, amongst other things, conferred the honours of the diaconate

* Basil is another writer who has been most strangely made to vouch for the identity of the deaconess and the widow. In one of his rules or canons (Epist. cc. can. 44), he enforces absolute chastity upon the deaconess. In another (Epist. cxcix. can. 2) he excommunicates a widow "inscribed in the number of widows, *that is, ministered unto by the Church,* (τὴν διακονουμένην ὑπο τῆς ἐκκλησίας), who marries again, admitting however, that, if she be inscribed under 60, "ours is the fault, not the woman's." In order to wrest this passage into an authority for the identity of the two classes, the expression διακονουμένην ὑπο τῆς ἐκκλησίας has actually been interpreted by some "exercising the functions of deaconess in the Church." It would, on the contrary, as it seems to me, be impossible to find a stronger instance than it supplies of the difference between the ministering deaconess and the ministered-unto widow.

upon one Nectaria, who had been excommunicated for breaches of confidence and perjury. Theodoret (Bk. iii., ch. 14) tells of a deaconess in the time of Julian, how she " evangelised " the son of a hea- then priest, encouraged him to stand fast under persecution, and to disobey his earthly rather than his heavenly Father, and sheltered him from his father's wrath. He subsequently gives a chapter to the story of " Publia the deaconess, and her godly boldness;" who, "being with the choir of the perpetual virgins, dwelt continually praising God the Creator and Saviour. Now the Emperor chancing one day to pass, they began more lustily with one accord to sing forth, deeming the wretch worthy of all contempt and ridicule; and chiefly they sang those psalms which deride the impotence of idols ; and with David they said, ' The idols of the nations are silver and gold, the work of men's hands.'   And after setting forth the uselessness of idols " (see Ps. cxv.) " they proceeded, ' They that make them are like unto them, and so is every one that trusteth in them.'   The Emperor, hearing these songs, and being thereby stung to the quick, bade them be silent while he passed. But she, holding cheap his commands, filled the choir with greater boldness, and again, as he passed by, bade them sing, ' Let God arise, and let his enemies be scattered ' (Ps. lxviii). When he, bitterly wroth, bade the mistress of the choir be brought before him, . . . and shewing neither pity for her gray hairs, nor respect for her virtue, ordered one of his guards to strike her on both cheeks, covering his hands with her blood. But she, taking this shame for sovran honour, withdrew into her cell, and still continually pursued him with her spiritual songs," —as David was wont to still the evil spirit of Saul, adds the author; an odd comparison, seeing that, by his own account, Publia irritated Julian's evil passions instead of soothing them. The function of the deaconess, as head of the Church-virgins, is referred to in other contemporary authorities.*

A deaconess named Romana figures again in the history of Pelagia, the famous actress of Antioch in the fifth century, who afterwards became a no less celebrated hermit and saint. In her life by James the Deacon, who seems to have been personally acquainted with her, this Romana, described as " the holy lady Romana, first of the deaconesses," is mentioned as having been deputed to receive Pelagia when she became con-

* Thus Gregory of Nyssa, in his life of his sister Macrina, speaks of one Lampadia, a virgin placed at the head of the virgins' choir, and in the rank of deaconess. Sozomen, in like manner, commends the modesty of Nicarete, a noble Bithynian lady, who declined the diaconate and the ruling over the Church-virgins, although often pressed by Chrysostom to undertake the office.

verted, and as having become her "spiritual mother."*

Epiphanius, earlier in date than either Sozomen or Theodoret, but treating of his own times, in combating the heresy of the Collyridians, who intruded women into the priesthood (Adv. Hær., Bk. iii., tom. ii., Adv. Coll. c. 3), and again in his "Summary of the Faith" (*Ibid.* c. 21), sets forth specifically the institution and certain of the principal functions of the deaconesses, declaring that they exist "in nowise for priestly purposes," (οὐχὶ εἰς τὸ ἱερατεύειν.) "It is to be specially observed," he says elsewhere, "that the needs of the Church system only stretched as far as the deaconess, and that it named widows, and of these the still older ones aged women, but never established elderesses or priestesses."† In his statement of the

---

* I quote from Cotelerius ("Patres Apostolici," vol. i., p. 290, note 2), who himself refers to Rosweyde, "Vitæ Patrum," Bk. i., ch. 8,—a work which I have not had the opportunity of consulting. I may mention here that a practice is said to have prevailed of ordaining deaconesses the wives of married priests, when the latter were promoted to the episcopate ; and Theosebia, the wife of Gregory of Nyssa, is quoted as an instance of the practice. I have been unable, however, to verify the fact.

† Ἄχρι Διακονιοσῶν μόνον τὸ ἐκκλησιαστικὸν ἐπεδεήθη τάγμα, χήρας τε ὠνόμασε, καὶ τούτων τὰς ἔτι γραοτέρας πρεσβυτίδας, οὐδαμοῦ δὲ πρεσβυτερίδας ἢ ἱερούσας προσέταξε. By supplying the pronoun αὐτὰς to the sentence χήρας τε ὠνόμασε, whilst overlooking the distinctive τούτων in the next, it has been

functions of the deaconess, especially as to the baptizing of women, Epiphanius agrees with the "Apostolical Constitutions."

But it is Chrysostom's history in particular which is interwoven with that of the female diaconate. As it supplies us with the most complete picture still extant of that institution during the second period of its existence, we may find it worth while to dwell upon the prelate's relations with his deaconess friends in some detail.

§ 5. *Chrysostom and his Deaconess Friends.*

No less than six deaconesses occur by name amongst those who appear to have enjoyed the intimacy of Chrysostom.

Nicarete has been named already in a note. On the persecution of Chrysostom's adherents under his successor Arsacius after his expulsion (404), Sozomen mentions, amongst other sufferers, this Nicarete, of a noble family of Nicomedia, famous for her perpetual virginity and holy life, who

construed as meaning "named *them widows*," and so turned into another of the stock authorities for the identity of the deaconess and widow. It will be seen from the story of Chrysostom how impossible it is to suppose Epiphanius to have been ignorant of the distinction between the two. His confining of the πρεσβυτίδες of St Paul to the ἔτι γραότεραι among the widows is indeed remarkable.

" sought always to remain hidden, so that she strove not to advance to the honour of the diaconate, nor, although often exhorted thereto by John" (Chrysostom), "to rule over the virgins of the Church."

Sabiniana, mentioned in Letter 13 to Olympias, is identified by Tillemont and by Montfaucon (in his " Life of Chrysostom ") with a deaconess of the same name, said by Palladius (see Montfaucon's note) to have been Chrysostom's aunt. "There came also," he writes from exile, "my lady Sabiniana the deacon, the same day on which we came there also, broken down indeed and worn out, as being at that age when it is painful to move; youthful nevertheless in mind, and feeling nothing of her sufferings, since she said she was ready to go forth even to Scythia, the rumour prevailing that we were to be taken away thither. And she is ready, she says, not to return yet at all, but wher-- ever we may be, there to tarry. She was received by those of the Church with much zeal and good-will."

Three letters are written to "*Amprucla* the deacon and those with her" (96, 103, 191). They turn chiefly on one of the staple topics of Chrysostom's correspondence, consolation under religious perse-cution, such as his adherents were subject to. "For we bear you about everywhere in our understanding," he says, "wondering at the immutableness of your mind, and your great manliness" (96). "Although distant," he says elsewhere, "we have heard of your manly virtue and excellence not less than if we were present, and greatly did we sympathise with your manliness, your patience, your immutable resolution, your steadfast and adamantine understanding, your freedom of speech and boldness" (103). The last letter (191), probably earliest in date of the three which have been preserved, whilst without historical bearing, is one of the pleasantest and most life-like in the collection. The lady, it seems, had been the first to open the correspondence, and was still confounding herself in excuses for having ventured to do so. Chrysostom writes back to her one of those caressing letters in which he is a master, and which go far to explain the extraordinary influence which he evidently possessed over the minds of women : " I say again the same thing to you, do not call it boldness, to have been the first to leap into a correspondence with us, neither deem that a sin which is your greatest praise." He then goes on to tell her what pleasure he derives from hearing of the welfare of his friends, and bids her "send him storms of letters" (νιφάδας γραμμάτων), giving tidings of her health.

The names of " *Pentadia* and *Procla* the deaconesses" occur in close connexion with that of Olympias. The former, who was the widow of the consul Timasius, had her share in the persecutions of Chrysostom's friends. Three of his letters are addressed to her, 94, 104, 185; and her name, moreover, occurs in one of the letters to Olympias (14), with reference to a certain Bishop Heraclides, whose case, writes Chrysostom, "although it did not do much good, yet I shewed to my lady Pentadia, that she might shew him all her zeal, if she could imagine any consolation to his misfortune." In his letters to her he takes very much the same tone as we shall see him do with Olympias : "Our greatest consolation, although dwelling in such a wilderness, is that of your manliness, your presence of mind, your immutable resolution, your great prudence, your freedom of speech, your lofty boldness, whereby you have both put to shame your enemies, and given a deadly wound to the devil, and have comforted '(literally, anointed)' those that fight for the truth,—raising, like a noble chief in war-time, a splendid trophy, and carrying off a brilliant victory,—whilst filling us with so much pleasure, that we think ourselves no longer in a strange and foreign land, neither in the wilderness, but to be present yonder, to be with yourselves, and to take pride in your soul's virtue. . . . For what artifice have they omitted? what manner of

engine have they not set in motion, endeavouring to
beguile your steadfast soul, true to God (γνησίᾳ
θεῷ?) yea, rather your noble and most manly soul?
They carried you away to the Agora, you who
knew nothing more than the church and your
room, from the Agora to the tribunal, from the
tribunal to the prison. . . . They set all in motion,
that they might compel and force you by fear to
say what was contrary to what you knew.   And
like as an eagle soaring on high, so did you, rend-
ing their nets asunder, rise to your due height of
freedom, suffering not yourself to be deceived in
these things, but shewing themselves to be false
accusers in this charge of the burning [of St
Sophia], whereon they, miserable wretches, seemed
most to pride themselves" (94).

In the winter following these events, Pentadia
seems to have wished to leave Constantinople.
Chrysostom's next letter dissuades her from so
doing : "Since I have learned that you meditate
expatriating yourself, and removing from thence, I
exhort your honour (παρακαλῶ σου τὴν τιμιότητα) to
think of or meditate no such thing.   First of all for
this, that you are a bulwark of the city where you
are, and a wide harbour, and a prop, and a firm
wall to those who labour wearily."   Health is
another consideration which he urges upon her :
" You know the weakness of your body, and how

it is not easy for you to move in such cold weather and such a winter."

In the third letter he complains of her not writing, which cannot be because she is cast down: " For I know your great and lofty soul, which can sail, as with a fair wind, through many tempests, and in the midst of the waves enjoy a white calm. And this you have shewn in these very affairs, and to the very end of the world has fame gone forth, bearing your achievements; and all loudly praise you for being able, fixed in one spot, to animate by your piety those who are afar off, and make them of a better courage."

But the most devoted of all Chrysostom's followers was *Olympias*, the Mathilda (shall we so call her ?) of one whose character offers perhaps more than one trait of resemblance to Hildebrand. She was an orphan of good birth, who had been married when young, but her husband died twenty months after her marriage. The emperor Theodosius then sought to marry her to Elpidius, one of his own kindred, and on her refusal (prompted by ascetic motives) he directed the prefect of the city to take her fortune in ward till she were thirty, and forbade her speaking to the bishops or going to church ; but after the war against Maximus, he ordered her goods to be

restored.* She is described by Sozomen (Bk. viii.,
c. 9) as having been, although a young widow,
ordained by Nectarius a deacon (διάκονον χειροτό-
νησε). Her unbounded liberalities drew upon her
the reproof of Chrysostom, who exhorted her to
moderate her alms as a wise steward; and this
counsel is assigned by the historian as one of the
motives for the deep hatred of the greedy priesthood of the metropolis towards the saint. On
Chrysostom's expulsion from the episcopate, he is
represented as going into the baptistery, and calling "Olympias, who never departed from the
Church, together with Pentadia and Procla, the
deaconesses, and Silvina, late the wife of the
blessed Nebridius, who adorned her widowhood
by her comely life," and exhorting them not to fail
of their goodwill towards the Church, and that
whosoever should reluctantly be brought to ordination, by consent of all, not seeking it, they
should bow their heads to him as to John himself;
for there cannot be a church without a bishop.†
During the persecution which followed, Sozomen
(Bk. viii., c. 24) praises the "manly" conduct
of Olympias, who, being brought before the prefect on a charge of having set fire to the church of

---

* See Palladius, Dialog. in Tillemont, Mém. Ecclés. xi. ;
and Montfaucon's Chrysostom, vol. xiii.

† Pallad. c. 10.

St Sophia, replied, by referring to her past life, and the spending of her large fortune " for the renewing of God's temples." But there being no witnesses for the charge, the prefect passed on to another, reproaching her and the other women for their folly in refusing the new bishop's communion, whilst they were yet free to repent, and be quit of the affair. The other women having yielded, Olympias held out, saying that it was not right that a woman taken through sycophancy in the multitude, and convicted in the court of no offence whereof she is accused, should be driven to defend herself on points not in issue, and claiming permission to bring forward witnesses as to the former accusation. The prefect remanded her under colour of letting her consult with counsel; but had her brought up again the next day, and fined her in a large sum, hoping thus to make her change her mind. But she refused to yield, and having left Constantinople, withdrew to Cyzicum. One letter of Chrysostom's seems to imply that she was expelled.

The relation of Chrysostom to Olympias appears to have been peculiarly intimate. She is represented by Palladius as having looked after his daily food whilst he was in Constantinople. No less than eighteen of Chrysostom's letters are addressed to " my lady the deaconess ($\delta\iota\alpha\kappa\acute{o}\nu\psi$)

Olympias, most worthy and beloved of God." It
would not be possible here to epitomise them all,
and most tedious if it were so, as there is great
sameness in them; but I shall give copious extracts, that from them we may realise the spiritual
portrait of the pattern deaconess of the fifth century, as sketched by the great Greek saint of the
age.

After saying that he will not dwell on her almsgiving, " whereof thou holdest the sceptres, and
didst bind on the crown of old," he proceeds :
" For who should tell thy varied, manifold, and
many-sided endurance, and what speech should
be sufficient for us, what measure for our history,
if one should enumerate thy sufferings from thy
earliest age until now : those from members of
thy household, those from strangers, those from
friends, those from enemies, those from persons
connected with thee by blood, those from persons
in nowise connected with thee, those from men in
power, those from the prosperous, those from the
rulers, those from the common people, those from
men reckoned in the clergy. . . . . But if one
should turn also to the other forms of this virtue,
and should go through no more thy sufferings received from others, but those which thou hast con-
trived for thyself,—what stone, what iron, what
adamant shall he not find conquered by thee?

For having received a flesh so tender and delicate, and nourished up in all kinds of luxury, thou hast so conquered it by various sufferings, that it lies no better than slain, and thou hast brought upon thyself such a swarm of diseases as to confound the physician's skill, and the power of medicine, ... and to live in perpetual fellowship with pain.*

" For thy self-control as respects the table, and thy continence, and thy steadfastness in night-watchings, if any should choose to set it forth at length, how many words will he need! Rather thou hast not allowed it to be called continence any more, nor yet self-control in thee, but we must seek out some other much greater name for these virtues. For we call that man continent and self-controlled, when he is pressed by some desire and conquers it ; but thou hast not what thou mayest conquer ; for having blown from the first with great vehemence upon the flesh, thou hast extinguished all its desires. . . . Insensibility alone remains to thee. . . . . Thou hast taught thy stomach to be content with so much food and drink as not to perish. . . . That desire being

---

* In other places indeed (see Bk. 4) he exhorts her not to "neglect taking care of herself,"—to "employ various and experienced doctors, and remedies capable of setting these things to rights."

quenched, the desire to sleep was quenched with it ; for food is the nourishment of sleep. And indeed thou didst also destroy sleep in another way, having from the beginning done violence to thy nature, and spending whole nights without sleep ; latterly, by constant custom, making a nature of the habit. For as sleep is natural to others, so is watching to thee. . . . But if any should examine the time, and how these things took place in unripe age, and the want of teachers, and the many that laid stumbling-blocks, and that from an ungodly house thou hast come now of thyself to the truth in thy soul, and that thine was a woman's body, and one delicate through the nobility and luxury of thy ancestors, how many seas of wonders will he find opening out at every point ! . . . Willingly would I tarry over these words, and sail over a boundless sea, or seas rather, following the many-branched tracks of each virtue of thine, whereof each track should bring forth a sea again, if I were to dwell on thy patience, and thy humility, and thy many-shaped almsgiving, which has stretched to the very ends of the world, and on thy charity, that hath outdone ten thousand furnaces, and on thy boundless prudence, full of grace, and surpassing the measures of nature. . . . But I will endeavour to shew the lion by his claw, by saying a few words of thy dress, of the garments that hang simply and at haphazard around thee. This indeed seems a lesser achievement than others ; but if any should view it diligently, he will find it very great, and needing a philosophic soul, which tramples upon all the things of life, and takes flight to the very heaven. . . . For I do not only marvel at the unspeakable coarseness of thy attire, surpassing that of the very beggars, but above all at the shapelessness, the carelessness of thy garments, of thy shoes, of thy walk ; all which things are virtue's colours."*

He then says that his object has not been to praise, but to console her, in order that, " ceasing to consider this man's sin and that man's fault, thou mayest bear in mind perpetually the struggles of thy endurance, thy patience, thy abstinence, thy

---

* Chrysostom indeed does not descend to such details as Palladius, himself a contemporary of Olympias, who tells us that " she abstained from animal food, and went for the most part unwashed ; but if she were compelled by infirmity to bathe (for she suffered constantly from the stomach), she descended into the water in her tunic." Her model in these respects is said to have been one Salvia or Silvia, who told the panegyrist of Olympias, when past sixty, whilst he was taking her from Jerusalem to Egypt, that she had never washed either her face or her feet, nor any other part of her body except her hands, which she washed to receive the sacrament ; that, though often ill, and ordered to bathe, she had never done so, nor had slept in a bed, nor been carried in a litter. Tillemont, Mém. Eccl., vol. xi. ; "Ste Olympiade," p. 417.

prayers, thy holy night-long watches, thy continence, thine almsgiving, thy hospitality, thy manifold and difficult and frequent trials. Reflect how, from thy first age until the present day, thou hast not ceased to feed Christ when a-hungered, to give Him drink when thirsty, to clothe Him when naked, to take Him in when a stranger, to visit Him when sick, to go unto Him when bound. Consider the sea of thy charity, which thou hast opened so, that by thy great efforts it hath reached the very ends of the earth. For thy house was not only open to all who came, but everywhere, by land and sea, many have enjoyed thy liberality, through thy love of strangers. . . . . Be proud (τρύφα) and rejoice in the hope of these crowns and these rewards." . . . .

Let it not be supposed that this " sea" of panegyric (to use Chrysostom's favourite image) was poured forth once for all. On the contrary, it flows again and again. " Rejoice and be glad," he exclaims in the next letter (3), " to have followed this gainful road, loaded with ten thousand crowns, from thy earliest age, and through constant and frequent sufferings. For bodily disease, various, of all kinds, harder than ten thousand deaths, hath not ceased constantly to besiege thee; and storms of insults and contumelies and calumnies have unremittingly been brought against thee, and frequent and constant faintings and fountains of tears have troubled thee at all times." Again he compliments her (Ep. 6) on her fortitude in time of persecutions : " And this is wonderful, that without rushing forth into the market-place, nor proceeding through the midst of the city, but seated in a small narrow room and on a bed, thou nervest and anointest those who stand. . . . A woman, clothed with a thin weak body,* after having borne so many assaults, not only hast thou suffered nothing like so much [as others,] but thou hast hindered many others from suffering." Again (7) : " Thou hast lost country, house, friends, relatives ; thou hast gone into banishment, thou hast not ceased to die daily." Again : " Thou hast known as well how to inhabit great and populous cities as the wilderness" (17). He finds a new subject of praise (16), in commending her for getting through legal proceedings without either giving way in an unmanly manner or suffering herself to be entangled with the mischief of litigation ; following a middle course, she has shewn in everything her great wisdom, and long-suffering, and endurance, and patience, and undeceivable prudence. The 15th letter is also stuffed with praise.

I do not wish to soften one line of this most

---

* Αραχνῶδες, an expression explained by that in another letter (17) : Ἐν γυναικείῳ σώματι καὶ ἀραχνίων ἀσθενεστέρῳ, *i.e.*, weaker than a spider's web.

painful picture. It is due indeed to Olympias to say, that she herself appears in one of her letters to have disclaimed Chrysostom's extravagant eulogies. But what hope was there for the Eastern Church, when self-complacency could thus be held out as the main ground of Christian consolation? Even the sword of the Mussulman, preaching that "God is God," carried with it surely a nobler gospel than this.

§ 6. *The Greek Female Diaconate in the Fifth Century.*

We see now what the female diaconate had become in the Greek Church of the fifth century,—how far it had departed from the model of the apostolic times, or at least of those early ages to which, by the very contrast, it will be felt now that the "Apostolical Constitutions" must surely belong. The days are gone when Phœbe travelled forth from land to land in charge of an apostle's letters. The days are gone when the deaconess went from house to house, carrying the good tidings into the seclusion of the women's apartments. The demon of ascetic self-righteousness has entered in, and is fostered by the preachings even of one of the greatest men, the most exemplary prelates of the age. The deaconesses do not "depart from the

Church." Profuse in almsgiving they may be, but how little can they be effectual "succourers of many," when by their austerities they ruin their health, when it is one of the features of Chrysostom's panegyric of Olympias, that she has brought upon her such a swarm of diseases as to defy all means of cure? No wonder that Epiphanius, Chrysostom's contemporary, mainly dwells upon that one duty of theirs, of assisting in the baptizing of women. Such easy, stay-at-home functions were the only ones now fit for them. No wonder that he adds a third to the classes from which the deaconesses are to be selected. They are to be, he says, either continent, by which he means virgin-wives, once married, or once-married widows, or perpetual virgins. The "Apostolical Constitutions" know of no such monstrosity as voluntary virgin-wives. They do not say that the "pure virgins" who may be made deaconesses are to be perpetual ones.

There has grown up, moreover, a real analogy of character, if not of position, between the deaconess and the apostolical widow. I say the apostolical widow; not by any means the person known by that name in the age of Chrysostom, one of whose achievements was the reform of the Church-widows, and from whose writings it is palpable that this class, instead of having been raised to the level of the deaconesses, had, on the contrary, fallen far below its own original station;* that the respectable almswoman had degenerated into the clamorous pauper; nay, that the still greater abuse had crept in of allowing the young and well-to-do to usurp the place of the aged and the destitute. In the third book of his work on the priesthood (c. 16), speaking of the difficulties of a bishop's work, he asks whether he shall first consider his duties towards the widows, or towards the virgins, or his judicial functions. The care of the widows, he says, is that which appears easiest; yet is it thought to be nothing more than looking after their maintenance? Not so; but in the first place, there needs much scrutiny before inscribing them on the register, as otherwise a thousand mischiefs have ensued. You may find that they have ruined

---

* "As there are now choirs of virgins," he says (on 1 Tim. v. 9; Works, by Montfaucon, vol. iii., p. 311), "so were there of old choirs of widows, nor was it lawful for them to be simply registered among the widows. He speaks not therefore of the one who liveth in poverty and needeth succour, but of the one who is a widow by choice." From which Tillemont blunderingly, but I believe not dishonestly, concludes that Chrysostom maintains the widows of St Paul to have been deaconesses. Such an idea, I believe, never entered Chrysostom's head. His younger contemporary Theodoret, at all events, expressly denies that the Pauline widows fulfilled any Church office :—Τὰς γεγηρακυίας οὕτως ὠνόμασεν, οὐ τὰς λειτουργίας τινος ἠξιωμένας (quoted in Suicer, Thesaurus, "Διακόνισσα et ἡ διάκονος").

their families, have broken their marriage-vows, have been guilty of thefts and other disorders. Not only must you not admit these, but none who are able to support themselves." Again and again he speaks of poverty as characteristic of them. "Widows," he says, "are a sort of persons who, both through poverty, and through age, and through their nature also, use a kind of un-bounded freedom of speech; . . . they clamour out of season, they make vain complaints, they lament themselves over things for which they ought to be thankful." He proceeds for a long time in this strain, and speaks even of their being obliged to beg their bread, and to beg it insolently.

Too many clergymen will surely have been re-minded by Chrysostom's details of scenes enacted week by week before their vestry-door. To con-found, up to this period, the " widows " so-called of the Greek Church with those women who en-joyed the "honour of the diaconate," is surely about as correct as to identify the receiver of bread and coal tickets with the lady-visitor who relieves her. But, on the other hand, the true pattern at this period of the apostolical widow, continuing in supplications and prayers day and night, was obviously exhibited by deaconesses such as Olympias or Pentadia. Nothing was more natural than that the laity at least should

confound the two, and should endeavour to impose upon the latter all the restrictions—as to
age for instance—which St Paul laid down for the
former.*

* Another of Chrysostom's reforms was the attempted
suppression of the practice of the spiritual brotherhoods of
the συνείσακτοι, both men and women ; denouncing, on the
one hand, men who took professed virgins to their homes to
live with them as their sisters,—and, on the other hand,
those women under the Church rule who lived with men as
such (see Pallad. Dialog., c. 18, and Montfaucon's Chrysostom, vol. i). This is the proceeding to which Gibbon apparently refers ("Decline and Fall," Bk. xxxii.), when he says
that "Chrysostom had condemned, from the pulpit, the domestic females of the clergy of Constantinople, who, under
the names of servants or sisters, afforded a perpetual occasion
either of sin or of scandal." There appears no colour whatever for the assertion that the women in question bore the
name of servants. The word συνείσακτοι has never been
so interpreted ; and the relation, as described by church
writers, is anything but a servile one on the part of the
women. On the contrary, they make merry with the man as
waiting on the woman, holding the distaff and the spindle.
But the use of the term by Gibbon has led some writers to
suppose that the deaconesses, the servants of the Church,
were the class spoken of. On the contrary, I find nothing
whatever to shew that the abuse in question had yet crept
into their body (though it certainly did at a later period).
They are never mentioned in Chrysostom's two treatises on
the subject, but the term πάρθενοι is used in those treatises
almost generally ; so that I am inclined to think that the
Church-virgins were really the class who, at this period, were
alone liable to the reproach in question.

§ 7. *The Greek Female Diaconate in the Codes and later Councils, till its disappearance.*

From the fifth century downwards, the female diaconate comes no more before us in the same life-like form which we have seen it assume in the days of Chrysostom. Its later history consists mainly of the efforts of the State to subject the institution to the disabilities of actual monachism. The Theodosian Code (438), plainly applying to the deaconesses the Apostle's words respecting widows, fixes at sixty, "according to the precepts of the Apostle," the age of their ordination (Bk. xvi., tit. ii., l. 27). On their entering into the diaconate, if they have children under age, a guardian is to be appointed, the mother retaining, however, the income of her lands, with full power to alienate them for value or otherwise, whether by deed *inter vivos*, or testamentary disposition. But she may not expend for religious purposes any part of her jewels, furniture, gold, silver, or family statues, all of which must be transmitted by her to her children, relations, or such other parties not under disability, as she may think fit. (This prohibition was, however, removed—by Ambrose's influence, Baronius says—scarcely two months later as to alienations *inter vivos*, by the very next law, which speaks of the former one as promulgated concerning " deaconesses or widows;" Bk. xvi., tit. ii., l. 28.) She cannot at her death institute for her heir any church, or any clerical or indigent person. No secret trust will avail for this purpose, whether by letter, codicil, donation, will, or otherwise ; nor will any appeal lie to justice, in case of any violation of the law in this respect, but the parties may at once enter into possession. From this stringent law of mortmain, if we may so call it, it may at once be gathered that the honours of the female diaconate had been already used by the growing spirit of priestcraft, as a means of diverting into the Church's coffers the fortunes of wealthy females.

It is worthy of remark that the above provisions, embodied in the Theodosian Code, are in reality those of a constitution of the Emperors Valentinian, Theodosius, and Arcadius, dated from Milan in the year 390. It is perhaps but reasonable to suppose that they bear the impress rather of Latin confusion respecting the two characters of deaconesses and widows, than of Greek accuracy respecting them. Certain it is that the Church at once protested against the confusion, and that it succeeded, in the long run, in overcoming it, and in fixing the age of admission to the female diaconate according to its own canons. For instance, the fifteenth canon of the Council of Chalcedon, almost contemporary with the promulgation of the Theodosian Code (451), enacts, that " the deaconess shall not be ordained before her 40th year, and this with the utmost deliberation; but if, receiving the imposition of hands, and remaining some time in the ministry, she gives herself over to marriage, doing despite to the grace of God, let her be accursed, together with her paramour." Clearly, since the Council cannot be presumed deliberately to have rescinded an apostolic command contained in a Pastoral Epistle, this fixing the ordination of deaconesses at forty is a proof that they were not deemed yet, by the heads of the Church, to be the widows of St Paul. By the time of Justinian, the State, after endeavouring for a while to split the difference as to the age of ordination of the deaconess, finally gives in, as we shall presently see, at all points to the Church.

In transferring to the new Code the provision of the Theodosian one, as to the age of ordination, the word fifty is substituted for sixty (the " precept of the apostle " being, however, absurdly retained as an authority), and the whole latter portion of the law, restrictive of alienation, is omitted (Bk. i., tit. iii., l. 9). Nor is this all. In a constitution (Bk. i., tit. iii., l. 20), ascribed to Theodosius and Valentinian (A.D. 434)—earlier than the promulgation of the Theodosian Code, and which therefore must be considered as having been tacitly abrogated by the former, but now revived— it is provided, that where a priest, deacon, deaconess, sub-deacon, or clerk of any other rank, monk or woman devoted to a solitary life, shall die intestate and without next of kin, their goods shall go to the Church or monastery to which they were attached. Another constitution includes gifts of yearly rents to monasteries, or to ascetic women, or to deaconesses, &c., amongst those which it was forbidden to compound for (*Ibid.*, l. 46). A later constitution of the year 455, ascribed to the Emperors Valentinian and Marcian, on "the last will of a woman devoted to God" (Bk. i., tit. ii., l. 13), enacts, that if any widow, or deaconess, or virgin devoted to God, or religious woman, or any other female bearing any name of religious honour or dignity, shall have made any bequest, by will otherwise executed in due form, of the whole or any part of her fortune to any church, shrine, clerk, monk, or to the poor, such bequest shall be valid. The clear distinction here exhibited between virgins, widows, and deaconesses, appears equally in a much later constitution of Justinian himself, A.D. 533 (Bk. i., tit. iii., l. 54), as to the capital punishment of heinous offences against the honour of "virgins, widows, or deaconesses, devoted to God." It is provided that where the offence is committed against a virgin living in a house of exercise or "ascetery," or in a convent, whether she shall have been constituted deaconess or not, the property of the culprit is to pass to the convent or ascetery where she shall have been consecrated, on the terms of giving her sufficient maintenance during her life.   But if the victim be deaconess of any church, but so constituted neither in a convent nor ascetery, and living alone, the offender's substance is to go to the church of which she is a deaconess, she, however, retaining the usufruct during her life.

The second edition of Justinian's Code was published, and the whole confirmed, in the year 534.   In the following year (535), by the Third of the " Novels" (or laws passed subsequently to the enactment of the Code), which has for object the limiting the number of the clergy of the metropolitan church, and of the other churches of Constantinople, in order to release the churches from the burden of debt which they had incurred by too large an increase of their clerical staff, the number of deaconesses in the church of St Sophia is fixed at 80, to 100 male deacons; whilst as respects the other churches, the then present number of priests, male and female deacons, subdeacons, &c., was not to be exceeded (cc. 1, 3). The Sixth Novel (same year), on the ordination of

bishops and other clerks, and on the expenses of
the churches, has a chapter specially devoted to
the ordination of deaconesses, not under fifty years
of age (c. 6).   They are to be neither young nor
in the prime of life, nor of an age of itself prone
to sin, but beyond the middle time of life ; either
widows of one husband or professed virgins ; of a
life not only well-famed, but not even suspected.
If any should of necessity be ordained before the
prescribed age, she is to remain in some ascetery.
The deaconess is to live either alone, or only with
her parents and her children, or her brothers, or
otherwise with such persons as to whom any suspicion of scandal would appear of itself silly and im-
pious, but not with any other relative, or any of
those persons who are called " beloved."   On her
ordination she is to be admonished, and to hear the
holy precepts in presence of the other deaconesses
already in functions.   If she leave the ministry to
enter into marriage, or choose any other mode of
life, she is subject to the penalty of death, and her
property is to be applied to the use of the church,
or convent, in which she is ; the same penalties
being incurred by her husband or seducer, with
the exception that his property is to be confis-
cated for the benefit of the State.

The 123d Novel exhibits the final surrender by the
State of the point still at issue between it and the

Church as to the age of the deaconess's ordination. Whilst the age of ordination is fixed for priests at thirty, for deacons or sub-deacons at twenty-five, and for readers at eighteen, " a deaconess is not to be ordained in the holy church below forty years of age, or who shall have been married a second time" (c. 13). In other chapters of this Novel, deaconesses are included in the provisions for giving the jurisdiction to the bishop in case of legal proceedings against clerical or (as our ancestors would have called them) religious persons, and for limiting the amount of fees payable by such persons in the above case (cc. 21, 28). A special chapter " on the deaconesses " (30) renews the prohibition of a former law against their living with any man, from whose company any suspicion of impropriety may arise.* On the admonition of the priest who is over her, the deaconess is to expel any such man from her house, otherwise to be deprived of her ecclesiastical functions, and of her emoluments, and to spend the remainder of her days in a convent. If she has children, her for-

---

* Whilst this chapter, and the 6th of the 6th Novel, before referred to, shew that the deaconesses were liable to the dangers of spiritual brotherhoods, the immediately preceding one (29) of the 123d Novel, "*Ne clerici mulieres subintroductas in propriis domibus habeant, episcopi vero nullas,*" affords additional proof that the two classes of women were generically distinct, though both characters might meet in one.

tune is to be divided between her and them *per capita*, and the convent is to receive her share, on the terms of maintaining and looking after her; but if she have no children, all her property is to be divided equally between the convent to which she is sent, and the church in which she formerly held office.

Another chapter (37) exhibits a remarkable instance of the way in which the ascetic spirit was overriding the old civil law. It provides, that where property shall have been left to a man or a woman on condition of marriage, and such person shall enter a monastery, or join the clergy, if a man, or if a woman, become a deaconess, or an ascete, the condition is to be void, and the clergymen or deaconesses of the Church are to enjoy the property, on condition of spending or leaving it to pious uses. Another chapter (43) somewhat increases the stringency of a previous law as to infractions of chastity by or against deaconesses or other consecrated women.

At this period, therefore (first half of the sixth century), the office of deaconess in the Eastern Church has become purely sacerdotal, forming a sort of connecting link between the secular and the regular clergy. The honour of the office has not departed. There is not, even at this late period of which we are treating, the smallest trace in the authorities of a generic difference between the ordination of the deaconess and that of the other members of the clergy, the word ordination (see for instance Nov. 6) being strictly rendered in the Greek version by the technical one of χειροθεσία, laying on of hands. The same terms of "most reverend" and "venerable" are applied to deaconesses, as to the bishops and other clergy (see Novs. 3, 6); the rules respecting them are comprised in the same ordinances of the civil power (Cod., Bk. i., tits. 2, 3 ; Novs. 3, 6), and their rank clearly fixed on a par with that of the deacons, and before the sub-deacons and other inferior clergy (Nov. 3); and they are the only class of females who are thus ranked in the clergy, the virgins, widows, nuns, being clearly not included with them in this respect, although assimilated to them in others. Their functions, as far as they are spoken of, are those of "coming to the holy ministry, ministering to the adorable ceremonies of baptism, and assisting at the other mysteries, which are lawfully celebrated by them in the venerable ministrations" of the Church (Nov. 6). On the other hand, the deaconess is included, in the heading of one law (Nov. 123, c. 43), under a name (*sanctimonialis*) which in later days is synonymous with "nun." So nearly does her condition approach to that of actual monachism, that the punishment, as we have seen, for the marriage of a deaconess is death against both parties, the legislator not being ashamed to quote as an authority the Pagan one of the Vestal Virgins,—though indeed the repeated provisions on this head seem to shew that there was considerable difficulty in enforcing these ascetic rules on the deaconesses.   There are now, moreover (see Cod., Bk. ii., tit. iii., c. 54), two classes of deaconesses, those residing in convents or in asceteries (the "skeets" of contemporary Russia), and those attached to churches, and living alone.   The former must obviously have become almost identified with the nuns among whom they lived ; the latter alone could have answered in somewise still to the old Church deaconess, "servant" of the Church.

From this period I am aware of but two or three scattered notices as to the female diaconate in the East.   The Synod of Constantinople in Trullo, 691-2, again enacts (Can. 40) that forty shall be the age for ordaining deaconesses, as twenty-five shall be that for ordaining deacons.   It still keeps up, in the clearest manner, the distinction between the deaconess and the widow, between the ordination of the one and the selection of the other.   After referring to St Basil's canon as to virgins, whose example, the fathers say, they have followed "as to widows and deaconesses," they proceed : " For it is written in the divine apostle, that a widow is to be chosen in the church at sixty years of age ; but the holy canons have decreed that a deaconess is to be ordained at forty years." The "Limon," or "Spiritual Meadow" of John Moschus, (end of seventh century), as quoted by Cotelerius, alludes to the deaconess's office in reference to female baptism. The monk Theophylact, of Gaza, who flourished toward 1070, mentions the existence of an interpretation of Titus ii. 3, which would apply it to the women-deacons, but holds himself to the simpler meaning of " aged women." *Balsamon, patriarch of Antioch, writing towards the end of the twelfth century, as quoted by Suicer, treats the office as nearly extinct. No deaconesses, he says, are now ordained, though some of the " ascetes " may be improperly so termed. And the way in which he speaks of them shews that the institution had become lost and stifled in female monachism. " As virgins," he writes, " they were received by the Church, and guarded according to the command of the bishop, as consecrated to God, except that they wore the garb of the laity, . . . and at

---

* Michael Attaliotes, Theophylact's contemporary, mentions, just before Nicephorus Botoniates' advent to the throne, the monstrous birth, at Constantinople, of a one-eyed, goat-footed infant, which was exposed "in the public porch of the Deaconesses," and cried (poor thing!) "like a child." —See his history, in Corpus Script. Histor. Byzant.

forty years old they received ordination as deaconesses, being found qualified in all respects." Matthew Blastar, a Basilian monk, who in 1335 completed an alphabetical collection of constitutions
relating to the Church, writes finally as follows:
"What ministry the women-deacons then fulfilled
in the Church, scarcely any one now knows; except that some say that they ministered in the
baptizing of women" (quoted in note to Cotelerius,
vol. ii., p. 290).   The same Matthew Blastar appears, however, to have preserved to us (I quote
from Moreri) the ceremonies used in the deaconess's ordination.   It was the same as that of the
deacon.   She was presented to the bishop in front
of the sanctuary, her neck and shoulders covered
with a small cloak called "Marforium."   After a
prayer, beginning with the words, "The grace of
God," she bent her head without bowing her
knees, and the bishop then laid his hands on her,
pronouncing the accustomed prayer.   Among the
Jacobites, however, the institution seems to have
lingered till a still later period.*   In modern Greek

* Augusti Derkwürdigkeiten — a not very trustworthy
authority. (See, however, now the preface to Dr Howson's
"Deaconesses," quoting Assemani, from whom it would appear that Jacobite deaconesses existed till the sixteenth century,—*i.e.*, till almost the period when, as will be seen hereafter, the institution was restored for a time by the Protestant
Churches of the Low Countries.)

parlance, I believe, the διακόνισσα is simply the deacon's wife.

§ 8. *Latest Notices of the Female Diaconate in the Western Church.*

If we turn now back from the Eastern to the Western Church, we cannot fail to be struck by the almost total absence of all mention of the female diaconate as a living institution, still more of individual deaconesses, in the writings of the Latin fathers. The passage of Origen before referred to, speaking of the ministry of women in the church as necessary, has indeed come down to us only in a Latin translation by Rufinus (fourth century), without a word of comment to modify its authority. But in the great Latin fathers of the fourth and fifth centuries—Ambrose, 340-397 ; Jerome, 340-420 ; Augustin, 354-436—the contemporaries of Basil, Epiphanius, Chrysostom, scarcely a word is to be found on the subject. That the existence of the institution in the East at least was familiar to them, we can have no doubt. Thus, Epiphanius, in a letter to be found amongst those of Jerome (60), and extant, I believe, only in the Latin translation there given, writes to the latter (probably as a " skit " against Chrysostom and his devoted deaconess friends) : " Never have

I ordained deaconesses, or sent them to other provinces, nor done aught to divide the Church." These fathers, at least, indicate no confusion between the deaconess and the widows. Jerome (see Letters 79, 123, &c.) treats frequently of widows, without ever referring to any diaconal function as exercised by them ; nay, with indications quite as clear as those of Chrysostom himself, of the position occupied by the widows of the Church, as objects of charity merely (Letter 123 ; Bk. 2, adv. Jovin., c. 14). " The widows spoken of by St Paul," he says, " are those who are destitute of all help from their own kindred, who are incapable of labouring with their hands, weakened with poverty, broken with age ; who have God for their hope, and whose whole business is prayer."

But the confusion above spoken of breaks out in a work, of the exact date of which I am not aware, but which I should suppose to be of the fifth, or at latest of the sixth century, the commentary on the Pauline epistles falsely ascribed to Jerome. The author (who is considered to have been a Pelagian heretic) plainly admits the existence of a contemporary female diaconate in the East, whilst by implication treating it as obsolete in the West. " As even now," he notes in reference to Rom. xvi. 1, " in the East women called deaconesses appear to minister in baptism, or in the ministry of the word, since we find women to have taught privately, as Priscilla." Again upon 1 Tim. iii., 11, which he understands correctly of the female deacons : " He orders them to be chosen as the (male) deacons. Whence we may understand that he says it of those whom even now in the East they call deaconesses." But he applies 1 Tim. c. v. expressly to the selection of deaconesses (" *eligi diaconissas—ministerio diaconatûs*").

But a curious feature now presents itself on the outskirts of the Latin church. The female diaconate, confounded with Church widowship, suddenly makes its appearance under its own name in the decrees of Gaulish Councils of the fifth and sixth centuries, but invariably to be denounced and prohibited. The Synod of Orange, 441, exhibits the first outbreak of Western aversion to the office, by absolutely forbidding (can. 26) the ordination of deaconesses (*diaconissæ omnimodis non ordinandæ.*) The Synod of Epaône, 517, interdicts wholly (can. 21) within its jurisdiction the consecration of " widows who are called deaconesses" (*viduarum . . . quas diaconas vocitant*); if they wish to be converted, they are only to receive the penitential blessing. The Synod of Orleans, 533, enacts the excommunication of " any woman, who, having received hitherto the blessing of the diaconate against the interdicts of the canons, shall have married again" (can. 17); a text, indeed, which shews that, in spite of previous prohibitions, the practice of ordaining deaconesses still existed.

The explanation of this prominence in Gaul of the female diaconate in the fifth century I take to be this: Southern Gaul was always one of the great battle-fields between Eastern and Western feelings. Massilia-Marseilles was an old Greek colony; the relations between "the Province" and Greece, intimate in the days of Cæsar, were intimate still in the early days of the Christian Church; Irenæus, one of the earliest Greek fathers, was Bishop of Lyons in the second century. New relations were opened between the two countries in the fifth century, through the settlement in Provence of the Basilian monks, and the foundation of the great monasteries of Southern Gaul (St Faustin, founded 422). Now the fifth century, as we have seen, was, in point of honour, the golden age of the female diaconate in the Eastern Church; and it would be almost unaccountable if, amidst the new tide of Greek influence brought in at this period into Southern Gaul, the female diaconate, in its then half-monastic state, should not have been sought to be revived or re-introduced.

At any rate, it is about this period, and even later than the last interdiction of the female diaconate (544), that we meet with the most interesting incident connected with it to be found in the annals of the Western Church. It occurs in the story of St Radegund, a Thuringian princess, wife of the Merovingian Chlothar I. of Neustria, forming the fifth narrative * in that most delightful of histories, most truthful of tale-books, Augustin Thierry's " Narratives of Merovingian Times." After a long period of domestic wretchedness by the side of a brutal husband, and after seeing at last her only surviving brother, a hostage at Chlothar's court, put to death by his orders, the queen fled to St Médard, bishop of Noyon.† As he was in his church officiating at the altar, " ' Most holy priest,' she cried, ' I must leave the world, and change my garments ; I entreat thee, most holy priest, do thou consecrate me to the Lord.' The bishop hesitated. He was called upon to dissolve a royal marriage, contracted according to the Salic law, and in conformity with Germanic customs, which the Church, while detesting them, was yet constrained to tolerate. . . The Frankish lords and warriors who had followed the queen began to surround them, and to cry aloud, with threatening gestures, ' Beware how thou givest the veil to a woman who is married to the king ! priest,

* Drawn from Venantius Fortunatus.
† The St Swithin of France, as respects rain-giving.

refrain from robbing the prince of his solemnly-wedded queen!' The most furious among them, throwing hands upon him, dragged him violently from the altar-steps into the nave of the church, whilst the queen, affrighted with the tumult, was seeking with her women a refuge in the vestry. But here, collecting herself, . . she threw a nun's dress over her regal garments, and thus disguised, proceeded towards the sanctuary where St Médard was sitting. . . . 'If thou shouldst delay consecrating me,' said she with a firm voice, 'and shouldst fear men more than God, thou wilt have to render thy account, and the Shepherd shall require of thee the soul of His sheep.' . . . He ceased to hesitate, and of his own authority dissolved Radegund's marriage, by consecrating her a deacon through the laying on of hands (*manu superposita consecravit diaconam*). The Frankish lords and vassals, carried away in their turn by the same feelings, durst no more take forcibly back to the royal residence one who in their eyes bore from henceforth the twofold character of a queen and of a woman consecrated to God's service." She subsequently formed, as we shall see hereafter, a sort of free convent, where the pleasures of literary society, even with men, were combined with devotional exercises and good works. The above narrative points us to a startling fact, which has no parallel in Eastern annals, that ordination to the female diaconate in the West was by this time considered equivalent to divorce.

In spite of all prohibitions, indeed, the idea of a female diaconate seems to have lingered nearly as long, within a century or two, in the West as in the East. According to Moreri (Art. " Diaco-nisse"), the institution subsisted longer in Spain than in Gaul. There seems, indeed, amidst the confusions produced by the barbaric invasions, to have grown up beside it the utterly uncanonical institution of female presbyters. Thus we find, in the canons of the Council or Synod of Rome (720 or 721), anathemas pronounced against who-soever should marry a female presbyter (*presby-teram*), deaconess (*diaconam*), or " nun whom we call servant of God" (*monacham quam Dei an-cillam vocamus*),—the last expression seeming to in-dicate that the true diaconal functions had by this time passed away from the deaconess, still invested with an honorific office, into the hands of a certain class of nuns. Again, the canons of the Council of Worms, in the ninth century, repeat an earlier canon against the re-marriage of deaconesses. In the Roman Ordinal, sent to Charlemagne by Adrian I. (772–795), and other rituals in use about the ninth century, will be found, it is said,

a service for the ordination of a deaconess.   This
is especially to be remarked, as otherwise, in some
of the latest mentions of deaconesses, the word
might be taken to be used, as Bingham shews it
to have been by one Gaulish Council, in the
modern Greek sense of wife of a deacon.

The Augustinian monk, Christian Wolf, who,
under the name of Lupus, published a Latin collection of the decrees of councils, refers to the
Life of Leo III., by Anastasius, as shewing that
there were still deaconesses at Rome under that
Pope (795–816).   Even in the tenth century they
seem to have subsisted in Southern Italy, probably
under Greek influence, since this part of Italy was
the one that remained longest subject to the By-
zantine emperors.   Baronius, under the year 991,
but treating of an earlier period in the same century, tells, from Leo Ostiarius, a story of a reproof
addressed by St Nilus to "a certain deaconess,
the head of a monastery" (of women), who came
to meet him with "her priest," a lusty young
cousin of hers, in the flower of his age, and the
convent virgins.   "What!" exclaimed the saint,
"are ye ignorant that this is a man? and is he
ignorant that ye are women?"   The very next day,
says the legend, the scandalous relations in which
the deaconess and the priest were living were dis-
covered.

We may perhaps conclude from this tale—which indeed fitly winds up the history—that the extinction of the office in the West must have nearly coincided with that great victory of the Romish system in the eleventh century, when God's order of the family was finally expelled from the ministry of His Church (Gregory VII., 1073–1085). Still, Richard, in his "Analyse des Conciles" (vol. iii. p. 627, Art. "Diaconesses"), writing a few years before the outbreak of the great French Revolution, notices some vestiges of the office then yet subsisting, according to him, in France; and in Milan also similar traces of it were, at an earlier period indeed, thought by Moreri to have survived. I must say, however, that the facts these authors mention, however curious, hardly seem to connect themselves with any orthodox tradition as to the functions of the deaconess.*

* The chief authorities with respect to the deaconesses of the early Church will be found collected in Bingham's Antiquities, Bk. ii., c. xxii. ; Suicer, Thesaurus, Art. Διακόνισσα et ἡ Διάκονος ; Christian Lupus, Councils, vol. ii. ; Richard, Analyse des Conciles ; Cabassutius, Notitia de Conciliis S. Eccles. (a work to which I have not had access) ; and in the Second Letter on "Sisters of Charity," in the *Educational Magazine* for 1841. They are also summed up in the Third Report of the Deaconesses' Institute of Echallens, and in the "Appeal" on behalf of the deaconesses of Paris,—in the latter with various misprints in the references. The confusion between deaconesses and widows appears, however, to pervade them all. Lastly, Dr Howson'

§ 9. *Conclusion: Lessons of the Historical Female Diaconate.*

There is surely a lesson for us in this history. Of what the female diaconate did, we know little. But knowing so little, it is sufficiently wonderful that we should find traces of its existence, both in the East and West, for from nine to twelve centuries—about two-thirds, in fact, of the Christian era. This strange obscure persistency indicates, either that it did far more work than is recorded of it, and lived thereby, or that its title to existence was in itself so unquestionable that even its own impotency barely sufficed to extinguish it.

Why did it perish? Evidently through the growth in the Church of the false ascetic principle, and in particular of the practice of religious celibacy,—to which, according to its original constitution, it must have been a serious obstacle,—by which it suffered itself to be overlaid. The scope of the female diaconate in the primitive Church was, as we have seen, to afford a full development to female energies for religious purposes; to asso-

work, referred to in my Preface, travels over much the same ground as mine. I have a strong impression that the subject is not exhausted, and that a closer investigation of Church-records and Church-literature, during the six first centuries at least, would add much to our knowledge, and clear many of our doubts.

ciate women, as far as possible, in rank and practice with men, while preserving to each sex its distinct sphere of activity; to the one the supremacy of the head, to the other that of the heart; to the one power, to the other influence; to the one the office of public preaching, exhortation, relief, to the other that of private exhortation, consolation, helpfulness; yet each acting under the inspiration of that Holy Spirit who was invoked alike over the head of deacon and deaconess at their ordination. True in this was the Church to the laws of man's being, as displayed progressively throughout Holy Scripture, from Genesis to Revelation. By a pre-ordained and eternal marriage, man and woman must be one, in order to fulfil the great destinies of humanity.* Genesis shews us how it is not good for man to be alone, how woman is made a helpmeet for him. The New Testament discovers to us the deep spiritual ground of this relation, by shewing us Christ as the Holy Bridegroom of His hallowed Bride the Church. History confirms the lesson from age to age, from country to country, by shewing how, if you deprive either sex of its free action, of its free influence

* The German language, in its greater richness, allows us to express this through its very forms. It is man and woman (*Mann und Weib*) that make up the complete human being (*das Mensch*).

over the other, the result is national sterility; the man a savage, the woman a fool.   Restore Eastern women to their rights, and the whole Eastern world will rise up new-born.

Now, there is one most subtle way of sterilising that eternal wedding. It is, without wholly debasing either sex in the other's eyes, to teach them to live apart, think apart, love apart, for the greater glory of God and of themselves—as if they were different species of one genus, the union of which could produce nothing but hybrids. Where thus marriage assumes in the eyes of the candidate for superhuman sanctity the shape of a fleshly pollution,—where woman ceases to be man's earthly helpmeet,—where, in violation of God's first ordinance, it has become good for man to live alone, —the familiar mingling of the sexes in the active ministrations of religion, unfettered and untrammelled, is impossible. The deaconess should be free as the deacon himself to leave her home at any time for those ministrations; she should be in constant communication with her brethren of the clergy. But place her under a vow of celibacy, she dare no longer forget herself in the abundance of her zeal; her seeming self-sacrifice is really an enthronement of self; her piety has a personal object, most contrary to active charity; every fellow-man becomes to her a tempter whom she must flee from; an enemy when near,—if a brother at all, a brother only when afar off,—to be loved, when present, only when most unlovely or least lawful to be loved, in age or loathsome sickness, or when morally cut off from her by a like vow with her own; by special permission, under jealous restrictions, beneath the Damoclean sword of tremendous penalties; but, above all, to be loved when absent, impersonally, in the abstract, with that vague humanitarian love so characteristic at once of effete piety and effete irreligion. Hence the high walls of the nunnery, in which eventually we find the deaconess confined; hence the vanishing away of her office itself into monachism.*

The further working of this falsehood we shall presently see. In the meanwhile, let us not overlook the wide difference existing between the Deaconesses' Institute of our days and what is recorded of the early female diaconate. That was essentially individual; and the only analogy to it lies in the "parish-deaconess," who goes forth from Kaiserswerth, or elsewhere, to devote herself to a particular congregation; although even she is far

---

* The monk Wolf (an honest and painstaking writer) thus naïvely accounts for the extinction of the female diaconate: "For the deaconess led an active life, of which it is certain that women are incapable" (*Cujus constat fœminas non esse capaces*).

from holding that position as a member of the clergy (*cleros*) which is assigned to her by the records of Church history.

In the gap between the two lies the "sisterhood" of later times. Let us now see how this grew up.

CHAPTER II.

§ 1. Church Virginship, and the Doctrine of the Spiritual Marriage of the Individual with Christ.

IN endeavouring to sketch out the somewhat dim history of the female diaconate in the early Church, I have shewn that it fell through the introduction of a principle inconsistent with its freedom and individuality, that of religious celibacy. Let us not attribute the introduction of that principle to the Church of Rome as such. It was in the institution of the Church-virgins that it took its rise.

Now it is indeed clear, as Bingham observes, and as a passage from Cyprian especially shews,* that long after the idea of professed virginity had

* Ep. lxii. ad Pompon. de Virg.

rooted itself in men's minds, yet the marriage of a
Church-virgin, with whatever disfavour it might be
looked upon, was yet valid in itself.   And it was
the State, and not the Church, which, if I mistake
not, first gave the example of the severe measures
against the marriage of professed virgins, which became afterwards the law of Romish monachism.

Nevertheless, I am bound to say that the institution of Church-virginship appears to me to have
borne, in what many would call the early Church,—
in the fourth and fifth centuries for example,—quite
as false a character as the later one of Romish
female monachism, without even producing those
fruits which the adoption into the latter of the principle of sisterhoods afterwards realised.   Everywhere the exceptional condition of the virgin is
made a character of special excellence; everywhere
the false centre of human self-will is set up by the
early Fathers, unconsciously to themselves, whilst
recommending an act of peculiar self-renounce-
ment.   They carefully disclaim speaking in dispar-
agement of marriage; frequently warn the virgin
not to boast herself against the wife; yet at the
same time they openly tell her how much holier is
her condition, urge her vehemently to persevere in
it, reprove her passionately if she decline from it,
declare virginity to be the choicest ornament, the
chief glory of the Church.   Athanasius for instance,

—the great Protestant saint, as he has been called, —in his Apology to the Emperor Constance, says of the virgins : "Whom therefore, when the Greeks see, they marvel at them, as being the temple of the Lord. For with no one truly is this reverend and heavenly doctrine practised, save with us Christians only. For this above all is a great sign, that with us is real and true piety." When, indeed, the subject falls into the hands of rough fanatics like Jerome, or coarse declaimers like Tertullian, their foul utterances in urging to peculiar sanctity are, I suppose, hardly to be exceeded in the pages of Peter Dens.

Now what was the pivot of these exhortations? A doctrine, as I verily believe, only second, in unscriptural falsehood, in social danger, to Mariolatry itself,—that of the marriage of the individual soul with Christ. The New Testament knows but of one Bride, the Church,—of but one marriage to the Bridegroom, the wedding of the Lamb,*— in respect of which every individual member of the Church, considered apart from the body to which he belongs, is but one of those "friends of

---

* I say this, not forgetting Rom. vii. 4, where the breadth of the original, "that ye should *belong* to another" (γίνεσθαι ἑτέρῳ) has been narrowed by our translators into "that ye should be married to another." See further on this point, Appendix C.

the Bridegroom" (John iii. 29),—those "children of the bridechamber" (Matt. ix. 15 ; Luke v. 34), who stand by, and hear, and rejoice to hear the Bridegroom's voice,—who have a right, with St Paul, to be jealous over the Bride "with a godly jealousy," knowing that she is espoused as a chaste virgin to Christ (2 Cor. xi. 2); or, in a lower type, one of those guests of the wedding (Matt. xxii.), gathered in from highways and by-ways, and who may be cast out for want of a wedding garment; one of those virgins (Matt. xxv.), wise or foolish, who have to wait the Bridegroom's coming. When once we feel that Christ belongs really to His Church, and to His Church only, we feel also as a usurpation, as a robbery, no less than as an impossible absurdity, the craving to have Him each for ourself alone. Can we fancy a living head, joined to an arm or a leg only? Or do we think that the highest type of bodily form is that of a star-fish, with every limb branching out from that miserable remnant of what is a head in higher creatures, a something made up of mouth and belly? But if we feel that we are really members of one another,—that it is through the Church and in the Church that we are joined unto Christ,—we shall feel also that there is no real remoteness from Him in that union,—nay, that we are far more truly His, and can fulfil His will far more perfectly by means of it, than by any individual and exclusive bond. If we look at this body of ours, the fearfully and wonderfully made, which our Lord and His apostles have consecrated as the earthly type of His Church, we shall see that the most distant joints are as really united to the head as the nearest, fulfil its behests as instantaneously—nay, are chosen as the special instruments of its will in touch and motion, far above those nearest; while all work together, none hindering, all helping one another. We have but to will it, and our finger moves without our being aware, in the slightest degree (whilst the body is healthy), of the transmission of the tide-wave of nervous energy from the brain to the extremity of the hand; so perfect is the harmony of that marvellous fellowship. But let disease once invade that fellowship, and then may indeed begin the day of individual action for the members, of individual union with the head. The finger may move at the head's bidding, and so inflict agony on the whole inflamed arm, or flash back a pang to the fevered head itself; one finger may move alone, and all its fellows drop powerless. Even so, I believe, is it with the Church, when its members are seeking individual fellowship only with its Head,—when the virgins waiting for the Bridegroom wait for their own sakes, and dream each of taking her place as bride at the marriage-

F

feast,—when by one little subtle change of a single word in a blessed utterance of deepest truth, it is no longer " the Spirit and the Bride," but " the Spirit and the Bridegroom," who say—Come ! The individual members may yet move in glad obedience to the Head ; this faithful soul or that may yet present a pattern of Christian piety and love ; but hundreds will wither around in palsy ; the holiness of the one will be the agony of the many.

This idolatrous worship of Christ as an individual Bridegroom, as it is more subtle and abiding than Mariolatry itself, so it is also more ancient. Indeed I look upon Mariolatry as having been rather its outgrowth and necessary complement than anything else. For, after all, the idea of the marriage of the individual with Christ is one which the ineradicable instincts of sex will prevent from ever being popular with men ; which, when taken in by them, will be found in general to stamp their character with a strange effeminacy ; which adapts itself especially to the nature of women. When once the feeling had crept in, that earthly marriage was not a sufficient emblem of the Lamb's wedding, that there was to be a spiritual marriage apart from it, the worship of a glorified female nature became for men a natural counterpart to the worship of a glorified male nature by women ;

perhaps a refuge from something unhealthier, un-holier even than itself.

Now we cannot open those pages of the Fathers which treat of virginity, without finding them insisting above all on the consideration, that the virgin is the spouse of Christ.* How attractively was this view presented, to youthful and enthusiastic minds, by writers like Chrysostom! Who can read without a momentary fascination passages like the following, taken from his description of one who is "a virgin indeed"—"For when she walks, it is as through a wilderness; if she sits in the church, it is in the deepest silence; her eye sees none of those present, women nor men, but the Bridegroom only, as present and appearing. When she enters again her home, she has conversed with Him in her prayers, she has heard His voice alone through the Scriptures. And when she is in her house, let her think on the longed-for One alone, let her be a stranger, a sojourner, a wayfarer, let her do all as becometh one strange to all things here below"?†

The first falsehood had been told, on which a whole edifice of falsehood was to be built up. The vow of virginity came thus to be considered

* See, for instance, Basil, Epist. cxcix., can. 2; Cypr., Epist. lxii. ad Pomp., &c., &c.

† Montf. Chrys. "Quod regulares fœminæ viris cohabitare non debeant," c. 7.

as answering precisely to the vow of marriage; espousing the woman to Christ, as to a spiritual husband; bearing the same consequences, to be guarded by the same penalties, as the human marriage-tie. A remarkable passage of St Basil* shews that it was with the female sex that this practice of vowing perpetual celibacy took its origin: "She is called a virgin," he says, "who hath willingly offered herself to the Lord, and renounced marriage, and preferred a life of sanctification. . . . One who is above sixteen or seventeen years old, being mistress of her thoughts, when she shall have been examined, and found steadfast, and shall have besought for admission with supplications, is then to be inscribed on the list of virgins, and her profession is to be held good." And after blaming the bringing of young girls to make profession by parents, brothers, and relatives, before the required age, and against their will, he goes on to say: "As to professions by men, we know nothing of them, except that if any have joined themselves to the monastic order, they appear, without word spoken, to have thereby adopted celibacy." †　It is certain, however, that long after Basil's time a monk's marriage was held valid.

* 2d Canon. Epist., can. 18.
† Ibid., can. 19.

§ 2. *Early Female Monachism as Compared with Church Virginship.*

Female monachism, therefore, not only must not be confounded with the institution of the Church-virgins, but was rather a reaction against it. The "perpetual virgins" almost lose themselves in antiquity; female monachism is not by its eulogists traced further back than Syncletica, contemporary with the Egyptian hermits of the third or fourth century, if not indeed herself an allegorical personage.* Whilst the Church-virgin belonged to a particular congregation, and was dependent upon the Church for support, monks on the contrary (I am speaking of both sexes) belonged to no particular church. They were essentially dwellers in the wilderness, men or women who fled wholly from the world to solitude; as is shewn in the saying of one of the early hermits, that " the wilderness was as natural to a monk, as water to a fish." Thus, even when recognised as a part of the Church system, monachism lay at first as it were only on its outskirts; and in the complete renouncement of the world which it embodied, celibacy, as the passage from St Basil shews, was a mere detail, implied rather than expressed in the embracing of the monastic life.

* See Baillet, Vies des Saints, vol. ii., 5th January.

Hence, in the enumeration of the different kinds of vows by St Augustin, the absence of all connexion between the vow of virginity, and the vow " to leave all one's goods for distribution to the poor, and to go into community of life, into the society of saints," by which clearly the monastic life is meant.*

I must say of *early* monachism, that whatever may have been its extravagancies, there was nevertheless throughout it a spirit of most real, unmistakable Christian piety, more alien than can be conceived, before it is examined, from the unhealthy sentimentalism, the calculating and often dishonest policy of later Romish times.   I believe that in monachism, more than anywhere else, the Church found the thews that threw the world of Northern barbarism.   The wild self-sacrificing energy, the dare - man, dare - brute, dare - devil strength of an Anthony or a Syncletica, going forth to live alone amidst the tombs,—not to consort with evil spirits and obscene creatures, like the possessed of old, but to baffle and subdue them, and make a mock of them through the cross of Christ,—was surely just the kind of religious heroism which would act most powerfully on those rude Northern minds, by the exhibition of a divine Berserk fury, as it would seem to some of them, in-

* Aug , Enarr. in Ps. lxxv. c. 26.

finitely nobler than their own. And I have no doubt that this influence very soon made itself felt. Chrysostom is contemporary with the great Gothic conqueror Alaric : the one sacks Rome ; the other is found writing a religious letter (ccvii.) to certain " Gothic monks."

But early monachism—the monachism of the wilderness and of the tombs—was above all the monachism of men ; and you will find a dozen Pauls, and Anthonys, and Pambos, for one Syncletica. Monachism was no eleemosynary institution at this time. The thousand monks of Serapion used to go out reaping in harvest-time for hire, and, after storing up enough for themselves out of the wheat which they received for pay, to give the rest freely to other monks who might be in need of it.* Women could not, in any number, face such labours, such a life. But whilst female monachism is at first completely overshadowed by male, we can discern in it already that ministering character which is its redeeming feature in all ages, whenever it can be brought out ; the need of manual labour being, nevertheless, as fully recognised for the nun as for the monk. I have already said that in the African Church the " sanctimonial virgin"—*i.e.*, nun—is found towards the close of the fourth century fulfilling many of

* Soz., bk. vi. c. xxviii.

the functions of the deaconess. Jerome, in one of
his letters (108) to Eustochium,—a poor girl who
figures frequently in his correspondence, and is the
object of some of his most notable outpourings of
holy filth,—speaks of a convent founded by Paula,
her mother, which was divided into three bodies,
each with a "mother" at the head, though all
wore one dress, and in which the inmates worked
to make clothes for themselves or others. Chrysostom* speaks of the young girls, not yet twenty
years of age, and richly brought up, who had taken
to a monastic life; how they worked far harder
than maid-servants, receiving the sick to be
tended, carrying beds, washing others' feet, and
even cooking. Augustin, in his book "On the
Manners of the Church" (bk. i., c. 68), says of
the "sanctimonial" women ("nuns" we may indeed call them already, since the word "nonna"
occurs in Jerome), that they "exercise and maintain the body by cloth-weaving, and hand over the
garments themselves to the brethren, receiving in
turn from them their necessary maintenance."
This passage points, I may observe, to a practice
of which traces occur again and again, and which
bears involuntary homage to the true relation between the sexes,—though carrying with it the most
awful temptations,—the establishment of monas-

* Chrys. in Epist. ad Eph., c. iv., hom. xiii.

teries for women in close proximity to, and connexion with, monasteries for men. Again, he says
of the monastic communities : " Many widows and
maidens, dwelling together, and seeking a living
by the weaving of wool and thread, have at their
head the most reverend and well-approved among
them ; women able and ready, not only to form
and regulate the conduct of others, but also to
instruct their minds " (c. 70). Lastly, in his celebrated letter to the nuns (*ad sanctimoniales*),—the
most abundant source of information as to the
condition of early female monachism,—the necessity of manual labour is incidentally pointed out
in the words that "in the monastery, as far as
possible, the rich become laborious." His chief injunctions are, however, to concord, the renouncement of private property, and submission to the
apportionment of food and clothing by the superior (*præposita*), who seems to have had a presbyter over her, like the director of a Romish convent.*

Thus, whilst one at least of the Fathers (Basil,
in his book on Virginity) would exclude the
younger virgins from all services of active charity,

---

* The term *præposita* occurs in the story of the tenth century quoted from Baronius, as applied to the deaconess, the
head of a nunnery, who forgot herself with her (*suo*) presbyter. Both names and organisation appear thus to have remained the same since Augustin's time.

for fear of the temptations of the flesh,—female monachism was at first active, self-devoted. It had, moreover, a further superiority over Church-virginship, in its social character. Not that this can have been wholly absent from the latter. The celibate girls attached to particular churches, and maintained in a special building, would scarcely fail to become, in some way or other, a community, — forming, in fact, the often-spoken-of "choir of the perpetual virgins." Those who were not so attached or maintained would find spiritual help, and material comfort and economy, in living together, and are indeed expressly recommended to do so by a religious writer of the time.* Female monachism, however, was social from the beginning. Syncletica, the earliest female hermit, was followed into the desert by other women, who sought to strengthen themselves by her counsel and example. So surely, under God's good providence, does brotherhood hunt out monachism into its wildest dens, and correct by social influences some at least of its evils and excesses! For strange it is, but true, that whilst by its title (*monachus, monacha*, solitary) monachism seems the breaking-up of the social principle, no set of men or women in the world have ever been so contagiously gre-

---

* The author of the treatise on Virginity, ascribed to Athanasius.

garious as these solitaries. The divine wisdom of
the words, "It is not good for man to be alone,"
cannot be more strongly shewn than by the fact,
that no hermit in the Christian Church ever attained to peculiar sanctity without drawing others
round him. In the deserts of Egypt, or amid the
perpetual snows of the Alps, everywhere we find
these flocks of solitaries, practically proving how
much mightier in man is the social principle than
the separating one, and under what difficulties
men will still endeavour to realise that idea of
brotherhood which is perpetually haunting them.
Accordingly, the greater Fathers, such as Basil
and Jerome (who had himself been a hermit),
soon declared themselves opposed to solitary
monachism* (for the pleonasm becomes indispensable). Thus monachism, which, I repeat it, seems
the breaking-up of the social principle, in fact soon
becomes one of the strongholds of that principle,
and carries it at once to its extremest consequences, by proclaiming all things common among
the brethren. For monks and nuns of all ages
have been, as we ought all to know, sad communists, and the rights of private property have
been most audaciously denied within almost every
convent door. From the earliest period, nothing

* See, amongst other things, Hieron. Epist. cxxv. ad Rusticum.

is more invariable than the renouncement of all private wealth by the monks of either sex,—those of the Egyptian *lauræ*, for instance, even when they did not dwell in a single building, but in an agglomeration of separate cells. Not a trace of this feeling, so far as I am aware, is perceptible in the notices which have been preserved to us of the Church-virgins, although I have endeavoured to shew how naturally they would become communities, and although it appears to me very likely that such was the origin of many of the Greek convents of later ages.

And thus all tends to shew that the idea of special brotherhoods and sisterhoods grew in a marvellous way—by a divine contradiction—out of the solitude of monachism. To confine ourselves to the special subject before us,—the Church-virgins sang together, walked together in procession, sat together in the church. The nuns might do all this, but, instead of being governed by the presbyter or bishop, they were governed by one of themselves; instead of being maintained by the Church, they maintained themselves; instead of being paupers, they had all things in common. Who can fail to see that the one institution had a bond of union, a living principle, which the other wanted, forced as it was to rely on the individual condition of its members, as professing virginity?

§ 3. *The Social Principle, the Mainstay of Monachism.*

The social principle, embodied in the effort to realise a brotherhood or sisterhood, is therefore the mainstay of monachism in either sex, and the question must not be thrust aside,—How far is the attempt a lawful one? Christ has told us, "Ye are all brethren;" how then can any number of men or women say among themselves, *We* are brothers,—*We* are sisters,—and define the conditions of admission to such brotherhood or sisterhood, as if it depended on them to fix them? Must there not at all times be something unnatural, artificial, meretricious, false, in any such system? There must indeed, if the aim of the community be to *make* a brotherhood, and not to manifest one. But if it be clearly felt that the whole human race is called in Christ to the adoption of sons, so that no outer and visible brotherhood can ever be but a type and shadow, a partial recognition and embodiment of that brotherhood which is spiritual and universal;—if the few who call themselves brothers or sisters do so in no spirit of exclusion towards the many, but simply in order to shew the many, by palpable marks and signs, the reality of that large family of which they are all called to be members, and to glorify the better the name of that Elder Brother who hath sealed the covenant of adoption with His blood,—then, I for one believe that such brotherhoods and sisterhoods *may* be used to strengthen and develop, instead of contravening, the universal brotherhood of the Church, to afford constantly a living witness for its truth. But they will bear that witness, just in proportion as they do not seek their perfection in themselves, but out of themselves; as, instead of raising walls of adamant between the brothers and sisters on the one hand, and the great world without on the other, they on the contrary devote the whole strength of their united efforts continually towards promoting the regeneration of that outer world, through all works of self-sacrifice and of love. The more secluded the cloister, the falser the brotherhood; the freer it is, the more perfect are its labours. And therefore the vow of celibacy, especially in the female sex, is most contrary to the healthy efficacy of the brotherly principle.

Corrupted by this falsehood, the history of female monachism becomes indeed, in great measure, the history of female idleness, of female sterility and uselessness, of the utter frustration through man's self-will of all God's gracious purposes with reference to one-half of the human race. But it is not wholly such a history. By the aid of the social and brotherly principle, it has rendered, and renders still, in spite of all perpetual vows, and galling observances, and doctrines which are but the traditions of men, many signal services to the Church. In other words, I believe that whatever good has been done, or has seemed to be done by female monachism, it is *sisterhood* that has done it, not monachism itself.

For, whilst the vow of celibacy must kill well-nigh altogether the freedom and usefulness of the ordained diaconate of the individual woman, it is obvious that it could yet consist with a large development in various directions of what I may call the natural diaconal functions of women, as soon as these were gathered together in communities. Over such, a *surveillance* could be exercised, both from without and from within,—the latter the more jealous of the two,—and by the creation of a little holy inner world, joined only perhaps to the great outer wicked one by a single grated door, it became possible for the caged saints to serve that great wicked world without receiving much pollution from it. Such is one whole side of the sad story of female monachism,—a great yearlong, life-long, agelong struggle of the loving female heart to be as useful as it can, without endangering that awful vow. And I think it will be found that, precisely in proportion as that vow is slackened or deferred, so does the work of women, even in the

Romish Church, become freer, wholesomer, more perfect in every way.

Female monachism therefore, under that aspect of its nature in which it develops itself as a *collective female diaconate*, becomes now the subject of our investigation. But its growth is so essentially connected with that of male monachism, that a short sketch of the progress of the latter becomes indispensable towards the due comprehension of its history. Before proceeding to trace such a sketch, I may, however, observe that, by the date of Justinian's Code in the sixth century, Church-virginship seems for all practical purposes to have melted into female monachism,—the virgin, to whose designation the epithet *sanctimonialis* seems joined or not indifferently, the widow, and the deaconess, being now the only three classes of women distinctly spoken of in connexion with the Church, or as dedicated to God, instead of the four which were known a century previously.*

§ 4. *Sketch of the History of Monachism till the Eleventh Century.†*

Monachism, as it first grew up in the so-called

* See, for instance, Code, bk. i., tit. iii., l. 54 (A.D. 533). See also Appendix D.

† See, for many of the views set forth in this chapter, Guizot's "History of Civilisation in France."

Egyptian *Laura*, was literally a collective hermit-hood—the first solitary being followed into the wilderness by others, who built their cells around his own, seeking to follow the example of his sanctity, and to govern their devotions by his teaching. There was no written rule. Obedience there was, and of the strictest, but obedience to a man, to the most worthy. It was the age, so to speak, of monastic hero-worship, when all the history of the institution was concentrated in that of the ruling saint of the day. The only point which made monachism a system as yet, was the simple fact of the building up of many cells in one place. Where men had lived, worked, prayed, fought beasts and devils for long years under the government of one holy man, there it was natural that they should still remain, and at his death seek out the next holiest to fill his place.

The first step onwards in the system was the creation of the Rule. The earliest rule is that bearing the name of St Basil—remodelled indeed, as we now have it, but which appears to have existed, in some shape or other, in the latter half of the fourth century. A very different rule, indeed, from the later ones; proceeding by question and answer, and thereby less a rule than a catechism, less a law than an instruction; but acknowledged by the Romish Church as one of the four great rules, and followed to this day, probably the most extensively of any,—throughout the whole Eastern world in particular, from Russia to Abyssinia. From the hour when it was given, the personal character of the abbot of the day was no longer all ; there was a written standard by which he and every member could be judged; there was a monachism independent of any individual monks.

The next step taken in the West was the establishment of the monastery or convent. I do not mean to say that the practice of dwelling under a common roof, instead of in separate hermitages, never obtained in the East before the Basilian rule went forth into Gaul. But whilst in the East monachism grew up of itself, it was transplanted thence full-grown into the West, together with the rule, and appears at once there under its conventual form. We do not hear first of particular hermits, but of the monastery itself,—and this not in the savage wilderness, but sometimes in cities, sometimes near them, or if far, in spots of agreeable resort, such as Lérins in the Hyères islands. Thus, whilst in the East men first became monks for the sake of solitude, they became such in the West for the sake of society. And while silence was a noted characteristic of the early Egyptian monks,—so that it was said of it as of the wilderness itself, that a monk lived in silence as a fish in water,—the early monasteries of Gaul (except, indeed, the two first, founded by St Martin on the banks of the Loire) became the great centres of intellectual activity in the religious world during the fifth and sixth centuries, or as Guizot calls them, " the philosophical schools of Christianity."* Hence a new work for conventual monachism, which will occupy it, say, till the thirteenth century; the preservation and communication of knowledge. So long as there is still some security for property and person, some exchange of thought, the monastery will be a school of learning, and such we see it to be both in the East and West during the fifth century. When the barbarians are everywhere abroad, and the ways are no longer safe, and there is much ado to provide food and shelter for the inmates, the monastery becomes a mere depository for such books and such knowledge as may chance to be stored up within it, with perhaps some poor chronicler (like Fredegarius) writing within it the sad tale of his own times in consciously barbaric language, and complaining sorrowfully that the lamp of knowledge has gone out.

* Not, indeed, that theological discussion and intellectual activity appear by any means to have been foreign to early Eastern monachism,—the Egyptian monks, for instance, being noted as specially addicted to the Origenic heresies. But in the East monachism became controversial ; in the West, amidst the society of the convent, it began by being so.

Perhaps, indeed, the early intellectual development of Western monachism was in part premature and factitious. At all events, the next great step in its history was taken only after it had sought renovation at its fountain-head of collective hermithood. The rule of St Basil having been felt to be unsuited in many respects to Western habits and to a Western climate, and, indeed, too austere, various alterations were made in it by different founders of monasteries, so that a great variety of particular rules appear to have grown up in the West, in the course of the fifth and beginning of the sixth century. These all were, however, gradually swallowed up in the first great rule indigenous to the West, that of St Benedict, the hermit of Subiaco. Given in 528, by 543 it had spread throughout a large portion of Europe; it had been carried to Sicily, to Spain, to Northern France. By the end of the sixth century most monasteries had adopted it. By the ninth, Charlemagne had to inquire whether any other were anywhere followed.

The Benedictine rule may be considered as the real starting-point of Western monachism as an organised system. It had produced hitherto clever disputants, orthodox or heterodox,—Faustus, Honoratus, Cassian, and the like. It now sent forth great missionaries, such as Austin and Boniface.

Issued between the age of the Gothic and Frankish invasions and that of the Lombards,—soon to
be followed (seventh to tenth century) by Arabs,
Hungarians, and Northmen,—the Benedictine rule
founded within its convents a discipline so strong
and stern, as to brace men against almost every
calamity. Not only is it characterised by the joint
obligation of manual labour and learning, but it
substitutes, for the mere Basilian " profession," the
three solemn vows of chastity, poverty, and obedience. It was now that the word " religion," as
Guizot observes, began to be applied peculiarly to
monachism, so that " to enter into religion" meant
henceforth to take the monastic vows, and monks
and nuns became emphatically " the religious " in
Christendom.

In the first half of the seventh century a new
change takes place, by the progressive incorporation of the monastic class into the clergy. For
the first few centuries, the monks had been considered as mere laymen. But as the system developed itself, a struggle commenced as to whether
monasteries, both of men and women, should not
be subject to episcopal jurisdiction ; which was now
decreed by councils, that of Arles, for instance, in
554, a few years after Benedict's death. At first
the investing the monks with the clerical character
acted as a restriction of their freedom; and Guizot

notes the beginning of the eighth century as a period of episcopal tyranny over the monasteries, which had (supported often by kings and popes) to wring charters from their bishops, as *communes* and boroughs had, a few centuries later, to wring them from their feudal lords. But the change sprang from the strength of monachism, not from its weakness. The time had come when the number of its followers, the endowments of its monasteries, the reverence of the people for its sanctity, the real services rendered by it as the great educator of the age, made it wholly unsafe to leave it out of the clerical pale. How soon, when once introduced, it leavened the whole ecclesiastical body, may be judged from the establishment* of the cathedral system, by which the canons or cathedral clergy were subjected to an actual rule, to a common discipline, and compelled to dwell and take their meals together, though retaining the use of private property. A like advance in power, shewing through a seeming curtailment of freedom, is visible at the beginning of the ninth century, in the establishment of monachism as a civil institution. These are the days of Charlemagne, or the early ones of his son Louis, when the union of Church and State is complete, and the latter, strong,

---

* By Chrodegand, bishop of Metz, A.D. 760, in the first instance.

enjoying the best earned title to Church support, exercises in turn over the Church a willingly-accepted control. Imperial capitularies now treat of monachism, as decrees of councils did erewhile; imperial commissioners (*missi dominici*) are required to receive complaints against bishops, abbots, abbesses; to examine whether in monasteries of men or women the religious live according to rule. The rule of the canons and canonesses is embodied in one capitulary (816); the first great reform of Benedictine monachism, by Benedict of Aniane, in another.

One other step, however, needs to be taken before the monastic system, as such, is complete. Celibacy—the Convent—the Rule—the Solemn Vows—the assumption of the Clerical character—State recognition—such has been the progress of its development hitherto. The Order remains yet to be founded. Although the rule of St Benedict may have been universally adopted in the West, as that of St Basil in the East, yet monastery has yet no definite relation with monastery; monks and nuns, out of their respective seats of discipline, form but a class, not an organised body. But in the beginning of the tenth century the reforms of Abbot Odo of Cluny (926-942), in his own monastery and others, are crowned by the uniting of all the reformed bodies, under papal authorisation, into one congregation. There is henceforth a Benedictine Order, as well as a Benedictine Rule. Monachism thus assumes the catholicity of the Church itself; nor is one surprised to find it, by the end of the tenth century, endeavouring on all sides to shake off episcopal jurisdiction, and to place itself in immediate spiritual dependence on the Pope.

Complete henceforth in itself, monachism has to achieve its last triumph; it has to transform the whole clergy into its own image. The monk Hildebrand, Pope Gregory VII., consummates that victory, by enforcing the celibacy of the so-called secular clergy itself. Henceforth we can only understand the Romish Church by viewing its clergy as a great monastic order, with the Pope for general. What other term could the early Church have used to designate their priests and deacons, vowed to estrangement from all family ties but that of μοναχοί—monks or solitaries? Monachism might seem conquered when the monks entered the ranks of the clergy, submitted to episcopal jurisdiction. Look at the Church three centuries later,—none but monks really remain in these ranks. The false centre has been fully set up; the exceptional condition has been made the rule; Christendom has organised its Pharisees; the priest, to be priest, must differ from other men.

Observe, however, once more how the social

principle has conquered the individual, in the bosom of monachism itself; how each successive triumph of the latter over the world without has only been achieved by the strength, not of separation and individualism, but of union and brotherhood. A man fled to the wilderness for solitude. Others follow his example, and the cells cluster together, and abbots are chosen, to whom obedience is to be paid. But separately-built dwellings are felt to interfere with the brotherhood of the monastic community; the great monasteries of the West rise up to embody a social purpose, and Western monks learn from the first to live under the same roof. Again, where obedience is paid only to a man, the tie of brotherhood seems to be dissolved with the death of every abbot; the rule is given, and the monastic community acquires a life of its own; allegiance is due to the law, not to the man. Then a claim is put forth on behalf of the community over the whole man, who must be bound down by solemn vows,—to chastity, which prevents his ever issuing forth from the monastic brotherhood into a wider one,—to poverty, which makes all the brethren equal by the world's great standard of wealth,—to obedience, by which at least a mockery of family life can always be realised. Lastly, the order is founded; the monastic brotherhood must not be confined to a single convent, it must stretch from city to city, from province to province, from realm to realm; it must reckon by the thousand, instead of by the hundred. Nay— last and worst juggle of all—the two sexes may be combined henceforth in this false brotherhood; a community of interests, of traditions, of government, may be wrought out between local brotherhoods here and local sisterhoods there, which shall call themselves by the same name, though every member of the one perhaps shall be forbidden to see any member of the other.

§ 5. *Female Monachism till the Eleventh Century.*

Until about the eleventh century, female monachism can hardly be distinguished from male. There are Basilian nuns and Benedictine nuns; nunneries, like monasteries for men, become schools or storehouses of learning, sometimes even centres of intellectual activity. At the beginning of the sixth century, the nunnery founded by St Cesarius at Arles contained two hundred nuns, mostly employed in copying books. Their rule bound them to learn " human letters " for two hours a day, and to work in common, either in transcribing or in female labours, especially in making cloth for their garments, so that they should not be obliged to purchase from without. Such a body was Benedictine before Benedict, nor can we be surprised at its later adoption of the Benedictine rule.*

In the seventh century (640) Bede shews us Earconberth, King of Kent, sending his daughter, to Abbess Fara at Brie, in the region of the Franks; "for at that time, many monasteries not having been yet built in the region of the Angles, many from Britain, for the sake of monastic conversation, used to go to the monasteries of the Franks or of the Gauls, and to send their daughters there to be taught, and to be married to the Heavenly Bridegroom."†

But two nunneries must be especially noted as instances of intellectual activity. One is that founded at Tours in the sixth century by Queen Radegund the deaconess, whose earlier story I have told ere this, to whom Fortunatus, *the* poet of the age, and the last Latin poet who has any title to the name, was chaplain, as well as almoner to the convent. Augustin Thierry has given us a charming account of this pleasant little community, and of the literary relations between Radegund and Sister Agnes, the superior of the convent, on the one hand, and the poet on the other; while the graver Guizot has not disdained to dwell on their

* Guizot; Hélyot, Histoire des Ordres Monastiques, Pt. IV., vol. v., c. iv.

† Eccl. Hist., Bk. iii., c. 8.

poetical intercourse, as indicating, perhaps, the origin of what we now call occasional poetry,—or, as the French say, *vers de société.* Fortunatus addresses his female friends in verse on subjects such as violets, flowers placed on the altar, flowers sent to the ladies, chestnuts, milk, eggs, plums, delicate little feasts. Not a shadow of scandal floats over the whole affair. Radegund was one of the most exemplary personages of the age, and closed in this pleasant monastic retreat a life of the severest trials. The gay verse-maker died a bishop at the beginning of the seventh century.

Again, in the Swabian nunnery of Gandesheim there flourished, in the latter half of the tenth century, the glory of female monachism during the Middle Ages, the poetess Hrotsvitha (whose dramatic works have been edited and translated into French, within the last few years, by M. Magnin*), herself not the first authoress of her convent. From her writings we find that she was instructed in all the Benedictine learning of the age, in the Holy Scriptures, and the works of ancient authors. Nay, in this German nunnery, which we have no reason to suppose peculiar in its constitution, it is clear that women in the tenth century were familiar with the works of Virgil and Terence, and able

* Théatre de Hrotsvitha, Religieuse Allemande du 10ᵉ Siècle, par Charles Magnin. Paris, 1845.

to converse in Latin metre; that it was considered in no wise contrary to the religious profession for a nun to write comedies, as she says herself, in imitation of Terence; that she did so amidst the universal applause of the learned; and, indeed, that, judging from internal evidence, her plays were actually performed in the convent. Let us tarry for a moment over this literary phenomenon.

Hrotsvitha composed eight poems : On the Nativity of Mary; On the Ascension of our Lord; On the Passion of St Gandolf; On the Martyrdom of St Pelagius; On the Fall and Conversion of Theophilus the Archdeacon; On the Conversion of a Young Slave, exorcised by St Basil; On the Passion of St Denis; and On the Passion of St Agnes. Her six comedies bear the titles of Gallicanus, Dulcitius, Callimacus, Abraham, Paphnutius, and Sapientia. All of them, although with the most delicate handling, turn upon the one subject of chastity and its temptations, and scenes of real pathos at times occur in them. In the " Abraham," for instance, which represents to us a hermit going in secular costume to rescue from perdition a niece whom he had brought up in a neighbouring cell, and who, having been seduced, had sunk to the lowest depths of vice, nothing can be more tender, more truly Christian in feeling, even when not in thought, than the old man's conduct towards the fallen one. "Why hast thou despised me?" he asks of her; "why hast thou deserted me? Why didst thou not tell me that thou wert lost, so that I and my dear Ephrem" (a fellow-hermit) "might do worthy penance for thee?" When she reproaches herself, he asks, "Who ever was exempt from sin, save only the Son of the Virgin?" he bids her believe in his love, reminds her of what he has done for her in leaving the wilderness, in giving up the rule, in mingling with the dissolute, and uttering jests" (*jocularia verba*). "Distrust not, despair not," he exclaims again; " . . . have pity on the fatigue which I have undergone for thee, lay aside that dangerous despair, —a heavier weight, I know, than all thy committed sins. . . . On me be thy unrighteousness, so only thou return to the place whence thou camest forth, and begin again that life which thou hast abandoned." When she yields at last to his entreaties, "Now art thou really mine own daughter, whom I nourished up ; now will I love thee above all things."* They start on their journey, and she says she will follow him. "Not so," he answers; "but I will go afoot, and place thee on my horse, lest the rough road cut thy tender feet." The treat-

* Nunc fatcor te vere meam, quam nutrivi, filiam, nunc censeo te per omnibus fore diligendam.

ment of the same subject in another piece, "Paphnutius," is less pleasing, owing to the severity with which the hermit behaves towards Thais, and the truly monkish horrors of the penitence which he imposes on her. But from the midst of these imperfections there bursts forth at last a glorious protest of Christian lowliness. Paul, a disciple of St Anthony, sees in a vision "a bed strewn splendidly in heaven with white garments, over which four radiant virgins preside, and seem to guard it by their presence." He thinks it must be for "his father and lord, Anthony;" but he is told by a divine voice, "Not, as thou hopest, for Anthony, but for Thais, the harlot, is this glory reserved." And the piece concludes by the prayer of Paphnutius for Thais at her dying hour, that at the resurrection "she may rise again a perfect man as she was, to be placed amongst the white sheep, and to be led to the joy of eternity." Could there be words which should cut more against the grain of all monastic self-righteousness? Hrotsvitha, at least, was no hooded Pharisee.

In the "Paphnutius," as well as in the last piece, the "Sapientia," there occur, along with much childishness, some equally noble and Christian passages as to the value of knowledge. "All knowledge that can be known," says Paphnutius, "offends not God, but the unrighteousness of him that know-

eth."*   "And to whose praise," he says again,
" can the knowledge of the arts be turned more
worthily and justly than to His, who made that
which may be known, and gave knowledge? For
the more wonderful the law through which we recognise God to have constituted all things by
number, measure, and weight, the more fervent
we grow in His love."

I have not dwelt upon the strictly speaking
dramatic merits of Hrotsvitha, which, perhaps,
only grow upon the reader, as he considers the
time and place of her writing, the difficulties of
writing in what must, after all, have been only an
acquired language to her, and the novelty of her
attempt to frame sacred dramas on classical
models. Perhaps the most striking scene is that
of her last piece, in which the aged mother, Wisdom, after witnessing the martyrdom of her three
daughters—Faith, Hope, and Charity—prays for
death, and receives it. The symbolic poetry of
this conception it is impossible to mistake, but it
is not to be attributed to the nun herself. She
found the legend ready-made to her hand, and
told the tale as of real flesh-and-blood martyrs.
But the real interest of Hrotsvitha's work lies in
this, that, amidst much of pedantry and awkward-
ness, a true woman's heart is felt beating in the

* Nec scientia scibilis Deum offendit, sed injustitia scientis.

nun's breast. The subjects which she has chosen shew the germs still dormant, but most living, of that charity which several centuries later will take visible form in many an asylum for the reformation of female sinners. The nun in her convent is yet engrossed with the spiritual miseries of her sex in the wide world, and the loving words which she puts in her heroes' mouths express the true spirit of a Christian penitentiary.

I have only to add, that in its development, as in its application, female monachism closely followed in the wake of male; receiving necessarily the rule, the solemn vow, the clerical character; entering with it into the order,—female Benedictines soon succeeding to male, canonesses springing up almost as soon as canons. There is evidence even that in the incorporation of the monastic body into the clergy the female sex often aspired to presbyteral functions; so that the Council of Autun, in 670, had to forbid women from ascending to the altar; the Council of Aix-la-Chapelle, in 816, which gave the rule to religious women, had to decree that abbesses should not give the veil, nor usurp sacerdotal functions; the Council of Paris, in 824, to forbid them again from taking the veil themselves, from serving at the altar, from giving the body and blood of Christ. In short, during the whole of this period, so far is female monachism from having yet found a place in the Romish system as a collective diaconate, that it seems in danger of being a mere mimic of the male.

§ 6. *The Béguines.*

A period, however, now opens (eleventh to thirteenth centuries) in which not only does woman's activity take the advance of man's, and make to itself a vast sphere of exercise in the field of charity, but the idea of fellowship is found striving, above all in the female sex, to set itself free from the grasp of monachism, and to stand forth in its simplicity before the world.

It was the age of the Crusades. The last of the barbarians, the Northmen, had ceased to be pirates, and had settled down into conquerors, in France, England, Sicily, Russia. The world had recovered from the fear of destruction which had overwhelmed it towards the end of the tenth century. Feudalism was beginnning to organise itself, and where the feudal lord was wise enough only to rob his neighbours, and not his own vassals, to shew here and there little patches of comparative security and civilisation. In the plains of Belgium and Northern Italy in particular, where security could only be obtained by the massing of numbers, where man had to rely on the wit and courage and good faith of his brother-men, rather than on the strength of the natural fastnesses of crag or gorge, centres of industry, trade, freedom, were growing up in the towns, under republican forms of government.

Above all, through the gradual evangelisation of all the Teutonic, and some even of the Sclavonic tribes, and in the face of Mohammedan conquests, there had sprung up the feeling of a Christendom, a fellowship among all Christian nations. In the Cru· sades that feeling found an object and a realisation, however imperfect, for the man. But the same religious fervour, the same instincts of fellowship, which threw Europe upon Asia, and united hostile sovereigns under the banner of the Cross, were at work in the breasts of women. Some went forth with their loved ones to the wars; many entered the cloister till their return;—what more natural than to pray Heaven for safety and victory on behalf of those dear ones, to unite in peaceful fellowships, as they in warlike?

But monachism, it cannot be doubted, had by this time fallen in general far in arrear of the religious fervour of the age. The Benedictines—the dominant order of the West—represent mainly the passive principle of monachism. Quiet, stay-at-home folk, very apt to settle on their lees, requiring frequent reform,* by these very reforms they

* Those of Benedict of Aniane, of Odo of Cluny, of

shew the difficulty they have in satisfying the wants of the time. From the latter part of the eleventh century other orders spring up to supply their deficiencies,—each combining convents of men and of women,—Carthusians (1086), Bernardins (1098), Trappists (1140), Mathurins (1197), Carmelites (1207)—most of them aiming at increased austerity, all eleemosynary in their constitution. As the Crusades proceed, each more hopeless, more ruinous,—as the patrimony of the lord passes into the hands of Jews, Lombards, enriched serfs, or burghers hardly less despised,—the dowerless widow, the portionless orphan, the ruined wife and daughters, and, still more, the families of the obscure dependents who perish in Syria or Egypt, find ever more and more difficulty in obtaining admission into the old-established houses,—rich, idle, corrupt, grasping. The new orders are indeed open to them, and their austerities may seem grateful to those who have lost all earthly hope. But what of those who seek only a temporary asylum during an absence which they fondly hope is but temporary? What of the unmarried daughters? What of all who, however willing to employ themselves with the utmost zeal for God's service, yet shrink from

Robert de Molême at Citeaux, the second reform of Cluny, and the great reform of St Bernard,—the last three all in the course of the eleventh century.

separating themselves wholly from their kind? The cloister will not suit these, even if rich enough to buy admission, or strong enough to bear all austerities.

There was a form of life already in practice, which answered this need, that of the *Béguine* sisterhoods, of which a full account is given in a posthumous Latin work of Mosheim's, on the "Béghards and Béguines."* The origin of their name appears clearly to be the Teutonic *beg*, or pray, used once in no unfavourable sense; so that béghards and béguines were simply "praying" men and "praying" women. The term "béguine" is the earliest, and Mosheim shews it to have been used in Germany and Belgium as early as the tenth century, to designate widows or unmarried girls, who, without renouncing the society of men or the business of life, or vowing poverty, perpetual chastity, or absolute obedience, yet led, either at their own homes or in common dwellings, a life of prayer, meditation, and labour. The example of these sisterhoods was followed about the twelfth century by young men in Belgium and France. In the thirteenth century these brotherhoods and sisterhoods flourished greatly. Matthew Paris mentions it as one of the wonders of the age for the year 1250, that "in Germany there rose up an in-

* "De Beghardis et Beguinabus Commentarius." Lips., 1790.

numerable multitude of those continent women, who wish to be called Béguines, to that extent that Cologne was inhabited by more than 1000 of them." Indeed, by the latter half of this century, there seems to have been scarcely a town of any importance without them in France, Belgium, Northern Germany, and Switzerland.

The first of these fellowships was composed of weavers of either sex; and so diligent were they with their work, that their industry had to be restricted, lest they should deprive the weavers' guilds of their bread. Wholly self-maintained at first, they rendered moreover essential service in the performance of works of charity. As soon as a *Béguinage* became at all firmly established, there were almost invariably added to it hospitals or asylums for the reception, maintenance, or relief of the aged, the poor, the sick. To this purpose were devoted the greater part of the revenues of the sisterhood, however acquired, another portion going to the maintenance of the common chapel. The sisters received moreover young girls, chiefly orphans, to educate; went out to nurse and console the sick, to attend death-beds, to wash and lay out the dead; were called in to pacify family disputes. In short, there is perhaps none of the natural diaconal functions of women which they did not fulfil.

Those who were received among the Béguines were required to be of blameless character; but girls were often received in childhood, and invested with the habit; they were not, however, called sisters, nor did they take any pledge of obedience to the mistress, till the age of fourteen. Great disorders seeming to have flowed from this practice, we find the Archbishops of Mentz and Magdeburg restricting to forty the age of admission; in one case (1310), remarkably enough, by reference to the first Pastoral Epistle respecting widows. The Béguine promised obedience to the mistress, and chastity, but not monastic, since she was free to marry at any time. The mistress delivered to each, on her reception, the Béguine's dress, and the veil with which she was to cover her head in public and at religious services: the dress scarcely differing from that in ordinary use by respectable women, but coarse and without ornament; in colour varying with each establishment, but generally blue, gray, or brown; the veil invariably white.

In France and Germany the Béguinage usually consisted of a single house, distributed into separate cells, but with a common refectory and dormitory; in Belgium, on the contrary, as we may see still, there were nearly as many small houses as sisters (thus recalling the clustered hermitages of

the early monks); the largest and highest buildings
being devoted to common purposes, and including
particularly the chapel, the hospital, and the infirmary for sick sisters, which was distinct.   The mistress had usually a sub-mistress under her; in the
larger béguinages, numbering thousands of inmates,
there were two or more mistresses.

The Béguines had no community of goods, no
common purse for ordinary needs.   Nevertherless,
those among them who were wholly destitute, or
broken down with infirmities, were maintained at
the public expense, or out of the poor fund; mendi-
cancy was never allowed, unless in the extremely
rare case of the establishment not being able to
relieve its poorest members.

As contrasted with the deaconess, it will be seen,
the Béguine formed no part of the clergy; received
no imposition of hands; took no part in baptism.
Her office was merely the general diaconal office of
the female sex, but carried on by means of a fellowship, and no longer typified in the individual; yet
fulfilled with a singular amount of individual freedom, as contrasted with the nun.   For if we find
many female monastic orders, properly so called,
engaged in works of charity, either within or without the convent, it will be by virtue of a rule, of
a vow, at least of a fixed engagement.   Now it
scarcely appears that, under any circumstances, the

Béguine was compelled to go out visiting the sick, by the rule of the béguinage. If she did so, it was rather by virtue of a general understanding that, in order to entitle herself to public countenance, respect, and assistance, she was to shew herself really helpful to the needy; or it was as a public functionary, nominated, and presumably paid by the town; whilst again, the striking feature occurs of her self-maintenance by labour, thus recalling the healthiest days of early monasticism.

It would thus appear that the Béguine movement really offers the first complete realisation of the idea of a collective female diaconate, in the shape of free sisterhoods of women. Nor can I omit to point out amongst what populations the institution arose and took root; precisely in those great cities of Northern Europe, the original nurseries of its freedom, its trade and industry, the very centres of the civilisation of the age; spreading over the low countries—Flemish and German France, North Germany, Switzerland; almost the whole range of those populations over which Protestantism spread itself two or three centuries later; almost the whole family of our proper continental kindred.*

* I owe to the writer of the papers on Sisters of Charity in the *Educational Magazine*, already referred to, both the idea of the importance of the Béguine movement, in connexion with my subject, and the use of Mosheim's somewhat rare posthumous work. Mosheim's Protestant testimony is,

I should observe, moreover, that there is a body which appears to me to present remarkable analogies to the Béghard and Béguine brotherhoods and sisterhoods in the south of Europe, and which is treated of by Hélyot with a wariness so strongly suggestive of reticence, that I suspect its history would deserve at least as close a scrutiny as Mosheim has carried into that of the Béghards and Béguines. I speak of the Umiliati, who are said to have been originally Lombard gentlemen taken prisoners by the Emperor Henry V., and released on condition of penitence, towards 1117, about the same time, consequently, as the rise of the Béguines. Like the Roman monks and nuns spoken of by St Augustin, they are said to have established woollen factories, in which they both worked themselves, and employed many poor artisans, their wives also

however, quite confirmed by that of the Encyclopedist of Monachism, Father Hélyot, in his " Histoire des Ordres Monastiques, Religieux, Chevaleresques et Militaires," who opens with the Béguines the sixth part of his work, which treats of "Congregations of either sex, and military and knightly orders not subject to any religious rule," and tells us that, " of all secular congregations and communities, there are none older than those of the Béguines ;" although, indeed, he only traces them to Lambert le Bègue, a rich inhabitant of Liège, towards the end of the twelfth century,—an origin quite disproved by Mosheim. The good father, indeed, claims elsewhere all true Béghards and Béguines as Tertiarians (or, as the English translator of Mosheim calls them, Tertiaries) of St Francis.

working with them, and spinning the wool which the men afterwards wove into cloth. They lived upon the produce of their labour, and gave the rest to the poor. But in 1134, by the advice of St Bernard, they are said to have left their wives, and to have founded their first monastery at Brera. The order was finally suppressed by Pius V. in 1570.

We have here all the leading features of Béguine-ism,—industrious and charitable fraternities, without celibacy ; springing up, moreover, precisely in those busy, populous, warlike, independent cities of Lombardy, the very centres of civilisation in Southern Europe, as the Flemish cities in Northern.

CHAPTER III.

THE SISTERHOODS OF THE CHURCH OF ROME.

---

§ 1. *Early Romish Charitable Fellowships—Mendicants and their Tertiarians.*

THERE has now to be told the struggle of Romish monachism with the Béguine movement; how it overcame it, how it appropriated to itself the idea of charitable fellowship, and did it so completely that to this day we Protestants can hardly imagine of a religious fellowship that shall not be Romish.

To the end of the eleventh century, it would seem, we must ascribe the first, strictly speaking, charitable monastic foundation of the Romish Church, that of the Augustinian Hospitallers of St John of Jerusalem, fellowships both of men and women, established to provide for the necessities of poor pilgrims to the Holy Land. The example was largely followed, and the charity of the Hospitallers soon extended beyond the wants of pilgrims only. Cardinal Jacques de Vitry, who died towards the middle of the thirteenth century, says (as referred to by Father Hélyot, vol. iii., c. 22) that there were a great many congregations of men and of women, who, renouncing the world, lived, without property and in common, in leper and other hospitals, under the rule of St Augustin, to serve the sick and the poor, obeying a superior, and promising perpetual continence. The men dwelt apart from the women, not even eating together with them, but both sexes were present at religious services; and in large houses, when the number of brothers and sisters was great, they met together frequently in chapter, to acknowledge publicly their faults and to do penance. Books were read to them during meals; they kept silence in the refectory, and at other fixed times and places, and had several other observances. The cardinal especially remarks, that some of them suffered with joy the foul smells, the filth and infection of the sick, things so unbearable that no other kind of penance seemed to him fit to be compared with this martyrdom. Father Hélyot supposes that the cardinal must have had chiefly in view the nuns of the oldest Paris hospital, the *Hôtel-Dieu,* where there were in 1217–23 thirty-eight Augustinian monks and twenty-five nuns. But I think we can-not mistake here the results of the Béguine move-ment, nor fail to see here a class of stricter Bég-hards and Béguines,—the great charitable impulse of the age putting on, not unnaturally, looser forms in free, democratic Belgium, stiffer in feudal and regal France. At any rate, the long noviciate—at first of twelve years—indicates at least a protracted period during which the members were free to with-draw and marry, and differed only from the true Béguines in not earning their own livelihood ; and it is certain that in later times there were Hospi-taller foundations which could be distinctly traced to the Béguines. (See Appendix E.)

But the true parallel, and eventually the success-ful conqueror of the Béguines of the North, is to be found in the institute of the Tertiarians, or Third-rule Regulars. Let us stop an instant to survey the remarkable movement in the Romish world of which they formed a part.

The origin of the Franciscans and Dominicans (1208, 1215) is ascribed by the writers of the Middle Ages to two causes : to the necessity of combating heresy, on the one hand ; to the apathy of the clergy and monks of the day, on the other. "At this time," says a writer, speaking of the thir-teenth century, "there rose up two religions" (*i.e.*, orders) "in the Church, namely, of the Minor Brethren" (Franciscans) "and Preachers" (Dominicans), "which were perhaps approved of for this reason, that two sects had formerly risen up in Italy, which still subsist, of which the one calls itself the Humiliati, the other the Poor of Lyons."* In the Humiliati we recognise at once the woollen-cloth-weaving fraternities to which I referred above (p. 122); the Poor of Lyons, as is well known, are the Waldenses. Another writer says : "When priests and monks had, as it were, grown wholly cold to the love of God and of their neighbour, and had fallen away from their first estate, then came the better mode of life of St Francis and St Dominic."†

With them begins the new era of missionary monachism. Not that monks had never been missionaries; on the contrary, very many of the noblest missionaries of the early Church amongst

* Chron. Ursperg. ad ann. 1212, quoted in Charpentier, "Essai sur l'Histoire Littéraire du Moyen-Age:" "Eo tempore exortæ sunt duæ religiones in Ecclesiâ, videlicet, minorum fratrum et prædicatorum, quæ forte hâc occasione sunt approbatæ, quia olim duæ sectæ in Italiâ exortæ, adhuc perdurant, quarum alii humiliatos, alii pauperes de Lugduno se nominant."

† Quando clerici et monachi quasi ex toto a caritate Dei et proximi refrigerati fuerunt, et declinaverunt à priori statu suo, tunc melior fuit modus vivendi S. Francisci et S. Dominici. Mur. Script. rer. Ital., t. ix., p. 450; Charpentier ibid.

the barbarians,—Patrick, the apostle of Ireland; Columban, the Irish apostle of Northern France; Austin, the apostle of the Anglo-Saxons; Boniface or Winifred, the Anglo-Saxon apostle of North Germany—to quote two instances only of the mode in which every seed of Christianity bore fruit in that fertile soil, and the convert race of yesterday became a converting one on the morrow,—had all passed through the monastic training. But monachism itself was still spiritually, if not materially, a fleeing from the outer social world. St Benedict was a hermit, whom others sought unto; Francis and Dominic, on the contrary, went forth, as monks, to conquer the world for Rome, and trained their respective orders to do the same. The cloister was not suppressed; on the contrary, new and unheard-of austerities were practised. But the world was invited, called, almost ordered to enter into it. Even in the person of the holy Francis, monachism still behaved in the spirit of a conscious mastership over the Church; how much more so in the person of the persecuting Dominic! Thus, however different might be the characteristic modes of action of the two leaders, the one overflowing with boundless charity, the other with gloomy, persecuting zeal, both had the same aggressive mission; both, instead of preserving, as it were, in Christian receptacles, like the Benedictines, the depôt of ancient learning, went forth abroad to teach, and to teach in *the vulgar tongue,*—for this is the mark of the new movement.

During this, the aggressive period of its history, monachism will have to enter into wholly new relations with the outer world. The order will more and more take precedence of the monastery; a fellowship of work will substitute itself for the fellowship of outward life; the social principle will disentangle itself more and more from the conventual system. Monachism will thus receive its first great blow; for put the hermit among men, and he is but a man after all; and yet it will parry the blow so skilfully that it shall seem a triumph. As the first ascetic of the desert gathered round him a crown of tyros, eager to follow the pattern of his austerities, long unable to do so, but always looking up to him as their leader; so the strict monastic order will gather round it a number of " congregations," as they are mostly termed, only half or three-quarters monastic, bound perhaps by simple, *i.e.,* releasable vows, instead of solemn ; or by mere temporary engagements, or by engagements not involving the now essential monastic principle of celibacy; and yet always looking up to the stricter order, receiving from it their discipline, tending ever more and more to approximate to its

I

own; till every order almost shall have its Third-rule regulars, or Tertiarians. What we have seen of the Béguines and the Umiliati, however, must have shewn us that this softening of the more rugged features of monachism arose in reality from influences without, and not within ; that monastic brotherhoods only linked on to themselves non-monastic congregations, because non - monastic congregations had been in a fair way of growing up without them altogether. The first Tertiarians of St Francis are later, not by years, but by centuries, than the sisterhoods of Béguines, the brotherhoods and sisterhoods of the Umiliati ; although the most flourishing age for both Béguines and Tertiarians alike is the thirteenth century.

I abridge from Hélyot (vol. ii., c. 29) the following account of the foundation of the first Tertiarians, those of St Francis :—

When St Francis had instituted the order of Minor Brethren, and that of the Clarissans, or Poor Ladies (1212)*—doubting whether he should continue to preach, or withdraw into solitude—he asked his brethren to pray for him, and sent two of them to St Clara and to the hermit Sylvester,

---

* The rule of the Clarissans, who take their name from St Clara, was very strict. As is the case in almost all instances of genuine monastic reform, they were bound to labour in common.—(Hélyot, vol. vii., c. 25).

to solicit their prayers for his enlightenment, not deeming himself worthy to implore God on his own behalf.   On the messengers' return he washed their feet, kissed them, and kneeling down, with bended head and crossed arms, asked what was the will of God?   " God had not called him to think only of his own salvation, but also to labour for that of his neighbours, by preaching the gospel, and by a holy example."   St Francis rose up : " In the name of the Lord, brethren, let us go forth." So he and the two brethren went forth from Assisi, not knowing whither.   Reaching the small town of Camerio, two leagues off, Francis preached repentance with such effect that the people were about to leave their goods and their families, and to withdraw into cloisters and solitudes.   But he dissuaded them from doing so, promising to give ere long a form of life which they might follow without quitting the state to which God had called them.   This was the Third Rule of St Francis (1221), which spread rapidly through Tuscany, and soon formed congregations in Florence itself.

Before reception as a Tertiarian, male or female, the candidate was examined to see if there should be any scandal about him, if he possessed aught of another's goods, if he had any unreconciled enemy. The husband was not admitted without the consent of the wife, nor the wife without that of the husband, "*if* he were a faithful Catholic and obedient to the Roman Church." A noviciate of one year was required; after admission, none could leave the order, except to take the solemn vows of religion. The dress of the members was coarse and without ornament, neither quite white nor quite black. They were not to bear arms, except in defence of Church or country, or by permission of the superiors, who could also give dispensations as to dress. They were forbidden to be present at feasts, plays, balls, or dances, and were to see that no members of their family contributed to the expense of such entertainments. Besides various obligations as to temperance, fasting, and religious exercises, they heard every month in common a solemn mass and the preaching of the Word of God, and took the communion thrice a year, after reconciliation and restitution of unjustly-acquired property. They were to avoid solemn oaths, except for the pledging of faith, the repelling of calumny, the giving witness in courts of justice, and the authorising of sales. Every member was to accept and faithfully fulfil any office which might be assigned to him by the brotherhood, but all functions were temporary only. The brethren were to preserve peace as far as possible, both among themselves and with the world outside; to avoid and conciliate litigation. Sick brethren were visited once a week, and their wants supplied, if necessary, from the common stock; the funeral of one was attended by all. A general assembly and visitation was held once a year or oftener, when those who, after three warnings, were found incorrigible were expelled. The Tertiarians were sometimes officially charged with charitable duties. At Milan, a body of them, including members of both sexes, were invested with the administration of all pious foundations and the laying out of charitable legacies. And although the brethren " Del Consorte," as they were termed, were for a time deprived of their office, in 1477 the Milanese requested it to be given back to them.—(Hélyot, vol. vii., c. 45).

I cannot say whether St Francis knew anything of the Béguine fellowships; what he knew of the Umiliati. But it will be seen at once how nearly the Third Rule of St Francis answers to the former; goes seemingly beyond them in its social character. Active duties of charity are, as with the Béguines, closely connected with a religious life; marriage is not forbidden; men and women join alike the institution—are not even compelled to leave their homes. Some may think such monachism no monachism at all. No more it would be, if the Third Rule of St Francis had been the First. But the First Rule with all its austerities must exist, that the Third may become possible. The Third

Rule only subsists to subordinate brotherhood to monachism, charity to asceticism, and so turn the great danger of the age.

§ 2. *Struggle between the Free and the Monastic Charitable Fellowships.*

There was essential antipathy between the free fellowships and the monastic orders, especially the Mendicants.   Not only did they see the Béguines drawing to themselves a large portion of the liberalities which they would otherwise have monopolised, but a larger.   The people had taken into their heads that God would rather listen to the prayers of busy and laborious, as well as pious, women, whom they saw mixing with them in their daily life, freely submitting their conduct to the scrutiny of others, than to those of monks and nuns confined in cloisters, living upon charity, nor even seldom in vice.   So gifts and bequests came freely in from the rich, for the sake of the Béguines' prayers, whilst they shared with the religious orders their most important civil privilege—exemption from taxation.   The Béguine, indeed, as Mosheim observes, was exempt from almost all the inconveniences of a conventual life, whilst enjoying almost all its advantages.   Like the nun, she shared the economies of a common management, and to some extent of a common household. Unlike the nun, she retained her individual freedom; could purchase and hold property, and, subject to certain restrictions, could trade and make money. The authority of the mistress only extended to the maintenance of order and decency, and to the providing for the care of the poor and of the chapel. Was it in human nature for the cloistered saints not to feel jealous of these free lances, so to speak, of ecclesiastical charity? Still worse was it when the Tertiarian fraternities grew up, so closely resembling the Béguines in their discipline. There was, indeed, no friction at first, for the Béguine movement belonged mainly to the North, and Italy was the theatre of Francis's reforms. But as the new tide of monastic fervour swelled by the establishment of new orders—Dominicans (1215), Celestins (1270), Augustinians (1276), &c.—all eleemosynary, all with affiliated female communities, all with more or less the same proselytising missionary character,—several of them (Dominicans, Augustinians, and other minor bodies, such as the Carmelites, Servites, Brethren of the Redemption of Captives, Brethren of our Lady of Mercy, &c.), with Tertiarian congregations clustered round them,—collision between the free and the monastic fraternities became imminent, and a conflict indeed broke out about the middle of the thir-

teenth century, which lasted till the middle of the
fifteenth.* Council after council, bull after bull,
now denounced and excommunicated Béghards
and Béguines as heretical. And with every allowance for monkish jealousies and Romish intoler-
ance,—with all due abhorrence for the stake and
the rack, and other coercive means by which the
extermination of Béghards and Béguines was pursued,—I cannot but feel that the institution fell,
like every other, by its own fault. The free fellowships departed from the spirit of their own foundation. In place of the self-supporting industry and
active charity which at first characterised them,
there crept in the very opposites of these,—reli-
ance upon others' alms, and indifference to good
works.† So complete was the change, that the

---

* The Augustinians must have especially distinguished
themselves in this struggle as the Béguines' opponents, for
in a German wine-song, apparently of the early part of the
fourteenth century, the poet, addressing the "wine, wine of
the Rhine, clear, bright and fine," says : "Thou reconcilest
those who are wont to be always foes—the Augustinian and
the Béguine. Thou canst part them both from sorrow and
pain, that they shall forget German and also Latin." (See
Vilmar's "Geschichte der deutschen National-Literatur,"
vol. i., p. 403).

† Two bulls of Pope Clement V., of the year 1311, the
one against Béghards and Béguines, the other against the
Béguines only, exhibit most plainly the extravagances which
had given an occasion to the persecution, and in some sense
an excuse for it. These are for the most part the excesses of

very name of " Béghard," *pray-er*, surviving in our " beggar," has come to designate clamorous pauperism, and the name " *Begutta*," synonymous with " Béguine," surviving in our " bigot," to designate narrow fanaticism.

Thus, in the first condemnation of these institutions by the Provincial Council of Mentz in its canons, 1259, we find it ordained " that the sect and habit, as well as the conventicles of Béghards, who cry in the squares and streets of cities, towns, and villages, ' Broth dorch Gott,' that is, Bread thro' God, or Bread from God, or Bread for God's sake, and whatever other singularities are not received in God's holy Church, be wholly reproved ;" the Council going on to require all rural deans in the province of Mentz to admonish the Béghards publicly on three Sundays or fast-days, and to expel them in default of their obeying such admonition ; concluding, " and we do ordain the same concerning the pestiferous Béguines." A bull of John XXII. (1317 or 1318) renews the interdicts in a more specially ecclesiastical spirit, and is chiefly directed against the uncanonical

gnosticism and mysticism ; a belief that man can become wholly impeccable in this life, so as to require no more prayer nor fasting, nor obedience to any law ; good works being considered as a mark of imperfection, and the indulgence of natural instincts on the contrary as not being a sin, especially if given way to under temptation.

assumption of a new religious habit by Béghards and Béguines, the formation of congregations and conventicles, the election of superiors, the reception of numerous members, the construction or acquisition of places where they might live in common, and the begging in public, "as if their sect were one of the religions" (*i.e.*, orders) "approved of by the apostolic see." Observe this latter clause, which is very characteristic. To make religious begging a privilege, to license for its own benefit a great economic evil, to muster and discipline a whole army of social Arabs, detached not only from family ties, but from all the cares and decencies of a home and an honest industry; ready for any mission, hardened by a rough and roving life; accustomed to live by their wits and by their tongue, with all the obedience of a cloistered monk, and all the *check* of a sturdy beggar, has been—not the master-stroke, that were hard to fix—but one of the master-strokes of policy of the monastic Church; yet, like all master-strokes of policy, one most likely to fall back on the designer's head, when met by any earnest living assertion of God's righteousness. A strolling friar like Tetzel was the fittest instrument for the dirty work of selling indulgences; but that dirty work gave the signal for our glorious reformation, and Tetzel's infamy is for ever bound up with the brightness of Luther's most blessed name.

But the Béguine sisterhoods of the North were too numerous, too useful, too much in harmony with the spirit of their age and country, too deeply rooted in the affections of the people, to perish before the canons of a council, or a Papal bull. Nor, indeed, it was soon seen, did Rome's safety require that they should perish. The existence of free brotherhoods was, indeed, inconsistent with that of Romanism itself; for every community of men, not bound by rule or vows, not subject to a clerical head, must be, of necessity, an asylum of free thought, such as a monastic church with an infallible head could not, without the greatest danger, allow. Sisterhoods, on the other hand, although equally unbound by vow or rule, might safely be tolerated; since, through the priestly director or confessor, generally an essential part of the organisation of any béguinage, they could be kept in dependence, tempted on into monachism.* And thus, parallel with the current of censure against Béghardism and Béguinism as a system, there begins to flow another current of toleration, and even, as the danger diminishes, approval, for

---

* See appendix F for a translation of one of the later Béguine rules (end of the thirteenth century), where the sisterhood is under Dominican direction.

those "faithful women, who, having vowed continence, or even without having vowed it, choose honestly to do penance in their hospitals, and serve the Lord of virtues in the spirit of humility" (Bull of Clement V., 1311).*

By little and little the Béguine sisterhoods are

---

* So a bull of John XXII. (1318), after denouncing Béguine errors, absolves, in like manner, "many women," who, in many parts of the world, "being in like manner commonly called Béguines, either secluded in their parents' houses, or their own, or sometimes also in those of others, or living together in common houses which they have hired, lead an honest life, frequent churches devoutly, and reverently obey the diocesans of the place, and the rectors of the parish church, in nowise arrogate to themselves curious disputations, or any kind of authority or rather temerity," &c., adding, however, with curious wariness, that this exemption is not to be construed into an approval of their condition. See also a letter addressed by the same pope in the same year to John, bishop of Strasburg, who had complained to him that as well prelates as rectors, by reason of the Clementine bull, were ejecting recluse women from their seclusion, in which they had dwelt for about fifty years in a praiseworthy manner, and were compelling them to lead a secular life, to the gross scandal and disturbance of the faithful. Another bull of the same pope, dated 1326, is addressed to the patriarchs, archbishops, and bishops of Italy, for the special protection of the orthodox Béguines in Lombardy and Tuscany—shewing how far the institute had spread. A bull of Boniface IX. (1395), addressed to the German clergy, and letters of Albert, archbishop of Magdeburg, add further injunctions against disturbing the orthodox Béghards or Béguines. The Béguines were finally absolved from censure by the Council of Constance, 1414.—(See Mosheim, op. cit. passim.)

adopted into the monastic system; in the course of the thirteenth and fourteenth centuries they are found growing up in close proximity to Franciscan and Dominican monasteries, taking Dominicans and Franciscans for spiritual directors, receiving rules from them, and becoming mere Tertiarian bodies in connexion with the monastic orders, till Hélyot, as before observed, at last claims them all as Franciscan Tertiarians. The name, indeed, grew to be applied in common parlance to all religious bodies existing for purposes of active charity, and thereby almost necessarily living under a larger rule. Hélyot relates that in France some bégui-nages subsisted as late as the beginning of the seventeenth century. There was in his days (first half of the eighteenth) a flourishing one at Amsterdam, besides a large one at Malines, containing more than 1500 or 1600 sisters, not reckoning boarders; whilst almost every traveller in Flanders has visited one or both of the two surviving ones at Ghent or Bruges.

§ 3. *The Tertiarian Nuns—Hospitallers—Alexians.*

And now, when the danger of the free charitable fellowships had been turned by means of the Tertiarian fraternities, there appears the inevitable tendency of these latter sham-free bodies, in a monastic church, to become monastic, by pronouncing the three solemn vows. The Third Rule of St Francis soon had its professed nuns, of whom St Elizabeth of Hungary is reckoned as the founder, though she is admitted not to have observed strict seclusion, since from the cloister, where she span wool, she was wont to go forth to tend the poor in the hospital which she had established. Here, indeed, we travel on that border-line between monachism and pure fellowship, where so much of usefulness mingles with the falsehood of professed celibacy, that we know not often whether to blame or praise. When we read of these communities of Tertiarian Hospitaller nuns,—some leaving their convents to succour the sick, to console the dying, to bury the dead; others exercising hospitality without leaving the cloister,—we may think that all this devotedness might have found another field, might have been exercised in another manner, without spilling all abroad that very precious ointment of spikenard, the family affections of a woman's heart,—without those fearful vows which are, as it were, the breaking of the alabaster box itself. But still a voice whispers, "Why trouble ye the woman? for she hath wrought a good work upon Me." The worship of these nuns may not be the highest and best, but it is surely genuine. Not upon them be the blame, but upon that Church which misdirects it, and offers them up as holocausts to its idol of Heaven-conquering pride.

To the end of the thirteenth and to the fourteenth century, I suspect, belong mainly the Tertiarian convents proper, and the chief foundations of Hospitaller nuns. At Paris, for instance, Hélyot tells us, at the " Hôtel-Dieu de Sainte Catherine," there were, in 1328, nuns as well as monks for the service of the poor. The chief duties of these nuns, as they were finally established in 1558, were to receive, for three days running, poor women and girls coming to Paris, and to bury the bodies of persons dying in certain prisons, or found murdered in the streets, or drowned in the river. At the " Hôtel-Dieu de Saint Gervais" there were four professed nuns as early as 1300, whose charitable obligations were the same towards men as those of the nuns of St Catherine towards women. It would be idle, indeed, to enumerate the various communities of women bound to charity under the general name of Hospitallers, or popularly, " Filles-Dieu." Their mission is simply told in the words of the beautiful vow of the Hospitaller nuns of Pontoise : " To be all their life, for the love of Christ, the servants of the sick poor, so far as in them lay, to do and to hold until death."—(Hélyot, vol. ii., c. 43).

But the real successors of the Béguines were the

so-called Alexian brotherhoods and sisterhoods; and the passage from the one to the other is so gradual, that in one bull of Boniface IX. (1395) we are in doubt which are meant. Its design is to screen from the penalties denounced on the Béghards and Béguines "poor persons of both sexes," who live " apart, that is, the men together in their houses, and the women in theirs, without mutual communication, humbly and honestly, in poverty and continence, under the spirit of humility; devoutly frequent churches; reverently obey the Roman Church, and their prelates and curates, in all things; receive poor and miserable persons, on request, into their hospitals, and exercise other works of charity according to their power, —that is, visit the sick, and, if need be, keep and nurse them in their sickness, when haply required so to do; and carry, on request, the bodies of the faithful departed to church-burial, in the places where they live." The careful repetition of the words " on request," &c., in the above passage, is strongly characteristic of the Béguine institute, as pointing out that the diaconal charities of these brotherhoods and sisterhoods were customary and spontaneous, and not compelled by rule; the statement that they lived "in poverty" varies, however, from the Béguine character. A bull of Eugenius IV. (1431) exhibits, on the other hand, the Alexian fellowships in their full-developed type, under the name of the " poor of voluntary poverty." They live, it says,—in terms but slightly varying from those of the last-quoted document,—" the men by themselves, and the women by themselves, in separate houses, without mutual intercourse, in poverty and continence ; frequent churches devoutly in humbleness of spirit ; reverently obey the Church of Rome, and their ordinaries, prelates, rural deans, rectors, and curates in all things ; freely receive distressed and other worthy persons into their houses, for hospitality's sake ; take charge of the sick, on request ; carry the bodies of the faithful departed to church-burial, even in time of furious pestilence, and exercise other works of piety and charity ; give to the poor out of the fruits of their labour and of the alms which they receive ; live in common ; and, through their faith in Christ, are surrounded with much popular zeal, favour, and affection." Although we have here the new feature of a community of life, we can hardly doubt that we have before us still Béguines, only become stricter and more monastic.

At a later period, these Alexian (or Cellite) sisterhoods are treated of by Hélyot as Tertiarian nuns or Hospitallers, under the still familiar title of " Grey Sisters." Without revenues of their own, they lived by alms, and served the sick out of doors,—the name of " Hospitallers " belonging properly* to those who merely exercised hospitality at their convents, whether towards the sick or towards pilgrims. The Grey Sisters, properly so called, were so named from their grey-white dress. In 1483, common statutes were received by the Grey Sisters of most of the Flemish and Northern French houses. They were to be kept to work whilst in the house ; to go out two and two together, without separating; not to watch more than three days in the same house. By Hélyot's time several houses—Amiens, Montreuil, St Quentin, Mons, &c.—had become cloistered, though some still exercised hospitality towards the sick or towards pilgrims. Sometimes the change was not effected without a struggle. At Beauvais, in 1627, the municipal authorities tried to prevent the claustration of the Cellite Sisters, which, however, was authorised by the provincial parliament, the nuns retaining their convent-house, an old béguinage. At Nancy, in 1696, the Bishop of Toul tried to compel the claustration of the Grey Sisters of the city. This time, however, on appealing to the provincial parliament, they obtained leave to re-

* But not invariably. Thus, the " Hospitalières de la Faille" of St Omer, Hesdin, Abbeville, and Montreuil, went out with a round hood (*un rond de chaperon*) over their faces to take care of the sick, and especially of the plague-stricken, at their homes.

main as they were (Hél. vii., cc. 38, 40.) It is impossible to doubt that the bulk of Hélyot's "Grey Sisters," and of some "Black Sisters," whom he also speaks of as Cellites or Collestines, —uncloistered nuns, who made a vow to assist the sick even in time of plague, and in some cases took care of penitents; some having hospitals of their own, whilst others went out to private houses to nurse; most of them being under the rule of the Alexian provincials (vol. iii., c. 54),—are monasticised Béguines. The works on which they are engaged, the localities in which they flourish, are the same; and surely it was the old healthy Béguine spirit which spoke out in that successful protest of the Nancy Grey Sisters against claustration, and in their appeal for help to the civil power.

§ 4. *Early Educational Fellowships—the Gerardins.*

It is observable that, although the mission of the male Franciscans and Dominicans was specially one of preaching and teaching, the religious impulse given by Francis and Dominic took shape among women in offices of physical charity rather than of instruction. No doubt the stricter female communities in connexion with the new missionary orders, especially when cloistered, took in young girls to educate; for the strictest claustration generally allows in the long run this outlet to the affections of the nun's poor heart. But educational labours did not form in the thirteenth century, as they did two centuries later, a prominent part of the nun's or Tertiarian sister's vocation. Perhaps the first indication of an educational impulse occurs in the foundation by Nicolas Orsini, Count of Spoleto, towards 1354, in a Clarissan convent at Genoa, of a " college of canonesses," to bring up young girls in piety till they should be in a condition to choose their calling. The community appears to have consisted of three classes —the canonesses, the scholars educated by them, and " convert sisters" (a class frequently found in Romish convents), for the ordinary household labours (Hélyot, vol. vii., c. 48).

But it is a remarkable fact that the origin of the great educational movement of the fifteenth and sixteenth centuries, as that of the great charitable movement of the twelfth and thirteenth, belongs to free religious fellowships, which flourished in the same regions as those of the Béghards and Béguines, and took up their work,—the Brotherhoods and Sisterhoods of the " Clerks of the Common Life," or Gerardins, founded in the fourteenth century by Gerard Groot of Deventer. The male members of this institute lived together in common houses, took no vows, but had a common table, a community of goods, and earned their livelihood by teaching the young and copying manuscripts. The sisters lived under the same rule, teaching young girls, and occupied in other womanly labours. In course of time, these "Clerks of the Common Life" divided themselves into two classes—the Lettered Brethren or Clerks, properly so-called, and the Illiterate Brethren, the two bodies living separate, but under the same rule. The Clerks then devoted themselves to study and education, composing works, and establishing schools; whilst the Illiterate Brethren worked with success in the mechanical arts. It was in the fifteenth century that these bodies chiefly flourished in Holland, North Germany, and the adjacent provinces, and from their schools proceeded the leading restorers of letters of those countries during this and the next century, Erasmus, Alexander Hegius, John Mummelius, &c.*

The fact of these persons living together a religious and industrious life was enough to make the people call them Béghards and Béguines; enough also to draw upon them the hostility of the regular clergy to those names. Mosheim's work on the Béghards and Béguines contains in its appendices

---

* Mosheim, Eccl. Hist., vol. iii., fifteenth century, pt. 2, c. ii., § xxii. ; the same, "De Beghardis et Beguinabus," p. 70, &c.

some curious details on this point, shewing us how, in 1398, the Gerardins consulted the jurists of Cologne to know if their institute were legal ; how some years afterwards the Dominican, Matthias Grabon, who had lived at Groningen, and had seen them surrounded with all the consideration which a monk might desire, without vows or rule, denounced them to Pope Martin V., asserting that none but a monk, and one subject to a rule which had been approved of by the Holy See, could embrace without sin the three " Evangelical counsels," as he called them, of "poverty, obedience, and chastity ;" that, consequently, "those women who lead a common life and dwell together, commonly called Beguttæ" (synonymous with Beguinæ), " whilst holding or preaching no erroneous doctrine, or otherwise suspected of error or heretical wickedness, are daughters of eternal damnation, and their state is forbidden and damned."   But the great Gerson took up the defence of the Gerardins, and the Council of Constance (1414) finally acquitted them, in common with the Alexians, and the true Béghards and Béguines (now mere mendicant fraternities), of the accusations brought against them.

And now came the era of the Reformation, and of the prodigious intellectual development which accompanied it, growing always more and more away from Romanism, until that intellectual de-

velopment was in part turned again to the profit of
the monastic church, through the rise of the Jesuits,
and of the female educational orders.

§ 5. *The Jesuits and Female Educational Orders, Ursulines, &c.*

With Ignatius,—whose work, in fact, bears the
same protest against monastic ignorance in the
period immediately preceding the Reformation, as
that of Francis and Dominic against monastic sloth
and corruption in the eleventh and twelfth centuries,—the tree of monachism, I firmly believe,
bore its last fruit.   How marvellous, indeed, its
growth, from the Egyptian Laura, planted deep in
the wilderness, to the fellowship of the professed
Jesuit, distinguished by no outer garb, subject to
no seclusion, freed from all monkish penances and
observances, mingling freely in the world, bound
to his monastic brethren only by the invisible link
of the common order!*   How the principle of
fellowship has fought its way, as it were, even to
the very centre of the monastic citadel!   The
change seemed vast, when the hermit, surrounded
against his will by imitators of his sanctity, was
succeeded by the vast material organisation of the
convent, by the catholic federation of the order.

* See "Constitutions des Jésuites."   Paris: Paulin, 1843.

The change seemed vast, when, from the secluded convent, offering still in the bosom of its visible, every-day fellowship, a refuge from the outer world, the Franciscan or Dominican went forth to conquer that world for the Church.   But now all brick-and-mortar signs of outer fellowship have disappeared, or if they remain, they remain no longer for the sake of the professed Jesuit himself, but of those upon whom he labours; the seminary has succeeded the monastery.   He is free to encloister others; except at the bidding of his superior he is no longer bound to cloister himself.   The sole barriers henceforth between him and his fellow-men are, celibacy, which is the ground of his separation, and common obedience, which links the seceders together.   Is there anything more which can be given up?   Can men, who are separated from others on one point, approximate to them more closely upon others?   Can the essential falsehood of their separation be exhibited more nakedly?   Why is it, that of all forms of monachism, Jesuitry has alone become a universal byword?   Why is it, that from country to country, Jesuits have been followed by execration, and suspicion, and contempt, beyond all monastic orders put together?   Why is it, that from country after country, they have been expelled by Romanist sovereigns and Romish popes?   And yet, why are they found at work still on all sides, bound up more and more with the fates of the Romish Church itself, leavening it more and more, more and more identified with it in the popular mind, crushed with it when it is crushed, rising again with it when it lifts its head once more?* Why, but because Jesuitism is at once the only form in which monachism can henceforth make head, and the form in which it is most certainly unbearable? Why, but because every shape of social and family order is slipping on all sides from the grasp of the monastic church, and it can only maintain itself by perpetually invading every state, every community, every household? Why, but because, where men are united to a false centre by no other link than that of a common obedience, that obedience must be of the most awful, penetrating, demoralising, deadly character? The Jesuit is bound to obey, not as a living man, but as a dead body; not as an intelligent and moral creature, but as a stick in aged hands. It has been indeed well observed, that similar expressions occur in other rules, the Benedictine for instance. Why have they not produced the same effect upon other orders? Why do they not excite the same aversion in us, in the one case as in the other? Surely it is because this blind, un-

* See as to this, the remarkable French clerical novel, " Le Maudit." Paris, 1863.

reasoning obedience was not elsewhere the sole pivot of monastic life; because the practical fellowship of the monastery laid hold upon the monk's heart with a thousand ties of personal reverence, and affection, and courtesy, and custom, whilst the abstract fellowship of the Jesuit order, made only more hateful by the espionage of the single *socius*, only appealed to his intellect; because when the worst came to the worst, the Benedictine's obedience had to be exercised mostly within four walls, amidst a limited circle of temptations, whereas the Jesuit might be sent forth into the wide world, the wide beautiful world with all its witcheries, always calling him to forbidden pleasures, to forbidden duties, alas! with nothing but his vow and his *socius* to keep him from its snares; sent forth to fail wretchedly, if he do not conquer?

Heirs to all past monastic experience, the Jesuits did not forego the means of aggrandisement of which the Franciscans had set the first example, by the affiliation of laymen as "coadjutors," perhaps even as "professed;" at least as members of "congregations" formed around or in connexion with Jesuit "houses" or "colleges." What is perhaps most remarkable, it is only as members of some affiliated congregation, or of some female religious order closely analogous to, but not identical with, that of the Jesuits, that women have been found able to serve the purposes of Jesuitism. Twice were Jesuitesses established, and twice in vain. Ignatius confessed that "the governing of these women gave him more trouble than all the company; for there was no end of perpetually solving their questions, curing their scruples, listening to their complaints, and terminating their differences." So that the first community of Jesuitesses, founded in 1545, was put an end to in 1547; and when the attempt was renewed in the next century, Pope Urban VIII. had again to put them down in 1631 (Hélyot, vol. vii., c. 61). In other words, Jesuitism in its typical form—monachism in its last development—is so utterly inhuman, that woman cannot be moulded to it.

But the true counterpart to the rise of Jesuitism is to be found in that of the female educational and missionary orders. The "Angelicals" of the sixteenth century used at first to accompany the regular clergy in their missions, seeking to convert women, as the latter, men,—thus recalling the labours of the early deaconesses. Cardinal Ximenes, at the beginning of the same century (1504, 1511), founded in Spain, at Alcala and Toledo, convents composed of a limited number of nuns, with annexed communities of young girls, who were to be brought up till marriage or profession, and endowed in case of marriage. Another similar institution was founded by the Count of Afuentes, at the place of that name; and many others rose up in Spanish America, for the benefit of the young Indian girls, who were educated by four and five hundred at a time (Hélyot, vol. vii., c. 48). The first great female educational order is, however, that of the Ursulines, founded in 1537 by Angela of Brescia, though not, in fact, for educational purposes. She insisted that all the girls of her congregation should remain in the world each in her parents' house, from whence they should go forth to seek out the afflicted for comfort and instruction, to assist the poor, visit the hospitals, tend the sick, and for any work of charity which might offer. Although the founder soon died (1540), the order spread rapidly. It seems to have first assumed its educational character in 1575, when the Ursulines of Parma and Foligno were established to instruct little girls gratuitously in reading, writing, and the catechism. By 1715, there were 350 Ursuline houses, divided among several "congregations," each with a history of its own,* each with some peculiarities of

---

* *E.g.*, when Françoise de Saintonge founded the first Ursuline educational establishment at Dijon, she was hooted in the streets; and her father called together four doctors learned in the law, to make sure that the teaching of females was not a work of the devil. Twelve years after, through those same streets, she was almost carried in triumph. See Mrs Jameson's *Sisters of Charity*, &c., p. 26.

constitution and discipline. Thus the " Paris Congregation," numbering more than eighty convents, had sprung from the gathering together at Avignon, in 1574, of some twenty to twenty-five young women for purposes of instruction. In 1594, they began to live in common; fell into disorder; were reformed by Madame de Ste. Beuve; transferred to Paris; erected into a monastic body in 1612, under a bull of Paul V. They pronounced, besides the three solemn vows, a fourth, to instruct little girls. Nuns were admitted at fifteen, after two years' noviciate; and each house received as many as it could support, and as many more as could guarantee their expenses. In the smaller Toulouse congregation, numbering eight or ten houses, the nuns used to employ part of their Sundays and holidays in the instruction of female servants and working people. Both this and the large Bordeaux congregation (one hundred houses) had affiliated fellowships (also called "congregations") of ladies, for visiting and succouring the sick, the poor, and prisoners, the instructing of servants in the fear of God and in the principles of Christianity, or the teaching of trades to poor girls. The congregations of Lyons (seventy-four houses) and Tulle (six) took no vow of instruction. ·The Ursulines of the county of Burgundy, approved of by Innocents X. and XI. (1648, 1677), were not even nuns, as making no solemn—*i.e.*, perpetual—vows, but only simple—*i.e.*, releasable—ones of chastity, poverty, obedience, and "stability." All were bound to labour for the sanctification of their sex; they brought servants together on Sundays and holidays for religious instruction. A three years' noviciate was required; and the directors were Jesuits. The Ursulines of Santa Rufina and Santa Seconda, at Rome, lived in like manner uncloistered, and without vows (Hélyot, vol. iv., pt. iii., cc. 20-32).

Augustinians and others soon followed in the wake of the Ursulines, as might be shewn in tedious detail. Of the educational establishments thus founded, several are (as above shewn in reference to the Ursulines) uncloistered, or free from perpetual vows; others are distinguished by a long noviciate; most are connected with the outer world by means of secular associates for out-of-doors purposes. As an instance of the pure sisterhood, I may mention the " Daughters of the Infant Jesus," founded at Rome, in 1661 (Augustinians), who were limited in number to thirty-three, (in memory of the years of the Saviour's life). They underwent three years' probation, and might withdraw for any just cause, including marriage. They instructed boarders in manual labour, needlework, drawing, painting, music, and singing; prepared girls for confirmation, and for the monastic life, and afforded "retreats" to girls and women. Another, but cloistered, Augustinian body, founded at La Rochelle in 1664, under the strange and blasphemous title of " Congregation of St Joseph of the Created Trinity" (*i.e.*, Jesus, Mary, and Joseph), consisted of houses limited in like manner to thirty-three members each. Its purpose was that of teaching poor girls from the age of eight or nine to that of fifteen or sixteen, when they were put out to service; supernumerary members were received at 400 livres a year for maintenance, half of which went to the objects of their charity. The secular associates of this institute, who were bound to give half their goods to the orphans instructed by the congregation, were admitted at the age of twenty, after three months' probation and two of noviciate. (Hélyot, vol. iv., c. 54, &c.) To the nun, be it observed, belongs generally the home-work of teaching; to the secular associate, the out-of-door work of relief. Thus monachism uses the lever of free fellowship to move the world.

Existing female orders, if reformed in the sixteenth century, generally adopted education for their purpose, or new foundations were established with this view. When a convent of Capucines or strict Clarissans was founded at Rome in 1575, on the old Franciscan basis of manual labour, it was made at the same time a school for young girls

(Hélyot, vol. vii., c. 27). When the order of "Our Lady," ranked as Benedictine, was founded at Bordeaux in 1608, its especial object was the education of young women, and the counteraction of the mischief caused by the schools of the heretics, whilst the order itself was modelled on that of the Jesuits. Indeed from this period, whatever be the primary purpose of any female religious order, education comes almost invariably to be super-added to it. Thus the Philippines of St Filippo Neri, in Italy, originally Franciscan Tertiarians, took, on their reformation, for office, the bringing-up of young girls till marriage or profession. About 1647, the celebrated abbey of the " Daughters of the Holy Sacrament" at Port Royal was reformed for the (to us) blasphemous purpose of the perpetual adoration of the Host. Yet, in addition to many works of charity which he enumerates, their contemporary historian, the French poet, Racine, particularly specifies the excellent education given by the nuns, who sought to render their pupils equally capable of becoming "perfect nuns or excellent mothers of families."* And one of the most ruinous blows afterwards aimed at them by their Jesuit persecutors was the forbiddance to take

* The readers of Victor Hugo's "Misérables" will recollect the precisely similar instance of the Benedictine-Bernardines of Piepus, whose economy he has so vividly described.

in young girls as boarders. It should, indeed, be observed that in time a distinction grew up, which still subsists, between those foundations for religious education, which exist really for the sake of the poor and the destitute, and those which are simply religious boarding-schools,—sometimes very costly ones,—for the education of girls, not only of the middle but of the very highest classes.*

§ 6. *The later Charitable Sisterhoods and Reformatory Orders—Sisters of Charity, &c.*

At the beginning of the seventeenth century,— whether stimulated or not by the example of a short-lived Protestant society of women, of which rather too much has, I think, been made by Protestant partizans of the female diaconate, the "Damsels of Charity" of Sédan, founded in 1560, by Prince Henry Robert de la Mark, for succouring at their own homes the aged and sick poor (seemingly only a somewhat strongly-constituted Ladies' Visiting Society),†—a new tide began to

---

* Such are at Paris, for instance, the celebrated convents of the "Sacré Cœur" (an institute modelled on that of the Jesuits), of the "Oiseaux," &c.

† This society had neither rule, vow, cloister, nor distinctive dress. Its members were chosen amongst the unmarried, took the engagement to spare no pains for the relief of misfortune, and, subject to certain general regulations, exer-

flow in female monachism. Education was no longer alone considered; physical suffering reasserted its claim; and there shone forth a spirit of womanly tenderness to the fallen, embodying itself in the female reformatory orders. To this period belong the development or reformation of various houses of hospitallers, and, above all, the foundation of the Sisters of Charity, "servants of the sick poor."

Vincent de Paule, preaching at Châtillon-les-Dombes in Bresse, recommended a poor family so strongly to his hearers that many persons went to visit them. Hence arose a charitable fraternity for the succouring of the sick (1617), with which he was so much pleased that he resolved to found congregations for the like purpose wherever he should go, or should send missionaries—(he was already the founder of the "Missionary Priests" *Prêtres de la Mission*). Though the plan was at first devised for the country alone, a congregation was founded at Paris, and soon the example was

cised their duties of active charity in the localities specially assigned to them. Though I once, when less conversant with the subject, thought otherwise, I cannot now conceive this foundation to have established any claim of priority for Protestantism over Romanism in respect of diaconal sisterhoods. If anterior by some seventy or eighty years to the bodies founded by Vincent de Paule, the "Damsels of Charity" were certainly anticipated by centuries by the Teritarian fellowships, as these had been by the Béguines.

followed in so many towns that, in spite of all the visiting of Vincent and of his priests, the "Confréries de Charité" would have wanted direction, but for the exertions of a widow lady, Mademoiselle Legras,* to whom, by 1629, he was obliged to delegate the charge of them.

Mademoiselle Legras had originally wished to enter a convent, but from seeing Vincent de Paule's example had resolved to devote herself wholly to the poor. It is related of her that, before starting on any of her visitation tours, she always took written instructions from him, and received the sacrament on the day of her departure. She was generally accompanied by some pious ladies, all together travelling roughly and faring poorly, in order the better to sympathise with the poor. At first, in the villages and small towns where the "fraternities of charity" originated, the female members relieved personally the wants of the poor, made their beds, and prepared their food and medicines. But when several had been established at Paris,—ladies of high rank entering into them, "who could not," says Hélyot, "render personally to the poor the required services,"—country girls were sought out as "servants of the poor," of whom many offered themselves for life. Vincent de

---

* It will be remembered that at this period the term "Madame" was confined to ladies of rank.

Paule sought to form them into a community, and placed several with Mademoiselle Legras, who now organised a system which spread far and wide.

A few extracts from Hélyot, some of which may provoke a smile, will enable us better to realise the progress of this movement. He tells us that Mlle. Legras's first thought was to relieve the sick at the " Hôtel-Dieu" (lately "improved" away), who were found to want many comforts. She therefore got together meetings of ladies, who resolved to give every day to the sick of the hospital jams, jellies, and other sweetmeats by way of collation, to be distributed by each lady in turn, together with spiritual consolation. After some time, however, Vincent de Paule observed that it was difficult for the same persons to employ themselves in works of bodily and spiritual mercy, and so—making divorce between religious consolation and the jams and jellies—he had fourteen ladies selected every three months to visit the poor, two by two, on appointed days of the week, and to speak to them on religious matters. Mlle. Legras, on the other hand, gave some of the young women, whom she was bringing up as "servants of the poor," to make purchases, prepare the articles required, and help the ladies in visiting and distributing their collations. What between the sweetmeats and the religious exhortations, we are told, this new female mission converted 700 heretics and some infidels. The same ladies subsequently undertook not only the carrying out of the system throughout all the kingdom, but also sent missions to heathen countries.

Whilst this general society of ladies from all quarters of Paris was occupied at the "Hôtel-Dieu," the particular fraternities of ladies which were formed in the different parishes to visit sick and poor artisans at their own homes, composed of the ladies of the parish, under the direction of the parish priest, had also recourse to the girls of Mlle. Legras's community.*

Thus the work divided into two branches : these communities of women, mostly of the working classes, the true "Sisters of Charity, servants of the poor," and the visiting societies of ladies, mostly employing one or more "Sisters of Charity" under them. The former institute was, however, as such, quite independent of the latter. As the number of the "Sisters" went on always augmenting, Mlle. Legras bought a house at La Chapelle, and established herself there in May 1636. She was in the habit of teaching the catechism herself to women and girls on Sundays and holidays, and

---

* Before, indeed, being formed into a community, the "servants of the poor" had been at first solely dependent on the ladies of the parish fraternities.

had schools besides, where her girls taught children of their own sex. In 1641 she came into Paris, to the Faubourg St Denys, opposite St Lazare, where Vincent de Paule had his priests (now known as "Lazarists").

The "servants of the poor" received successively the charge of the Foundling Hospital (another creation of Vincent de Paule), and of two other charitable establishments in Paris, and, through their branches, of several provincial hospitals; were sent to the army, for the care of the sick and wounded soldiers; or, on the Queen of Poland's request, as far as to Poland, where they received the charge of the plague-stricken in Warsaw (1652), and afterwards that of an asylum for orphan or deserted girls. When Hélyot wrote, in 1719, they had 290 establishments in France, Poland, and the Netherlands, comprising more than 1500 women. The sisters had generally no property; their very lodgings were held consecrated to the poor. They were maintained by the hospitals where they served, and received a very trifling sum for extra expenses. Candidates were admitted to the seminary of the establishment, after strict inquiry into their character, on payment of a small sum for dress and furniture; being entitled to take away whatever they brought in, should they leave the institution. At the lapse of six months they received the sisters' dress, and began to be instructed ; when deemed competent, they were sent out as required. After five years' probation, they took simple vows, renewable annually. From time to time they were called back to the seminary, for an eight days' "retreat." The superior, elected for three years, was re-eligible for three more. But Mlle. Legras was elected for life. (Hélyot, vol. viii., pt. 6, c. 14).

I have dwelt upon the institute of the "Sisters of Charity" at greater length probably than its intrinsic merits required. But, confounded as it generally is by Protestants with many other similar bodies, although itself forming but a prominent detail in the history of Romish charities, it embodies probably for many all that they know of those charities. Viewed in itself, with its class-distinctions,* it seems to me far inferior in spiritual beauty to Béguinism, or to several forms of Romish sisterhoods. It exhibits, indeed, a further disentanglement in the Romish Church of the principle of fellowship from the monastic system. The Sisterhoods of Charity do not, like the Tertiarian fellowships, look up to a First or a Second Rule. The very ground of their formation is found in the recoil of Mlle. Legras from the temptation

---

* Which have, indeed, disappeared in modern times, when many of the sisters are ladies by birth.

of the cloister. And thus, instead of the charitable fellowship being a mere outside appendage, bulwark ornament, and at the same time highway to the cloister, it becomes a centre itself, round which clusters again the larger growth of a visiting society.

Second only to the " Sisters of Charity " is the " Congregation of the Sisters of St Joseph," founded by the Bishop of Puy in 1650. The purposes of this institute included all works whatsoever of charity and mercy; the management and nursing of the sick in hospitals, the direction of refuges for penitents, the care of houses for poor orphan girls; schools for the education of little girls, wherever no sisterhoods bound by solemn vows were at hand to hold them; the daily visiting of the sick and of prisoners. In most of their houses they had a pharmacy, containing the most usual and needful drugs. The sisters looked especially after poor girls in danger of losing their honour, trying to find lodgings and work for them; sought to establish charitable fraternities (" Congrégations de la Miséricorde ") of married and unmarried women where none existed; held once a month a ladies' meeting for the visiting of the sick poor of the parish; besides private Sunday and saints' day meetings, of widows, married women, and girls separately, to converse on religious or charitable subjects. After two years' noviciate, the sisters made simple vows of poverty, chastity, obedience, humility, and charity. They were authorised to form in villages small communities of three or four affiliated sisters, who only pronounced the three first vows, and were dependent on the superior of the nearest house of their congregation (Hélyot, vol. viii., pt. vi., c. 24).

The " Hospitallers of St Joseph,"—distinct from the above sisterhood of that name,—were at first a secular congregation, formed by a few women who went to the hospital of La Flèche to take care of the poor. After they had been working for eight years, they pronounced, in 1643, simple vows of chastity, poverty, and obedience, and of devoting themselves to the service of the poor, taking engagements for three years, or some other definite time. Amongst the ladies of rank who joined them is mentioned Mlle. de Melun, Princess of Epinay, whose father was Hereditary Constable of Flanders, and Seneschal of Hainault. They had hospitals in several large French towns, a large establishment in Canada, at Montreal, and others besides, and exchanged their simple vows for solemn ones, under a bull of Alexander VII., in 1667, although continuing to take in "associate sisters" under simple vows. If any house of this institute became poor, it was part of the rule for the others to assist it rather than found another, and all the houses were to correspond from time to time with one another.

Observe that the two great sisterhoods of " Charity " and of the " Congregation of St Joseph " pronounced only simple—*i.e.*, releasable—vows, and the former only from year to year and after a long noviciate.   It will be found, I think, almost invariably, that female monachism in its strictest form only exercises Christian charity within the four walls of its convents ; that its sphere of usefulness is mainly confined to the education of infants and young girls, the reformation of the erring, perhaps the care of the female sick ; that as soon as its charity, even towards the sick, expands to reach the other sex, a long noviciate becomes indispensable, simple vows are substituted for solemn.   In other words, as the usefulness of female monachism extends, so must its monastic character sit the looser upon it, and the " sisterhood " take more and more the place of the " order."   Would you know how the two principles struggle together ? In 1628, the Hospitallers of Toulouse wished to found a hospital for receiving the sick.   The council of the order forbade them.   It was enough for them to share in the charity which the Knights, to whom they were affiliated, practised with so much edification at the hospital of Malta.* So these poor souls, longing to devote themselves to active charity, were put off with the dry husks of a fictitious participation in the merits of others' good works. Would you note the superior efficacy, for active duties, of the comparatively free sisterhood? A secular congregation, that of the Hospitallers of Dijon and Langres, under simple vows, and with a five years' noviciate, was placed in charge of the hospitals of Dijon in 1668, after a body of nuns (those of the Holy Ghost of Montpellier) had failed to give satisfaction. (Helyot, vol. viii., pt. vi., c. 31). Would you see how the free sisterhood gradually loses its efficiency by becoming monasticised? In the order " of the Visitation of our Lady," founded by François de Sales at the beginning of the seventeenth century, the sisters, whilst uncloistered, and pronouncing simple vows, used to devote themselves to ordinary works of mercy, such as visiting, relieving, and nursing the sick. In 1626, they became, as the term is, a " religion," changing their simple vows for solemn ; attempted the reformation of women, and were intrusted with the direction of the prison of the Madelonnettes at Paris, for female offenders ; and they were received in Poland

* Hélyot, vol. iii., c. 15 : "Le conseil de la religion s'y opposa, et on leur répondit qu'il suffisait qu'elles participassent à la charité que les chevaliers pratiquaient avec tant d'édification dans l'hôpital de Malte."

upon similar terms.   Yet in Poland the purpose of
their institute was eventually changed to the mere
instructing of little girls; in France, they had to
give up the charge of the prison which had been
intrusted to them, and in Hélyot's time their main
work had sunk to the almost passive one of giving
an asylum to infirm women and girls (Hélyot, vol.
ii., c. 50; vol. iv., cc. 43, 44).

Not, however, that solemn vows themselves
could altogether stifle the active charities of women in this age, although undoubtedly the main
strength of the Romish charitable movement
lay in the "congregations," as distinct from the
"religions." Several orders of Hospitaller nuns
were founded in the seventeenth century; the
Hospitallers of St Thomas de Villanueva, Tertiarians of St Augustin (latter part of the century), who had charge of most of the hospitals of Brittany (Hélyot, vol. iii., c. 11); the
Hospitallers of Loches, Augustinians (1621), who
took, besides the three vows of charity, poverty,
and obedience, a fourth to serve the poor uncloistered (Hélyot, vol. v., c. 49); the Bethlehemites
of Guatemala (1668), (Hélyot, vol. iii., c. 48); the
Hospitallers of the Charity of our Lady (1624), for
the reception of sick women only, and these only
under certain limitations, including that of their
not being unconverted heretics (Hélyot, vol. v., c.

48). To the beginning of the seventeenth century belongs also the great reform by " Mother Geneviève Bouquet," a goldsmith's daughter, of the Paris Hospitallers. Of the Hospitaller nuns of the Hôtel-Dieu, Hélyot says, with an emotion beyond his usual gossipy manner : " There is no one who, seeing the nuns of the Hôtel-Dieu not only dress and clean the sick and make their beds, but in the midst of winter break the ice of the river which passes through the midst of the hospital, and enter it as far as their middle to wash clothes full of filth and horror, will not consider them as so many holy victims." It should not, however, be overlooked, that the noviciate in this order, although reduced, after 1636, from twelve years, which it had been in the old Béguine days, to seven, was still unusually long (Hélyot, vol. iii., c. 22).

The new charitable work of female monachism in the seventeenth century was, however, that of the reformation of erring women. Of the female orders founded for this special purpose I will only mention a few.

That of " Our Lady of the Refuge " was established in 1624 by a lady, Marie Elizabeth de la Croix, whose history, a romance in itself, comprising a forced marriage with a husband whose cruelty to her was incredible, the passion of a physician who used sorcery to obtain her affections, and a period of demoniacal possession, is given at length by Hélyot. She began by taking two women from the streets into her own house, then others, till the number rose to twenty; she herself with her three daughters waiting upon them, one cooking, another serving at table, the third reading to them. When the establishment was finally organised in 1634, the honourable and the penitent formed still but one body, alike in dress and life, except that the virtuous were always to be chosen as superiors, and for offices of responsibility; but lest the institute should ever degenerate into an ordinary convent, the penitents were always to form two-thirds of the whole number. The community was thus divided into three classes: those sisters who devoted themselves entirely to the work of reformation; the penitents, who, being deemed really converted, were admitted to the same profession as the virtuous sisters; and those who were not yet deemed awake to religious feelings. No maried woman was admitted unless separated from her husband, or with his consent (Hélyot, vol. v., c. 47).

Very beautiful also is the institute of the " Daughters of the Good Shepherd," a much later foundation, established by Madame de Combé, for penitents of all countries, who were freely maintained, beyond the expense of the first dress. The sisters were received at twenty-three, after two years' probation, wore the same dress as the penitents, and were lodged and fed the same. Every sister on her reception kissed all the penitents, waited on them at dinner, and kissed their feet afterwards (Hélyot, vol. viii., pt. vi., c. 32).

There is somewhat less of absolute self-abnegation in the order of "Our Lady of Charity." Father Eudes, brother of Mézerai the historian, collected a few penitents together, and placed them with a woman named Madeleine L'Amy, who instructed them, taught them to work, and supplied their wants out of the funds which were collected for her. She incited Eudes to establish at Caen a House of Refuge, where the penitents were at first instructed by young women who did not leave their families. As the zeal of these, however, soon fell off, a community was established in 1642 by royal letters patent, and afterwards confirmed by a bull of Alexander VII. in 1666. The members took, besides the three solemn vows, a fourth to labour for the instruction of penitent women and girls. But no penitent was ever to become a nun in the order (Hélyot, vol. vi., c. 53).

Many other bodies—mostly of a mixed character, partly educational, partly for purposes of physical relief, or again, of moral reformation—were founded during the seventeenth and eighteenth centuries, most of them under simple vows only, the history of whose establishment offers often noble instances of female self-devotion.*

The community of the " Santa Croce " of Rome was founded for the reception of dissolute women, and the instruction of young girls, the sisters, however, having power to marry (Hélyot, vol. iii., c. 51). The congregation of the " Filles de la Croix " took its origin in the infamous crime of a schoolmaster of Roye in Picardy, on the person of one of his female scholars (1625), when four poor seamstresses offered themselves to the parish priest to teach girls under his direction. After some time they seem to have been persecuted, took refuge at Paris (1636), and were placed at Brie-Comte-Robert by a lady, Madame de Villeneuve, who soon joined them, as well as the original director, the Curé Guérin. But soon a difference arose between the patroness and the director on the management of the house, and especially on the question of vows, of which the priest was sensible enough to disapprove. They were, however, established as a congregation by Archbishop Gondy in 1640, and by royal letters patent in 1642, and Madame de Villeneuve and the young women who sided with

---

* It is a remarkable fact, that if a list of Romish female sisterhoods contained in "Hospitals and Sisterhoods " can be trusted, all such sisterhoods founded since 1685 are " active," none contemplative.

her took simple vows of charity, poverty, obedience, and stability ; others, however, remained with Guérin at Brie-Comte-Robert, without taking vows. Both branches of the congregation appear to have spread in France and in Canada. Their common rule was to exercise spiritual charity towards women, especially towards the poor, and to keep open house for their reception, both towards spiritual instruction and exhortation (Hélyot, vol. viii., pt. vi., c. 17).

Somewhat similar to the above is the institute of the " Filles de la Providence de Dieu," founded by Mme. Polaillon, widow of a councillor of State, and established by royal letters patent in 1643, as an asylum for young girls endangered in their honour by their beauty, their poverty, the desertion or ill conduct of their parents. Their association was renewed in 1652. They laboured not only for the instruction of youth, but also for the conversion of female Jews and heretics. Sisters were received at twenty, after two years' probation, and took simple vows of chastity, of obedience, of serving their neighbour according to the constitutions of the institute, and of perpetual stability in the house. They received also, for a yearly sum, unmarried women of good character, without requiring them to engage themselves to the community. The girls received for instruction must be wholly destitute, and must not exceed the age of ten.   There was also an inferior class of " given sisters " (*sœurs données*) for the rough work of the house.   (Hélyot, vol. viii., pt. vi., c. 19).

The " Filles et Veuves des Séminaires de l'Union Chrétienne " were a community,—of which the first idea belonged also to Mme. Polaillon, — formed in 1661.   The duties of the institute — one of which (as in the case of the last-named body) recalls the old diaconal function of the " Angéliques " of the sixteenth century—were threefold— 1st, The conversion of heretic women and girls ; 2d, The reception of girls and widows of good birth who were without resources or protection ; 3d, The bringing up of young girls in virtue and piety, and the teaching to them reading, writing, and women's work generally.   Many houses of the institute were soon founded ; a branch of it, called " La petite Union," devoted itself specially to the bringing up of servant-girls, and the receiving them when out of place.   The members of the congregation were bound to teach little girls gratuitously, to endeavour to reconcile women's quarrels, and generally to do all the good that might fall within their power.   The probation term was two years, after which they made simple vows of chastity, obedience, and poverty, and a fourth of union amongst themselves (Hélyot, vol. viii., pt. vi.,c. 20).

The "Filles de Ste Geneviève," or "Miramiones," were founded by Mme. de Miramion, a widow, born in 1629, who in her youth had been carried away by the notorious Bussy Rabutin. As a private person, she maintained twenty little girls in a house, and paid mistresses for their instruction, and would often wait on the sick at the Hôtel-Dieu. And here comes in a trait characteristically Romish. Her director, we are told, exhorted her to make a "retreat" for a year, in order to devote herself entirely to her own perfection, without exercising her charity towards her neighbour.* After this, as "treasurer of the poor" for a Parisian parish, she is related in time of civil war to have distributed more than 2000 cups of broth in a day. Her ordinary resources failing, she sold a pearl necklace for 20,000 livres, then her plate, and with the produce established missions, schools, charities for the sick poor of the country districts. She learned herself to bleed, to dress wounds, to compound salves, &c., and kept a pharmacy in her house. After the marriage of her daughter, she devoted herself entirely to pious objects, and, amongst other labours, founded

---

* " Son directeur l'engagea à une retraite d'un an, pour vaquer uniquement à sa perfection, sans s'adonner aux exercices de piété à l'égard du prochain, *dont on ne lui permit l'exercice qu'à la fin de l'année.*"

the community of young women above mentioned, who were to hold schools in the country districts, dress wounds, and assist the sick. There was already in existence a " Community of St Geneviève," founded in 1661 by Mlle. Blosset, to visit the sick, acquire religious influence over women, receive young girls for a yearly maintenance, hold elementary schools and conferences, and receive women to "retreats." The two bodies united in 1665, and were afterwards joined by other communities formed with somewhat similar objects. The Filles de St Geneviève, as definitively constituted, taught little girls to read, write, and work, and instructed them in their religious duties; received schoolmistresses to train, or went to train them in the country; held familiar religious conferences for women, received "retreats," helped the sick, the poor, and wounded of the parishes where they were established, and were able to bleed, and dress wounds. They were admitted at twenty, after two years' probation, and made no vows. Associate sisters were also admitted after one year's probation. (Hélyot, vol. viii., pt. vi., c. 29.) Let me mention also the congregation of the " Filles de Ste Agnès " of Arras, and of the " Holy Family of Douay," established to bring up deserted orphan girls till they should be of a marriageable age, and who pronounced only the three simple vows.* (Hélyot, vol. viii., pt. vi., c. 31.)

§ 7. *Persistency of Romish Diaconal Sisterhoods.*

I shall not attempt to carry down the story from where Hélyot leaves it, before the middle of the eighteenth century.† Since then, old orders have

---

* By the side of these various charitable communities stands out with an interest quite its own the institute of the "Rosines" of Turin (founded 1740, by Rosa Governo, who had been a servant), an account of which will be found in Mrs Jameson's "Communion of Labour," p. 124. These have no vows or seclusion; they are a genuine working association of women, only with a strong religious element infused in their work. Here Mrs Jameson found nearly 400 women, from fifteen years of age upwards, gathered together in an assemblage of buildings, where they carry on tailoring, embroidery, especially of military accoutrements for the army, weaving, spinning, shirt-making, lace-making, every trade, in short, in which female ingenuity is available. They have a large well-kept garden, a school for the poor children of the neighbourhood, an infirmary, including a ward for the aged, a capital dispensary, with a small medical library. They are ruled by a superior elected from among themselves; the work-rooms are divided into classes and groups, each under a monitress. The rules of admission, and the interior regulations are strict; any inmate may leave at once, but cannot be re-admitted. Finally, they are entirely self-supporting, and have a yearly income of between 70,000f. to 80,000f.—£2800 to £3200. No female organisation is more pregnant with hopes for the future than this.

† It may, indeed, be thought, that as Hélyot's details, at least of later foundations, are in great measure confined to

become decayed or been reformed : new ones have been founded. But I have yet to learn that any new development of monachism has taken place. On the contrary, the real wonder is to find such a general identity between the picture drawn a hundred and more years ago, and the original as we see it now. In vain did the great French Revolution remodel the whole of European society, and nearly the whole map of Europe. In vain did religion seem for a while dead in France and throughout much of the Continent. Still, throughout every Roman Catholic country is the educa-

France, the field of study would be greatly enlarged could we have as full a survey of the rest of the Romish world. I think not. France, especially since the Reformation, is the very heart of Romanism, even though Rome may be its directing head. When France is lukewarm, all Romanism languishes; when France is zealous, Romanism is aggressive. Where would the Papacy have been by this time, but for French piety, French eloquence, French gold, and French steel ? The semi-Protestantism of the Gallican Church has almost alone kept alive the intellectual activity of Romanism in the last three centuries, even amongst its most virulent opponents, and every brightest light of the Romish Church since Ignatius and Xavier has been, by birth or language, a Frenchman. In studying, therefore, female monachism in France, we may rest assured that we study it in its most typical and striking form. In Mrs Jameson's " Sisterhoods of Charity," and her " Communion of Labour," will be found, however, details as to German and Italian sisterhoods, especially as to the " Elizabethan Sisters " of Germany, who, with the Béguines, were excepted from the general suppression of religious communities by the Emperor Joseph II.

tion of girls mainly or wholly in the hands of female communities. Still are " Sisters of Charity" or " Mercy," of " St Joseph," &c., at work in almost every Romish hospital, and earning, by their self-devotion and skill, the praise of every English surgeon who studies in foreign wards. Still are " Grey Sisters " sought for as private nurses throughout all their olden haunts, from the Channel to the heart of Switzerland. Still is almost every Roman Catholic refuge, reformatory, penitentiary, prison (for females at least), under the control of religious sisterhoods—as, for instance, the well-known Asylum of the Good Shepherd at Hammersmith. The Papacy may tremble on its base, but the Collective Female Diaconate of the Romish Sisterhood is rooted in almost all lands.*

The evidence of the vitality of such institutions which is afforded by the general identity of the picture traced more than a century ago by the encyclopædist of monachism, with the original such as it may be seen at the present day, is so remarkable that it deserves to be illustrated by an instance or two.

---

* See, for instance, in the Appendix to "Hospitals and Sisterhoods," the list of houses of "Sisters of Charity" now in existence. It appears elsewhere, from the same work, that since the beginning of this century there had been founded, by the date of its publication, twelve new female sisterhoods, all for purposes of active charity.

In the year 1854 (apparently), an Anglican clergyman of decided Romanistic leanings, being compelled to leave his parish for change of air and scene, determined to examine into the practical working of the " sister Church "—*i.e.*, the Roman Catholic—in France. He has consigned the results of his experience in a little work, published in 1855, under the title of " A Glance beyond the Grilles of Religious Houses in France," in which will be found much curious and interesting detail on this little-known subject, mixed with many a most painful page to any reader of honest Protestant feelings, and some careless libelling of the French Protestant Church. His tour was one simple enough. Crossing to Calais, he reached Paris, *viâ* St Omer, Douai, Arras, and Amiens, returning by Boulogne.

At Arras, he finds seventeen sisters of St Vincent de Paule—*i.e.*, the " sœurs de charité " proper, in charge of the St Louis hospital, tending the sick as they might have done in the seventeenth century; in charge, again, of an orphan-house for the poorest children of both sexes, as they were at Warsaw in the eighteenth. He finds the Ursulines educating young girls—here indeed of the upper classes—in their convent, as they might have done towards the end of the sixteenth. Nuns of the Good Shepherd are engaged in their old work of receiving penitents, though they have added to it an orphanage. He finds branches of the Franciscan nuns,—of the community of the "Holy Family,"—of a seemingly new institute (of which more hereafter), the "Little Sisters of the Poor." By the side of these diaconal bodies the Benedictines of the Holy Sacrament keep up their perpetual vigil before the altar; the Clarissans adhere to their strict discipline of old. He goes on to Douai, and finds again a Fever-hospital and Poor-house under the charge of Sisters of Charity. He finds these sisters still under the direction of the missionary priests, now known as Lazarists, whose monastery he visits at Douai, and whose "Superior General" is the common head of both the male and female orders.

In Paris, lastly, he finds himself in the centre of Romish practical monachism. Sisters of Charity are everywhere,—at the Infirmary of the "Invalides," at the Foundling Hospital, the Hospital for Sick Children, &c., &c., with institutions of their own in each of the twelve arrondissements of Paris. In connexion with the sisterhood have been revived those charitable associations of ladies from which, as has been shewn, it in fact originally sprang. Thus, he tells us that in 1840 was founded a society of ladies under the general of the Lazarists, for visiting the sick at their homes, especially in the most densely-peopled districts, and those most distant from ordinary means of succour; only—by a change which shews the democratic tendencies of the day,—whereas formerly it was the ladies who ordered, and the "servants of the poor" who obeyed; the ladies now " associate themselves with the sisters of St Vincent, and go with them or under their direction, to carry assistance to the sick, in money, soup, medicine, and other necessaries, and at the same time to take advantage of their state of health to influence them for good ; to teach the Catechism to those who have never learned, or who have forgotten it." Another secular association of the " Ladies of Charity " is also in connexion with the sisters of St Vincent, and " there are associations of these *dames* in a great number of parishes in Paris, of which M. le Curé is always president," —just as in the days of Louis XIV. The sisters themselves are 12,000 in number (an increase, it will be observed, of 800 per cent. since Hélyot's days), scattered all over the world, carrying on their old work of nursing the sick, visiting the poor, instructing the young. — Cloistered Franciscans educate gentlemen's children, but remain faithful to their old habit of manual labour, so far as doing needlework for churches and for the poor.—Ladies of St Thomas of Villanueva have charge of another hospital for sick children, and (having seemingly coalesced with or revived the congregation of the " Good Shepherd ") of a female reformatory, with a preventive branch for educating young girls. . . . .

It would be tedious to go on with these details. Two recent foundations must, however, be noted, not, indeed, as shewing any new development of monachism, but as exhibiting the powers of self-sacrifice which it knows yet how to discipline, and to adapt to new social wants.

The " Little Sisters of the Poor" renounce all worldly possessions before entering the institute, so that every need whatsoever, down to the wearing apparel of the sisters, has to be begged for. Twelve of them have charge of one hundred and seventy-one poor people, all above sixty years of age, some utterly infirm and helpless. Three times a-day two of the sisters go forth, in all weathers, basket in hand, to provide for the maintenance of the whole community, — begging everywhere, at gentlemen's houses, at hotels, *cafés*, shops, market-stalls. Of the broken victuals which they receive, the best are dressed for the inmates of the house ; what remains they eat themselves, the very hardest crusts out of the special " crust-drawer" being saved for their own eating.*

* See in " Hospitals and Sisterhoods," p. 116 and following, the account of the rise of the " Little Sisterhoods," whose institute, founded, it would seem, in 1839, numbered

Another beautiful institute is that of the " Blind Sisters of St Paul," of which the objects are :—

1st. The reception as pensioners, subject to a rule of labour and study, of adult blind girls who have no means of livelihood, and who may eventually be received into the community ;*

2d. The education of blind children, six years old and upwards ;

3d. The education and teaching in some trade of a certain number of girls not blind, who may become the guides and instructors of the blind ;

4th. The reception, for a very moderate sum, as free boarders, of blind ladies ;

5th. The carrying on of all available efforts for the moral, intellectual, and physical improvement of the blind.

So much for the vitality of Romish diaconal monachism in the female sex within its old haunts. Let us see an instance of that vitality in a quite different field, in a land where it has no adventitious aids to rely upon, where it stands exposed to the fiercest glare of public scrutiny, where it must rely on its practical worth alone for support. Miss

in 1854 between five hundred and six hundred sisters, working in thirty-three houses.

* " The blind are thus," said the author's guide to him, " raised to the dignity of spouses of Jesus Christ " (*à la dignité d'épouses de Jésus Christ*). The old soul-destroying falsehood is thus rampant till now.

Bremer, in her "Homes of the New World (1853)," speaks thus of the Romish convents of St Louis, Missouri :—

. . . "I visited various Catholic asylums and religious institutions under the care of nuns. It was another aspect of female development which I beheld there. I saw in two large asylums for poor orphan children, and in an institution for the restoration of fallen women (the Good Herder's* Asylum), as well as at the hospital for the sick, the women who call themselves 'sisters,' living a true and great life as mothers of the orphan, as sisters and nurses of the fallen and the suffering. . . . . I must observe, that Catholicism seems to me at this time to go beyond Protestantism in the living imitation of Christ in good works. . . . . Convents are established in the New World in a renovated spirit. They are freed from their unmeaning existence, and are effectual in labours of love.

"These convents here have large, light halls, instead of gloomy cells; they have nothing gloomy or mysterious about them ; everything is calculated to give life and light free course. And how lovely they were, these conventual sisters, in their noble, worthy costume, with their quiet, fresh demeanour and activity. They seemed to me lovelier, fresher,

---

* Obviously the "Good Shepherd." The translator should have known better.

happier than the greater number of women living in the world whom I have seen. I must also remark that their nun's costume, in particular the head-dress, was, with all its simplicity, remarkably becoming and in good taste. . . . . I do not know why beauty and piety should not thrive well together. . . . . The sight of the sisters here would assuredly make a sick person well."—(Vol. ii., p. 344).*

Surely there is a meaning for us in all this, and especially in the permanence of an institution on one point so utterly at war with human nature itself.

I do not know if others feel as I do the strangeness of its history,—that curious interweaving of the false with the true in seemingly indestructible vitality,—that marvellous marriage of solitude with society,—the tremendous power acquired by that which is spiritually the very type of individualism, solely through the adoption of every means and appliance of practical fellowship. For at bottom monachism, in its most social form, monachism in the shape of a vast order of thousands of men and women spread over the whole world, gathered into common societies in each town, in constant communication with one another, subject to one rule,

* See also the Appendix to " Hospitals and Sisterhoods" for a list of the Sisterhoods of Charity in the United States.

obedient to one general freely elected by the suf-frages of all, is spiritually nothing but one collective hermit, who has made the wilderness his dwelling, who has fled the common brotherhood of humanity. And yet all the strength of that hermit lies surely in this—that he is a *collective* hermit; that the false monastic order mimics the true human order. How was it, for instance, that the monks ever triumphed over the secular clergy, but that they were united and the others scattered? Bishops, priests, deacons, had to be gathered into synods and councils before they could act in common; but each monastery was a perpetual synod, a perpetual council. So that whilst singly the monk was probably never a match for the priest, the monks as a class were always able to overbear the priesthood, even when not by the force of numbers, yet still by the habit of united action.

And how is it in like manner that convents and monastic seminaries, considered as places of edu-cation, have always, amongst a Roman Catholic population, that is to say, upon equal terms, taken the lead in the long run of private lay teaching, so long as it was not connected with the principle of a religious reformation? And how is it that mo-nastic or semi-monastic bodies of women (I do not say of men) have in like manner invariably outshone private nurses in the care of the sick, private matrons

or female turnkeys in the management and reformation of the female outcast or criminal ? Not surely
through this, that they were estranged in life from
the whole of the other sex, and in spirit from the
remainder of their own, by a vow of celibacy,—I
trust to have shewn ere this that by far the greater
portion of the active charities of the female sex in
the Romish Church are exercised either without
vows, or under releasable ones;—but through this,
that they were bound together as one body, by
common ties, common hopes, common objects, a
common life often, a common point of honour, and
perhaps the common stigma of a hated name and
a ridiculed dress. Surely, once more, it is the
brotherly principle which has done the work of
monachism, its really vast work, and not the selfish,
separating, individual one.*

* In the last appendix to Dr Howson's work will be found
a slight account of some existing " Sisterhoods of Mercy" in
the Greek Church, the origin of which, however, is not mentioned. I should suspect them to be copies of the Romish
ones, but owing to the far less monastic character of the Greek
Church, capable of much healthier life than the originals.
Their constitution appears to me quite unexceptionable.

CHAPTER IV.

DEACONESSES AND SISTERHOODS IN REFERENCE TO THE REFORMED CHURCHES.

---

§ 1. *Deaconesses and Female Monachism among the Reformed Churches in the sixteenth and seventeenth centuries.*

THERE would now remain to be considered what efforts have been made, in the Reformed Churches, to reproduce either the typical institutions of the early Church or the later developments of Romanism, or to substitute new forms for those older ones, towards the consecration of female zeal and usefulness to the service of the Church, either individually or in bodies. I shall not, however, attempt to do more than give a few hints for the purpose.

One of the most curious branches of the subject, though one which I have not had leisure to follow out is that of the connexion of female monachism with the Reformation.   Those who are at all familiar with the history of the sixteenth century, must be well aware by how much the spirit had preceded the practice of religious reform; how, when all the principles had been already proclaimed, which sapped at its base the old Romish world, the fabric of that old world remained still standing, and the "evangelical doctrine" was received by and preached in many a convent of either sex, without seemingly a suspicion that it was soon to be deemed incompatible with their existence.   As late as 1521, when the controversy as to celibacy was already beginning, we find Luther writing thus to Melancthon (9th September), in a letter which exhibits, with invaluable candour and openness, the struggle then going on in his own mind :—" If with a free and evangelical mind thou takest vows, and of thy free will makest thyself a slave, it is just that thou do keep and pay thy vow,"—thus admitting the possible compatibility even of perpetual celibacy with "a free and evangelical mind."

Of the Béguines, and of what remained of the Béghards untainted by Antinomian heresy, and unruined by persecution, it is related by Mosheim that they embraced almost everywhere the doctrines of the Reformation.*   The German Béguine

* See first appendix to Mosheim's work " De Beghardis "

sisterhoods (known in Germany under the name of *seelen-weiber*, " soul-women ") appear indeed to have disappeared, their hospitals passing into the hands of the State ; but the last notices we have of them are pleasant ones,—accounts by old Lutheran ministers of how, as children, they used to go to the Béguinage, and learn beautiful hymns from the aged Béguines, which they could still repeat with delight.

Monastic foundations however, strange to say, subsisted to a much later period in connexion with Lutheranism. Thus Hélyot, speaking of his own time (vol. v., pt. iv., c. 35), tells us of a Cistercian abbey of Fraunberg in Westphalia, partly Romanist and partly Lutheran, and of which the abbesses were of both denominations alternately ; adding that there were various other abbeys in the same country, both of men and of women, which were wholly Lutheran. Of the " secular canonesses,"—a body closely analogous to the Béguines,—he tells us (vol. vi., pt. iv., cc. 50–53) that at St Stephen of Strasburg they were Zwinglian from the middle of the sixteenth century to the year 1689; that at Gandersheim, Quedlinburg,* Her-

&c., with reference to the Béguines of Gorlitz and Rochlitz in Lusatia, and the seven Béguinages of Lubeck.

* So utterly perverted, however, were these institutions from their original purposes, that we find the notorious

ford (?), and elsewhere in Germany, they were Lutherans in his time. And he speaks in like manner (vol. vi., pt. iv., c. 55) of some Danish convents where the nuns had, although embracing Reformed doctrines, continued to live in community under a superior, such as those of St Dominic at Copenhagen.*

The Reformation, however, exhibits several attempts to revive the type of the early deaconess, and this amongst the bodies furthest removed from the Romish Church, least enslaved by its traditions. The authoress of a pamphlet on "The Institution of Kaiserswerth on the Rhine" (London, 1851) tells us, that "in the first general synod of the Evangelical Church of the Lower Rhine and the Netherlands, at Wesel, 1568, we find the office of deaconesses recommended, and in the Classical

Aurora von Kœnigsmark, the mistress of Frederic Augustus, Elector of Saxony, and afterwards King of Poland, obtaining a canoness's stall at Quedlinburg Abbey.—See "Maurice de Saxe," by M. St René Taillandier, in the *Revue des Deux Mondes* for May 1, 1864.

* I believe some of these lay abbeys for gentlewomen in Holstein formed, under the head of "Stiften," one of the elements in the late Dano-German imbroglio.

It seems not worth while to do more than mention the so-called "Protestant Nunnery," or "Arminian Nunnery," of Nicholas Ferrar (died 1637), at Little Gidding, Huntingdonshire, which was in fact nothing more than an attempt to subject a particular household to a conventual discipline.

Synod of 1580, expressly established." Amongst ourselves, we find recorded in Neal's " History of the Puritans" (vol. i., c. 6., edit. 1822), amongst the celebrated " Conclusions " of Cartwright and Travers, one " Of collectors for the poor, or deacons," which runs as follows :—

" Touching deacons of both sorts,—viz., *men and women*—the church shall be admonished what is required by the apostle ; and that they are not to choose men of custom or course, or for their riches, but for their faith, zeal, and integrity ; and that the church is to pray in the meantime to be so united, that they may choose them that are meet. Let the names of those that are thus chosen be published the next Lord's-day, and after that their duties to the church, and the church's duty towards them ; then let them be received into their office with the general prayers of the church."*

The Puritan doctors seem on this subject to have been considerably better read in ecclesiastical antiquity than Hooker, who thus alludes to it (Eccles. Pol., bk. v.), not only confounding, as indeed did Cartwright also, the widow with the deaconess, but utterly ignorant of the indisputable fact of the deaconess's ordination : " Touching

---

* It is obvious that Cartwright and Travers apply 1 Tim. iii. 11 to the female deacons.

widows, of whom some men are persuaded, that if such as St Paul describeth may be gotten, we ought to retain them in the church for ever; certain mean services there were of attendance, as about women at the time of their baptism, about the bodies of sick and dead, about the necessities of travellers, wayfaring men, and such-like, wherein the church did commonly use them when need required, because they lived off the alms of the church, and were fittest for the purpose. . . . Widows were never in the church so highly esteemed as virgins. But seeing neither of them did or could receive ordination, to make them ecclesiastical persons were absurd." Altogether a rather unfavourable sample of the "judicious" Hooker, and one on which, in consideration of the many wise and noble things he has elsewhere said, I shall forbear further comment.

The tough old Puritans however persisted, at least for a time, in their notions about the revival of a female diaconate; for we find in one of the memorials of the Pilgrim Fathers, Governor Bradford's Dialogue, a description (which has been often quoted of late years) of the Church of Amsterdam "before their division and breach," wherein we are told that there were three hundred communicants, two pastors and teachers, four ruling elders, "three able and godly men for deacons, one ancient widow *for a deaconess*, who did them service many years, though she was sixty years of age when she was chosen. She honoured her place, and was an ornament to the congregation; she usually sat in a convenient place in the congregation, with a little birchen rod in her hand, and kept little children in great awe from disturbing the congregation; she did frequently visit the sick and weak, especially women, and, as there was need, called out maids and young women to watch and do them other helps as their necessity did require; and if they were poor, she would gather relief for them of those that were able, or acquaint the deacons, and she was obeyed as a mother in Israel and an officer of Christ."—(Young's "Chronicles of the Pilgrim Fathers," c. 26.) With the exception of the "little birchen rod" and the "great awe of little children,"—Puritan attributes of which I find no trace among the records of the early deaconesses,—I must say that this appears to me a most faithful reproduction of most of the functions of the original office. Nor was the Amsterdam deaconess a solitary instance. It has been shewn by Dr Fliedner (I quote here from Dr Howson's work) that at Wesel, in the Low Countries, there was a female diaconate at least from 1575 to 1610, and that amongst other causes which led to its extinction were the restricting the appointment to women above sixty, and the employment of married women—in other words, that confusion between the deaconess and the widow, against which I have so often protested in these pages, and therewith a second departure from the practice of the early Church. All these various attempts, however, to inweave into the organisation of the Reformed Churches the agency of the diaconal functions of women appear in time to have died out, and, strange to say, without leaving anything in their place, at least in this country, beyond the exercise of private charity. For it is a remarkable fact, that the great development of visiting and other local charitable societies, mainly worked in practice, as we all well know, by women, is of very late date indeed. The Strangers' Friend Society, now chiefly Wesleyan, was founded towards the end of the last century; the first parochial visiting societies, I am assured, are scarcely more than thirty or forty years old; the Metropolitan District Visiting Society dates only from 1842–3.

§ 2. *Deaconesses' Institutes and Protestant Sisterhoods in the nineteenth century.*

It is only within the present century that the question of organising women's labours in the service of the Church has been seriously considered amongst Protestants.   It appears certain, indeed, that the subject was mooted at least as early in England as in any other country, though we have proceeded with characteristic slowness to act upon the appeals made to us, from more than one quarter, even before the French Revolution of 1830.   In the *Educational Magazine* for 1840, I find mention and strong commendation of a pamphlet entitled " Protestant Sisters of Charity," published in 1826, in the shape of a letter to the Bishop of London, and ascribed to the Rev. A. Dallas.   Two years after the date of the above pamphlet, Southey, in his " Colloquies," gave an account of his visit to the Ghent Béguinage in 1815, calling it an institution " in itself reasonable and useful, as well as humane and religious;" recording the fact that "no instance of a Béguine withdrawing from the order had ever taken place."   In 1840, a series of papers on " Sisters of Charity " appeared in the *Educational Magazine*, written by a valued friend of my own, lately principal of a great training college, and to which I owe many a hint that I have since endeavoured to work out.   But meanwhile Pastor Fliedner had already (in 1833) begun with his wife and a female friend that work of female reformation which was to result in the great Deaconesses' Institution of Kaiserswerth.   Pastor Fliedner acknowledges himself to have received his first impulse toward the reformation of erring women from Mrs Fry. She in turn, after witnessing in Germany the working of the Kaiserswerth Institute,—especially, one may conjecture, of its hospital,—was moved to set up, in conjunction with other ladies, the " Institution for Nursing Sisters," still in existence in Devonshire Square, Bishopsgate. The Paris Deaconesses' Institute next followed, in 1841; that of Strasburg in 1842; that of Echallens (now St Loup) in Switzerland in 1843. Dr Wordsworth, in his " Diary in France," 1845, seems to have been the first to mention the Paris deaconesses amongst ourselves.* An article by myself in the *Edinburgh Review*, on " Deaconesses or Protestant Sisterhoods," called attention to the general subject in 1848, dwelling chiefly on the Paris Institute, with which I was personally acquainted, but referring also to Kaiserswerth, Strasburg, and Echallens. (See Appendix G.) Whilst it was passing through the press, was established, under episcopal patronage, the " Training Institution for Nurses," known as St John's House, which comprises a class of " Sisters," being persons " willing to devote themselves to the work of attending the sick and poor, and of educating others for their

---

* I was unaware of this fact till I met with it in Dr Howson's book.

duties."* The Sisterhood of the House of Mercy at Clewer, and that of Wantage, both of them for the reformation of fallen women, were founded in 1849; Miss Sellon's "Sisterhood of Mercy," in which so much of folly has been mixed up with so much of self-devotion, about the same time or earlier. (See Appendix H.) The Paris Deaconesses' Institute was emphatically commended by the late Bishop of London in his charge of Nov. 2, 1850. Kaiserswerth and its doings were specially set forth to the English public (1851) in a pamphlet printed by the inmates of the London Ragged Colonial Training School, under the title of "The Institution of Kaiserswerth on the Rhine," by a lady who had spent some time there herself, and who was destined ere long to win for herself an imperishable name as Florence Nightingale; they have since formed the subject of one or two other special publications. The Crimean war, however, may be said to be that which first popularised the subject amongst ourselves, partly by bringing Englishmen

* I may observe that the head nurse of a ward in Bartholomew's, Guy's, and probably other London hospitals, is termed "sister." I have asked of medical men in vain hitherto the explanation of this fact, and believe it to be a tradition handed down from the days of Romanism, when hospital nursing in England was the work of religious sisterhoods. I cannot find that at present any religious import whatever is given to the name in these cases.

into contact with the flourishing colonies of German deaconesses in the East; but, above all, through the need which it shewed to exist for the ministering labours of women even in connexion with that terribly manly work of fighting, and through the special value which experience stamped there upon those labours, when prompted by unworldly motives and duly disciplined beforehand. Then Miss Stanley's " Hospitals and Sisterhoods " indicated to the English public the extent of the diaconal labours of Romish sisterhoods. Mrs Jameson's " Lecture on the Communion of Labour," 1856,* set forth that view of the relation between the sexes which appears to me indispensable as a groundwork to the wholesomeness of any diaconal work by women. Dr Howson of Liverpool mooted

---

* Strange as it may seem, both the works just mentioned only came to my hands whilst finally preparing the present one for the press in 1864, though I was aware of their respective purports. The few details which I have adopted from them I have inserted in notes referring to them, but I have not otherwise in the most trifling manner modified my text.

Agreeing as I do most heartily in the central idea of Mrs Jameson's "Communion of Labour," I do not think it worth while to point out here various inaccuracies (arising from a too implicit following of Romish authorities) in her " Sisters of Charity," especially as respects the Béguines. I cannot however but say that both authoresses, by starting from the Romish sisterhood, appear to me to have missed the true point of view from which " Woman's Work in the Church " ought to be considered.

in 1858 the usefulness of deaconesses in reference to the teaching of the poor, and in 1860 published in the *Quarterly Review* an article which, in an expanded shape, was republished in 1862, and which contains, so far as I am aware, the fullest extant account of modern deaconesses' institutes; whilst the Rev. W. F. Stevenson, addressing a wholly different public, wrote for *Good Words* (1861) these articles on the " Blue Flag of Kaiserswerth," which, expanded, form one of the most interesting portions of his volume entitled " Praying and Working " (1862).*

I shall not attempt to enumerate the various institutions which in the meanwhile have sprung up amongst us, with or without the use of the names of " deaconess " or " sister," for the better organisation of woman's work in the Church. Most of them, especially of those in connexion with the Church of England, will be found noticed in Dr Howson's work above referred to. A great difference, however, has till of late years been visible between such attempts abroad and at home.

* I do not pretend here to have given an exhaustive list of publications on the subject, but have simply pointed out a few of the most important. The bibliography of Miss Sellon's sisterhood would of itself form a chapter, and a very painful one, in any work which should aim at treating the subject with any degree of completeness. Some considerations respecting it will be found in Appendix II.

Whilst the Continental Deaconesses' Institutes have from the first endeavoured to bring together as many various branches of female charity as it was possible to compass, we, with a characteristic English lack of synthesis, started at first—with the unlucky exception, indeed, of Miss Sellon's sister-hood — only from single objects. Devonshire House and St John's House only dealt with the care of the sick; Clewer, Bussage, Wantage, with that of the penitent. From 1858 to 1861, however, the subject of woman's work was considered in the Convocation of Canterbury, and latterly with un-expected largeness; and, probably as a result of the growing ripeness of opinion amongst the clergy of the Church of England on the question, insti-tutions on the wider Continental plan have been founded of late years at Middlesborough in York-shire, and again at the North London Deaconess Institution (1861).

Kaiserswerth, of course, remains still at the head of the movement—the true Protestant counterpart of the Vincent de Paule sisterhoods of the Romish Church. "At present," writes Mr Fleming Steven-son, "the colony (for such it must be called) con-sists of an hospital for men, women, and children; a lunatic asylum for females; an orphanage for girls; a refuge for discharged female convicts; a Magdalen asylum; a normal seminary for governesses; an infant school; a chapel; two shops; a publishing office; a museum; a residence for the deaconesses; and a home for the infirm. . . . Besides, as the property of the institution, there are — a home for maid-servants in Berlin; an orphanage at Altdorf; the deaconess home at Jerusalem; the seminary at Smyrna; the hospital at Alexandria; and the seminary at Bucharest. The number of these Christian women is about 320, of whom upwards of 100 are at Kaiserswerth, or at private service, and the rest scattered over 74 stations in Europe, Asia, Africa, and America. Upwards of 800 teachers have been sent out to educate many thousand children." And the growth of the work at large is sufficiently shewn by the statement quoted by Dr Howson from the " Jubilee Report " of Kaiserswerth, that there are now 27 motherhouses, with a total of 1200 sisters, carrying on their labours in all parts of the world.

§ 3. *Special Characteristics of the Protestant Deaconesses' Institute.*

The Protestant Deaconesses' Institute has, it is obvious, much more in common with the sisterhood of the Church of Rome than with the original female diaconate of the Church, and the term " deaconess " has been, perhaps, rather hastily employed in reference to its inmates. Freed, however, as it is, or should always be, from the vow or obligation of celibacy,—and thereby, it is to be trusted, from the aspiration to a perfection higher than the holiness of ordinary life, and, above all, from the deadly dream of a special union of woman with Christ as a Bridegroom,—it assumes a new character of its own, as a normal school of female charity and moral usefulness.

Considered in this light, a Deaconesses' Institute will be seen to derive its value, not from the magnitude of the charitable foundations connected with it, nor from the number of resident sisters at the "mother-house," but from the extent of the field which it offers for the due training of women in those ministering functions which have their root in woman's own nature as the best of nurses, the gentlest of almsgivers, the tenderest of educators for the young of both sexes, the great trainer and moral reformer of her own. The Protestant Deaconesses' Institute, therefore, instead of in anywise estranging its members from the common life of mankind, should simply and solely aim at fitting them the better to take part in it; it should glory rather in sending better women out, than in taking the very best in. Like the Church of which it is an instrument, it exists for the world and not for itself; it has to help in conquering the world for its true King, not to open secure refuges where a few of that King's subjects may pay their respects to Him undisturbed.

The Deaconesses' Institute of our days is therefore, I repeat it, a new thing in the history of the world, a new development of the Church's energies under the influence of the Holy Spirit. Yet, if it keeps steadily before it the essential truth, that the ministering functions of woman are only then truly and wholesomely fulfilled, whilst she remains wedded to man by the perpetual wedding of constant communication, free intercourse, the fullest interchange of the gifts and graces of each, it will not be in vain that such institutions will have recalled to mind the name of the female diaconate. Although I would fain see the name of deaconess reserved for those women who are officially called by the Church to minister to its diaconal purposes, it is such that the Deaconesses' Institute aims at sending out as the finished results of its training ; and the female deacon of the early Church has indeed, as I have before observed, been virtually re-evolved from the Protestant institutes, in the person of the so-called " parish deaconess," sent forth from Kaiserswerth or elsewhere to minister in particular parishes.*

* The so-called High Churchmen amongst ourselves have been the first to reproduce a similar type in the "sisters" attached of late years to certain parishes, and their example

If the early Church selected deaconesses without previously training them for their functions, that is no reason why the Church of the nineteenth century should not so train them. It would be pure pedantry to condemn Kaiserswerth because Phœbe was never trained there.

For the Present only can be propagated by slips and grafts; the Past, only by seedlings. We shall lose time and pains if we plant the dead sticks of the Past, and expect them to grow; yet the driest boughs will often bear the ripest seeds. Let us sow these in faith, and let God give them a body as it shall please Him, and to every seed its own body. I believe myself that the old Church-lore will afford us many a hint, if we study it lovingly, faithfully, and freely, amid the perplexities of the present. But if some should think to revive the female diaconate by investing it with the precise functions, limiting it by the precise restrictions, which it had and was bound by of old, they will be merely planting a dead stick, which cannot grow. If, however, we feel that it is the duty of the Church to call forth the ministering energies of its female members, to give them regular direction, to invest

has extended to other fractions of the English Church. The use of the word "sister" is, however, in such cases, quite a misnomer, and, where there is no "sisterhood," singularly absurd.

them with solemn sanctions,—if we cannot rest
satisfied with the dry schemes of ladies' committees
and penny clubs, with the casual labours of women
otherwise engaged, bestowing upon the Church the
mere crumbs of their leisure, taking up the work
and then setting it down again, sometimes as a
source of religious excitement, sometimes as a
mere praiseworthy and perhaps hereditary occupation, sometimes as a means of introducing themselves into a particular society;—then perhaps
we shall find a seed of life in the idea of the old
Church deaconess, the unmarried female, or the
widow, devoting herself for the time being freely
but wholly to the needs of others, solemnly consecrated to her office by the invoking upon her of
that Holy Spirit which alone can enable her to
fulfil it, whether in the care of the rich, the visiting
of the poor or the prisoner, the reformation of the
erring, or the training of the young ; and we shall
rejoice to think that institutions like Kaiserswerth
or Paris, Strasburg or St Loup, Middlesborough or
London, afford such varied and admirable fields of
training, and selection for labourers so efficient and
precious.

Nor shall we, I think, stumble over the circumstance that some such institutions may adopt the
title, or may reproduce many of the characters, of
the "sisterhoods" of the Church of Rome. If, as

I trust to have shewn, the sisterhood, though indispensable to the charitable machinery of that Church, yet belongs to her no more than the individual female diaconate, but has, on the contrary, been persecuted by her whenever it has sought to exist as a free organisation, then are both institutions freely open to adoption by Protestant churches: the real question being, as it seems to me, how far they should be combined, how far modified, in reference to the wants of the time. For indeed the seeds of the Past can only bear fruit if planted with a full knowledge of the Present, of its wishes and of its needs, of its good and of its evil. The poverty, vice, ignorance of one age are not the poverty, vice, ignorance of another. The source may be the same, but the form is wholly different. As I am told it has been observed in India that, at each successive visitation of the cholera, the treatment has to be varied, the specifics of former days proving powerless now, whilst other remedies, before inoperative, take effect,—so it is with the successive visitations of moral evil. No stock remedies will avail; no closet treatment can be devised; we must go and meet the evil face to face, study it, grapple with it, fail repeatedly, till we wring its secret from it at last; and when we have succeeded for the time, know yet that the subtle foe will reappear under another form, and that new energies will have to be exerted, new powers of observation applied to wring out a new secret, new remedies employed with success, which we perhaps have had to throw away as useless.

And yet, if we have faithfully laboured, our labour, we know, will not be vain before the Lord. The branch we are tending with such care, which is now so green and flourishing, may,—nay, *must* wither; but it may bear fruit a hundredfold. What remains at Joppa in visible shape, of the good works and alms-deeds which Dorcas did? What a picture is presented to us by the events of late years of the material and spiritual state of Syria! Fierce bigotry between Mussulman, Druse, and Christian,—the fierceness surviving in the first, even when the bigotry is dead. Fraud and bigotry, mutual hatred, and too often treacherous cowardice, among the various Christian communities as between themselves. Yet who shall say that the seed which Dorcas sowed has not borne fruit even a thousandfold? Who can say how many Christian women, in every age, in every communion, under every sky,—in continents unthought of when Dorcas lived,—have not been incited by her example to spend themselves for the good of their poorer brethren?

§ 4. *Conclusion.*

Let me now endeavour to sum up the conclusions of the above inquiry.

1. The early Church, from the apostles' own times, set the seal upon the ministering functions of women, by the appointment of a Female Diaconate, strictly excluded from the priestly functions of public teaching and worship, but nearly coequal with the male diaconate as respects the exercise of active charity, and to which, in the records of the second century, we find women solemnly ordained. The individual female diaconate, however, languished and disappeared with the growth of professed celibacy, which makes the familiar mingling of the sexes impossible.

2. The Individual or typical Deaconess is, like the deacon, attached to the service of a particular congregation. As primary objects of her charity at once and her authority, it may be observed, there are to be found beside her in the early Church two classes of persons of her sex,—aged widows, destitute of all family support, who, having deserved well of their fellow-parishioners by a life of active piety, are in their old age provided for by the church,—and young girls, often probably equally destitute of support, and maintained in like manner.

3. Though the Individual Female Diaconate dies out with the monasticising of the Church, the need for the diaconal activities of women does not. On the contrary, as the family life of the congregation languishes, and the members of each particular church cease to be of one heart and of one mind, the field of destitution—physical, intellectual, moral—must widen on all sides, requiring the Church more and more to concentrate her energies, multiply and develop her appliances for its counteraction; whilst with the growing inequality of fortunes amongst the members of Christian congregations, and the compulsory or voluntary celibacy of many, there is set free a mass of active charity, especially in the female sex, peculiarly available for the purpose of such counteraction. But, deprived of its pivot and fitting place in the constitution of the Church, this charity has to seek its standing-ground in the Church principle of fellowship; and there grow up thus fellowships of either sex, but particularly of the female, devoted to one or more works of religious love. Among the early Béguines in particular, these charitable Sisterhoods, free from the vow of celibacy, adequately fulfil the office of a Collective Female Diaconate, after the disappearance or suppression of the individual one.

4. These Free Sisterhoods, being wholly incom-

patible with the Romish Church-system, are by that Church suppressed or reduced into subjection, whilst others are established for similar purposes, but in connexion with its monastic orders.

5. Even in the Romish Sisterhoods proper, however, it is found that in proportion as the diaconal functions are active and many-sided, so they require to be free; the monastic principle is nearly as poisonous to the collective, as to the individual female diaconate, and always tends to drive the former back upon such works of charity as can be carried on within four walls, more especially the education of girls.

6. After the restoration of the Bible to the laity, and the abolition of the vow of celibacy, or, in other words, after the unmonasticising of the Church, the need of a Female Diaconate soon manifests itself—with us at first, chiefly among the Puritans.

7. That need asserts itself with renewed energy in our own days, in various attempts either to restore the early Deaconesses, or to copy the Romish Sisterhoods. The attempt meets with signal success on the Continent, among both the Lutheran and Reformed (or Calvinistic) bodies, till the so-called Deaconesses' Institutes spread over nearly the whole Protestant world, and even

succeed at last in establishing a footing amongst ourselves.

8. Closely examined, these institutions are found to represent a new principle, that of the Training of Women for works of charity, whether as recognised members of the staff of the Church or not; a principle involved indeed in all the freer Romish sisterhoods, but crushed there by the monastic tendencies of the Church to which they belong.

9. They are thus fit nurseries for a genuine Female Diaconate kindred to that of the early Church, and have proved the fact by the sending out of the so-called "parish deaconesses" of Germany.

10. The chain of Catholic tradition, in respect of woman's work in the Church, which the Church of Rome had snapped, has thus by Protestant hands been practically restored, and the new Female Diaconate needs but a franker and more general recognition, and a more solemn consecration, at the hands of the Reformed Churches of Christendom, to bear, as I believe, yet more abundant fruit.

APPENDIX A.

The Coptic Apostolical Constitutions. *   (See p. 23.)

THE remarkable feature of the Coptic Constitutions
—in the earlier portions especially—is the prominence given to the Widow.   She is introduced in the
very first page, where Christ is represented as
directing His apostles to " appoint the orders for
bishops, stations for presbyters, and continual service for deacons; prudent persons for readers,†
and blameless for widows."   After the provision
relating to the appointment of bishops, presbyters,
and deacons, the following passage occurs (c. 21):

* See "The Apostolical Constitutions ; or, Canons of the
Apostles in Coptic, with an English Translation.   By Henry
Tattam, Archdeacon of Bedford.   London: O. T. F., 1848."

† I may observe that the least genuine portions of the
Greek collections contain, to my knowledge, nothing so
audacious as this ascribing to our Lord Himself the appointment of the " Reader's " office,—valuable though I deem
it in itself.

" Cephas said, Let three widows be appointed;
two, that they may give their whole attention to
prayer for any one who is in temptations, and that
they may render thanks to Him whom they follow.
But the other one should be left constantly with
the women who are in sickness, ministering well"
(the original is *esdiacōnin*); "watching and telling
to the presbyters the things which take place.   Not
a lover of filthy lucre ; not given to drink ; that she
may be able to watch, that she may minister in the
night.   And if another one desires to help to do
good works, let her do so according to the pleasure
of her heart; for these are the good things which
the Lord first commanded."   This is followed by
another provision concerning deacons, and one
concerning the laity ; after which, we meet with the
following singular passage (c. 24) : "Andrew said,
It is a good thing to appoint women to be made
deaconesses."   (c. 25) "Peter said, We have first
to appoint this concerning the Eucharist, and the
body and blood of the Lord : we will (then) make
known the thing diligently."   (c. 26) "John said,
Have you forgotten, O my brethren, in the day that
our Master took the bread and the cup He blessed
them, saying, This is my body and my blood? You
have seen that He gave no place for the women,
that they might help with them.   (Martha answered
for Mary, because He saw her laughing : Mary
said, I laughed not.)   For He said to us, teaching,
that the weak shall be liberated by the strong."
(c. 27) "Cephas said, Some say it becomes the

women to pray standing, and that they should not cast themselves down upon the earth." (c. 28) "James said, We shall [not?] be able to appoint women for a service, besides this service only, that they assist the indigent."

In the second book, after provisions respecting bishops, presbyters, deacons, confessors, readers, and subdeacons, there occurs one respecting widows (c. 37), who are not to be ordained, but chosen by name, if their husbands have been dead for a long time, and are to undergo a probation even when old. The widow is to be appointed, it is repeated, by word only, without laying on of hands, "because she shall not put on the Eucharist, neither shall she perform public service; but . . . is appointed for prayer, and that is of all." The next chapter in like manner (c. 38) provides that "they shall not lay hands on a virgin, for it is her choice alone that makes her a virgin." It is provided further on that widows and virgins are to fast often, and pray in the church (c. 47); and a provision occurs similar to one in the Greek collection, as to giving a supper to the widows by way of charity (c. 52).

The fourth book contains a provision that, "concerning the subdeacons, and readers, and deaconesses, we have before said that it is not necessary to ordain them" (c. 67); it repeats, in nearly the same terms, the former provisions as to the non-ordination of virgins and widows (c. 69, 70), using as to the latter the words, that if "she has lived prudently, and they have not found any fault against her, and has taken care of those of her house well, as Judith and Anna, women of purity, let her be appointed to the order of widows." The fifth book, on the other hand, repeats the provisions already quoted from the third and eighth books of the Greek as to the deaconesses not blessing, nor doing any of those things which the presbyters and the deacons do, but helping the doers only, and ministering to the presbyters at the time of the baptism of women; as to their excommunication by a deacon, but not by a subdeacon; and their sharing a quarter of the eulogies with the subdeacons, readers, and singers (c. 73, 75).

The passages above quoted from the first book are the only ones on the subject which appear to me to have any mark of originality. But I think it is difficult to resist the impression that they have been tampered with. Nothing can surely be stranger than the discussion between Andrew, Peter, and John on the appointment of deaconesses; and the sentence about Martha and Mary seems hopelessly corrupt. With reference to the widows also, the limiting of their number takes us very far away from the apostolic view; since, if widows are objects of charity, as St Paul treats them, it is impossible *a priori* to fix how many of them there shall be in the church.

B.

Canons of the Councils of Nicea, Laodicea, and Carthage. (See p. 26.)

The nineteenth article (Labbé, vol. ii., p. 677) of the Canons of the Nicene Council, "concerning the Paulianists, who afterwards have taken refuge in the Catholic Church," after providing for the re-baptizing of bishops, &c., or their deposition if unworthy, proceeds as follows, in a passage which has been the subject of much controversy, and which I translate literally : "Likewise also as to the deaconesses, and generally as to all who are ranked in the clergy (ἐν τῷ κανόνι) the same form shall be observed. But we bore in mind those deaconesses who are ranked in the habit (ἐν τῷ σχήματι), since they have not even any ordination, that they should be ranked wholly amongst the laity." There is clearly here an opposition between deaconesses ἐν τῷ κανόνι and ἐν τῷ σχήματι, which appears to me to indicate that the Paulianists had honorary deaconesses (analogous to certain of the Romish canonesses of later times), who put on the dress without binding themselves to any duties, and consequently received no ordination.* Yet

---

* The above use of the word σχῆμα is, I think, illustrated by c. 44 of the 123d Novel, forbidding the use of the monastic garb (*uti schemate monachi, aut monasticæ*) by laymen, and especially on the stage. Compare the earlier

the passage has been construed as a general forbiddance of the ordination of deaconesses, by the
unscrupulous Romanist Baronius and others—a
class of writers indeed to whom the idea of a female
diaconate is essentially repugnant. The older in-
terpreters, as Balsamon and Zonaras, Bingham
justly observes (Antiq., Bk. ii., c. 22), confine the
article, according to its title and natural construction, to the Paulianist deaconesses.

I am almost ashamed of referring to the Canon
of the Council of Laodicea, Περὶ τοῦ μῆ δεῖν τὰς
λεγομενας πρεσβυτίδας, ἤτοι προκαθημένας, ἐν ἐκκλησίᾳ
καθίστασθαι, " That one ought not to establish in the
Church the women called πρεσβυτίδας or presidents,"
—rendered in the Latin, both by Dionysius Exiguus,
and the later Hervetus, "presbyteræ," "præsiden-
tes," whilst only the untrustworthy Isidorus Mercator
gives the gloss, " Mulieres quæ apud Græcos presbyteræ appellantur, apud nos autem *viduæ seniores.*"

The Canons of the fourth Council of Carthage
are certainly remarkable for the prominence they
give to the religious virgin (sanctimonialis virgo)
and widow, whilst omitting all mention of the
deaconess. The virgin, when "presented to her
bishop for consecration," is to "wear such raiment
as she is to wear always hereafter, suited to her
profession and sanctity" (c. 11). On the other
hand, those widows or religious women (viduæ vel
sanctimoniales) who are selected for the office of

Code, Bk. i., Tit. iv., l. 4, forbidding the use of the virgin's
dress (here termed *habitus*) by the same classes of persons.

baptizing women, are to be qualified for their functions, so as to be able to instruct by apt and wholesome discourse any ignorant and rustic women at
the time of baptism, how they should answer the
questions of the baptizing minister, and what life
they should lead after receiving baptism. This
passage is one of the main authorities relied upon
by later writers for the complete identity of the
widow and deaconess. To be consistent, it should
be argued that it proves equally the identity of both
with the *sanctimonialis*, the nun (*monialis*) of later
days. But it is clear from history that the canon
is absolutely valueless as respecting the practice
of the whole Eastern Church at least, at the very
period to which it belongs.

By later canons of this Council it is provided
that " young widows, infirm of body, are to be
maintained at the expense of the Church of which
they are widows" (c. 101). Again, that " widows
who are maintained at the expense of the Church
are to be so assiduous in the work of God as to
help the Church by their merits and prayers" (c.
103). Another lengthy canon is against their
second marriage. Widows who, whether so left in
youth or in mature age, have devoted themselves
to the Lord, and, throwing off their lay dress, have
appeared in a religious garb under witness of the
bishop and the Church, if they contract a "worldly"
marriage, are treated as guilty of a worse adultery
than the unfaithful wife.

I should infer from the above passages, that any

clear perception of the office of a female diaconate had by this time died out in the African Church. We see instead of it, as I have said, widows and consecrated virgins invested with a peculiar garb, devoting themselves to God in the presence of the bishop and of the Church, fulfilling some diaconal functions, but receiving no imposition of hands, and subject, not directly to the bishop, as in the Apostolical Constitutions, but to some member of the clergy; since the ninety-seventh canon bears that " the person " (in the masculine) " to be put at the head of the religious women shall be proved by the bishop of the place." (Qui religiosis fœminis præponendus est, ab episcopo loci probetur.) The confusion between the widow and the deaconess, which is evinced in the requirement, that the " widows maintained at the expense of the Church should be assiduous in the work of God, so as to help the Church by their merits and prayers," has led to the direct infringement of the apostolic command, in burthening the Church with the maintenance of younger widows, and again in forbidding them to marry, although left widows in their youth. The whole spirit of later Romish conventualism may be traced in these canons, and especially in that most offensive passage, which treats as adulterous the second marriage of a widow consecrated to God.

(Two passages from Lucian and Libanius, of very doubtful application to the female diaconate, but

which are among the stock quotations on the subject, I merely mention here, to shew that they have
not been overlooked).

C.

*The marriage of the soul with Christ, a doctrine not
countenanced by St Paul.* (See p. 79.)

Nothing is more remarkable than the divine cau-
tion, for I can use no other term, with which St
Paul shuns the idea of the marriage of the individual with Christ, even when seemingly led naturally on to it by the current of the illustration he
may happen to be following up.

Take, for instance, that chapter (vii.) of the
First Corinthians, which chiefly recommends virginity: " He that is unmarried careth for the things
that belong to the Lord, how he may please the
Lord (ver. 32). . . . The unmarried woman careth
for the things of the Lord, that she may be holy
both in body and in spirit" (ver. 34). Here,
although the contrast is actually with the husband
who "careth for the things of the world, how he
may please his wife" (ver. 33), and the wife, who
"careth for the things of the world, how she may
please her husband" (ver. 34), the Apostle, as it
were, pointedly refrains from suggesting that the
Lord is in any special manner the husband of the
human being who thus becomes devoted to Him.

Take another passage, in which the idea of marriage to Christ is actually set forth, 2 Cor. xi. 2 : "For I am jealous over you with godly jealousy : for I have espoused you to one husband, that I may present you as a chaste virgin to Christ." How carefully the idea of the unity of the Church is preserved! We are "espoused to one husband," but "as a chaste virgin," not "as chaste virgins." True, it is only the Corinthian Church which is spoken of; but who does not see that the part is here taken in the name of the whole? that if St Paul were addressing a "Catholic" epistle to all the Churches throughout Christendom, he would still speak of presenting them, one and all, "as a chaste virgin" to the One Bridegroom of the One Bride?

Take again Rom. vii. 4: "Wherefore, my brethren, ye also are become dead to the law by the body of Christ; that ye should be married to another, even to him who is raised from the dead, that we should bring forth fruit unto God." I have already pointed out that "married to another" is a very narrow interpretation of γένεσθαι ἑτέρῳ—in fact an unconscious begging of the question now at issue. But is it for nothing that the plural is used? Is it—let the expression be allowed me—a polygamic plural? or does it not express essentially the idea of the marriage of the *Church* with Christ? It is "ye"—the disciples in general—who have been married to the law, who have to "be married to another" (γένεσθαι ὑμᾶς ἑτέρῳ); it is "we"—St Paul with them—who have to "bring forth fruit unto

God." Surely St Paul well knew that the idea of the marriage of the individual with Christ would be a dividing of Christ Himself, as well as of His Church; a profaning of the one eternal wedding, as it were by a thousand petty acts of spiritual polygamy, as false to man's glorified nature in Christ Jesus as the divided caresses of a Solomon or an Ahasuerus. I shall be grieved if these words give pain; but I believe the evil to be a deadly one, and I cannot deal gently with it. Face the idea in itself, and you will see that the worship of Christ as an individual bridegroom is in reality the worship of Him, not as the representative of humanity, but as a male human being, capable (to repeat words just used) of spiritual polygamy. Many a time have I sickened over the expressions of Romish writers, speaking of nuns as " the spouses of Christ," so completely did their language remind one of an Eastern harem, from which was wanting not one of the precautions of Mohammedan libertinism, even to the eunuch, spiritual at least, in the shape of a Father Confessor. And I know that this foul prurient talk is being now dinned into the ears of many and many an English girl by Romanists, conscious or unconscious, open or concealed, then most dangerous when they least mean it, and that many a one already has been prevailed upon to leave father and mother, and friends, and fellow-creatures, and to plunge herself into the depths of a convent, in hopes of uniting herself there, by the most solemn of marriage vows, to a

Bridegroom who will never forsake her. And I feel that every such act is a contemning of Christ's earthly body and heavenly bride, the Church, a real offence against her unity, since we cease to love our fellow-creatures as we ought, when we grow to believe that we can be united to Christ otherwise than with them, and as members of that common body.

As respects women, indeed, although more natural in a sense, the idea of the marriage of the individual with Christ is still more unscriptural than as respects men. St Paul is express to this point. See 1 Cor. xi. v. 3: "The head of every man" [παντὸς ἀνδρός, not ἀνθρώπου] "is Christ, and the head of the woman is the man" [ὁ ἀνήρ], "and the head of Christ is God." If the relation of the head to the body is here treated as identical with that of marriage (a position which would involve the utterly repugnant one of Christ being married to God), then all the spiritual marriages of Romish nuns fall to the ground, since Christ is only the head of the man, and the woman cannot be united with Him except through the man.

Yet whilst to Romanism belongs the peculiar form of this error which has reference to the female sex, and all the material developments of that form in art and in daily life, from a Raffaelle's "Marriage of St Catherine," to the latest reception of an English nun, such as we see advertised in our newspapers sometimes cheek-by-jowl with a lecture by Gavazzi, Mr Spurgeon, or Mr Bellew,

—the doctrine is one, as we well know, as rife in Protestant as in Romanist countries,—pervading English and German hymn-books alike,*—often characteristic of the most fervid forms of devotion amongst the Dissenting bodies,—and which can be carried without violence or difficulty, as I shall presently shew, quite out of the pale of all Christian orthodoxy.

Now I can understand the argument: If the whole Church be married to Christ, then must every member of Christ be married to Him also. It needs, I believe, to be completed by the words "as such member," in order to shew that not an individual marriage is meant, but a participation in that of the Church itself. But it should be observed that what is celebrated by mystics of all creeds is simply the marriage of the *soul.* Where is there a hint of such a marriage in the Bible? Surely it is the whole human nature which is united with Christ,—body, soul, and spirit. Christ is said to be the Head of *man*, not of man's soul, —the Head of "every man," not of this or that soul of man which chooses to accept His headship. In this view, I do not hesitate to say that the materialistic Romanist error of the marriage of the *woman* with Christ, does not so far depart from the truth as the more specially Protestant one of the marriage of the *soul* with Him.

* See for instance the beautiful German hymn, "Seelen-bräutigam," composed by Adam Drese, 1630-1718.

Now it is a remarkable fact that this tenet has never been more seductively set forth in our days, than by a writer who fully admits himself to have travelled quite out of the region of orthodox Christianity. Let me quote a passage or two from the chapter on the "Loves of the Soul," in Part III. of "The Soul, her Sorrow and her Aspirations," by Professor F. W. Newman :—

"If thy soul is to go on into higher spiritual blessedness, it must become *a woman;* yes, however manly thou be among men. . . . . Spiritual persons have exhausted human relationships in the vain attempt to express their full feeling of what God (or Christ) is to them—Father, Brother, Friend, King, Master, Shepherd, Guide, are common titles. . . . . But what has been said will shew why a still tenderer tie has ordinarily presented itself to the Christian imagination as a more appropriate metaphor, that of marriage. . . . . Those in whom these phenomena have been sharply marked, so as to make a new crisis of the life, seem instinctively to compare the process which they thus undergo to a Spiritual Marriage. We have seen the longings of the soul to convert God's transitory visits into an abiding union, and how it is eager above all things to make this union *indissoluble.* On getting a clear perception that it is asking that which He delights to grant, it believes that its prayer is answered. . . . . It is therefore very far indeed from a gratuitous phantasy, to speak of this as a marriage of the soul to God : no other metaphor in fact will express the thing."*

It is then certain that the doctrine of the soul's marriage is compatible with the most avowed heterodoxy. There needs hardly to be pointed out that it is no less so with sheer heathenism. Those who are in anywise conversant with Hindooism, must be aware that it is really the cardinal idea of the worship of Krishna. And although one leading Hindoo myth illustrating the doctrine cannot well be repeated here, it is certain that page after page of professedly Christian utterances in reference to it, both in verse and prose, would be accepted as strictly orthodox by the most learned worshippers of the glorified spouse of the Gopis.

To decaying Hindooism, I own, I would fain consign a doctrine which seems to me utterly false to the spirit of the Bible,—avowedly emasculating to its professors,—utterly offensive to all who have obtained but one glimpse of that greatest mystery of the social life of humanity, the Marriage of the Lamb with the Bride.

* With his characteristic candour, Mr Newman admits that "the Hebrew prophets, especially of the latter school, habitually represent the relation of the Israelitish Church collectively to Jehovah as that of a wife to a husband ; but this does not seem to be applied to individuals." He speaks of St Paul (2 Cor. xi. 2) as having "first set the example of concentrating the similitude on parts of the Church." I have shewn above that the verse in question, instead of warranting the further application of the idea to the individual soul, testifies most strongly against such an inference.

D.

*The Church-Virgins and the transition of the institu-
tion into monachism.*   (See p. 96.)

The history of the Church-Virgins appears to me
to have been far less clouded by commentary than
that of the female diaconate.   Those who are
curious on the matter, I will refer to *Bingham's
Antiquities*, where it is, so far as I am able to
judge, treated of with the author's usual soundness
and candour; observing, in the first place, that I
cannot find any trace of any special offices having
been assigned to the professed virgins as a body.
I have shewn already how naturally the virgins
would grow to fulfil all the characters of destitution assigned by St Paul to the "widow indeed,"
and thereby acquire similar claims on the Church
for support; and accordingly we find that there
was a register of such virgins, similar to that of
the widows; that they were supplied with victuals
like the widows and the ministering clergy, at the
expense of the Church at first, and after Constan-
tine of the state, unless when Pagan or Arian
persecution interfered to stop their maintenance
(see for instance Theodoret, Bk. i., c. 11; or
Athanasius, Encyclic to the Bishops, c. 4).   There
was, at least sometimes, a special residence or
Parthenon assigned to them; thus, the author of
the life of Anthony, ascribed to Athanasius, speaks
(c. 3) of his having placed his sister in a Parthenon

to be brought up, before embracing the monastic life. A certain number of Church-Virgins, as well as of Church-Widows, appear throughout the East to have made part of the organisation of every individual church; and the outrages and violences exercised towards such virgins, as well as towards the ministers of the Church, form—in the works of Athanasius for example,—an invariably recurring detail in the history of every fresh persecution against the Church. Of the identity of position which thus grew up between the Church-Widow and the Church-Virgin, a single instance will suffice. Chrysostom, in a letter (207) to Valentinus from his exile at Cucusum, begs his correspondent to forward some money, on the ground that "the most honourable presbyter Domitianus, who has the direction of the widows and virgins of this place," had informed him that they were well-nigh reduced to starvation (A.D. 404).

In the early Church, it is clear that the profession of virginity, like that of widowhood, was not by any means essentially connected with the relinquishment of home or family duties, or with dependence on the Church. The two subjects, of widowhood and virginity, are generally treated of together, or in close sequency, by the Fathers, the two vows frequently mentioned as it were in the same breath (see for example August. Enarr. in Ps. lxxv., c. 16). The connexion between the two ideas is instanced in a striking manner, in a treatise on Virginity, attributed falsely to Athanasius, of which the author exhorts a virgin to good works, by telling her that she will receive "the honour of the good widow," τιμὴν τῆς καλῆς χήρας (Athan. de virg., c. i.), referring at length to 1 Tim. 5, 6, and the following verses, so as clearly to imply that the virgin is to be "well reported of for good works," to "lodge strangers," to "wash the saints' feet," &c. But in the praises of virginity and of widowhood which occur in the works of perhaps every church father—in Cyprian and in Ambrose, in Augustin, in Jerome, in Chrysostom,—the profession itself is treated as something altogether individual, and neither giving *per se* a claim on the Church for support, nor requiring the professor to embrace either the solitary or the cenobitic life.

Of the process by which the Church-Virgin passed into the Nun, it would serve no purpose here to give the detail. It will be sufficient to say that the Codes and Novels exhibit that process actually going on, and to shew it from them by a few samples.

Up to the middle of the fifth century, the distinction between the Church-Virgin and the Nun is clear at law. Thus a constitution of the year 455, referred to in the body of this work, and ascribed to the Emperors Valentinian and Marcian, speaks of the widow, the deaconess, the virgin devoted to God, and the *sanctimonialis* or religious woman, as separate classes : Sive vidua, sive diaconissa, *vel virgo Deo dicata, vel sanctimonialis mulier.*—Cod. Lib. i. ; Tit. ii., l. 13.

By the time of Justinian, although the distinction reappears at times, there is, to say the least, a tendency to consider the " sanctimonialis virgo " as the general type, of which the " monastria," "ascetria," and even the deaconess, are individual specimens, and in which the Church-Virgin is merging; see for instance Cod., Bk. i., Tit. iii., c. 54 (A.D. 533). The notion of the distinction between the Church-Virgin and the *sanctimonialis* had not however died out; see Cod., Bk. ix., Tit. xiii. The last passage that I am aware of in which the Church-Virgin is spoken of as distinct from the nun is the 79th Novel; though even here it seems implied that she resides in a monastery, and the title includes her under the term "ascetria" as generic :

"Apud quos oporteat causas dicere monachos et *ascetrias*. C. I. Propterea igitur sancimus, si quis quamcumque habuerit causam cum aliquibus venerabilibus *sanctimonialibus,** *aut sacris virginibus, aut mulieribus omnino in monasteriis consistentibus.* . . . . Epilogus. Hac valente lege, si quis cum aliquo reverendissimorum monachorum *aut virginum aut mulierum omnino sacrarum et in venerabilibus monasteriis habitantibus* habuerit causam." . .

It is difficult to imagine in what the distinction between the two classes of women at this time may have consisted; except that perhaps the Church-Virgins, although residing in convents, were

---

* This word seems here to apply to " monks " of both sexes, if we may so use the term.

according to tradition maintained by some particular Church, whilst the ordinary *ascetria* or *monastria* depended on the resources of the convent itself. I notice at least that in a law forbidding composition being taken for rent-charges bequeathed to pious uses, the deaconesses and *ascetriæ* are the only two classes of females referred to as objects of special charity (Cod., Tit. iii., c. 46); but the word may have been used here also as including the Church-virgins.

After this no distinction occurs but between the Deaconess (sole remnant of the old Church-system as respects females) and the *ascetria* and other types of the new monastic Church-system which was growing up. Thus in the 123d Novel: "Si quis contra aliquem clericum, aut monachum, *aut diaconissam, aut monastriam, aut ascetriam* habeat aliquam actionem (c. 21). . . . . Sportularum viro nomine omnem personam in quocunque ecclesiastico officio constitutam, et ad hoc *diaconissam et monacham, aut ascetriam, aut monastriam* (c. 28). . . . . Sancimus, si personæ talibus conditionibus subjectæ, sive masculi, sive fœminæ, monasteria ingrediantur, aut clerici, aut *diaconissæ, aut ascetriæ* fient (c. 37). . . . . Si quis rapuerit, aut sollicitaverit, aut corruperit *ascetriam, aut diaconissam, aut monacham,* aut quamlibet aliam fœminam venerabilem habitum habentem" (c. 43). . . . .

What was the difference between the *ascetria* and the *monastria*, and whether the latter was in all points the same as the *monacha,* it is difficult to say. Compilers of ecclesiastical digests use "monasterium" and "asceterium" as synonymous, which I feel strongly convinced they were not. Judging from etymology, the "monastery" was a mere depôt of monachism, the "ascetery" its field of battle. In the one monks or nuns simply resided together, in the other they "exercised" their faith by privations and austerities. But there might be "ascetes" in a monastery; thus the 123d Novel forbids the dragging of a "monastria" or "ascetria" from the monastery (non tamen *monastriam, aut ascetriam* monasterio abstrahi; c. 27), in the case of judgments involving execution against the person.

The "most reverend" canonesses, *canonicæ*, are another class of religious females who make their appearance in common with the *ascetriæ*, in one law only (Nov. 59),—a sumptuary law for funerals. It appears from it that these *ascetriæ* and *canonicæ* had some duty to perform in relation to funerals in the *xenodochia*, or hospitals for the reception of strangers: " Eo quod *ascetriæ* ad hoc ministrantes opus sub xenodochiis per tempus memoratorum venerabilium xenodocorum constitutæ sunt" (c. 3) These women used to precede the bier and chaunt: "Sancimus singulo lecto gratis dato unum asceterium dari, *ascetriarum aut canonicarum* non minus octo mulierum præcedentium lectum et psallentiim" (c. 4).

E.

The Hospitallers of St Martha in Burgundy. (See
p. 126.)

An admitted offshoot from the tree of Béguinism
was the congregation of the Hospitallers of St
Martha in Burgundy, founded at Beaune in 1445
by the Chancellor of Duke Philippe le Bon, with
six Béguines from Malines. Hélyot gives a description of the noble foundation directed by them, such
as it was in his days. There was a very long ward,
common to the sick poor of all nations, with a
chapel at the east end, so disposed that all the
sick might hear and see the religious services.
Behind the altar was another ward for the more
dangerous cases, with its special offices; and behind this again the dead-room, with washing places
and great stone tables. Along the great ward to
the south ran a large square court, surrounded by a
higher and lower gallery. The higher gallery was
what we should call a sanatarium, containing
twenty apartments for persons in easy circumstances, to which gentlemen and rich " bourgeois"
would come in to be treated both from the town
and from a distance of several leagues. Each suite
of apartments consisted of a bed-room, ante-room,
dressing-room, and retiring-room, and contained
three beds, to change the sick persons, besides
being richly and completely furnished. The patients here had to provide themselves with food,

and to pay for medicine, but not for the furniture or the service of the sisters, although there were few who left no gratuity behind at their departure. The lower galleries contained rooms for poorer people, who were tended and treated at the expense of the hospital, like the sick of the common ward; although if they required fires, meat, or nurses for their special service, they had to pay for them. A small river ran through the courtyard, and was carried by conduits into all the services, so that all was kept fresh and sweet.* At a similar foundation at Châlons-sur-Saône, we are told that in winter it was the practice to burn perfumes in the wards to avoid bad smells, and in summer to have vases full of flowers suspended from the ceilings. I believe the introduction of flowers into hospital wards is still nearly a novelty amongst us, and one that has been found very beneficial. Christian charity in the sixteenth century was thus far beforehand with medical science in the nineteenth. In the Châlons hospital, also, there were four lofty rooms, tapestried and richly furnished, with private kitchens, for patients of rank. And "the two Burgundies" (the duchy, and the county) contained, we are told, many other hospitals, all served by sisters.—(Hélyot, vol. viii., pt. vi., c. ii.)

There is something, perhaps, which offends our

---

* It is most remarkable to find in Mrs Jameson's lecture on "Sisters of Charity Abroad and at Home," an account of the Beaune Hospital tallying almost precisely with the above. It remains still under the care of the same sisterhood.

feelings, in the aristocratic distinctions of treatment between the persons of rank and the poor in these hospitals. I cannot help thinking, however, that it is good to bring class with class together under one roof in a hospital, and that, let the rich patient's room be as splendidly furnished as it might, there was a lesson of humility for him in the near presence of his poorer fellow-sufferers, and in the sharing with them of the same Christian charity, which does not reach him so easily, to say the least, in our days, through two or three strata of nurses, flunkeys, and maids in a Belgravian or Tyburnian mansion.

F.

Translation of one of the later Béguine Rules (see p. 139).

The following is a translation of the rule of the Béguines of Innenheim at Strasburg, given by Mosheim. It will be observed that it belongs to the latter period of the Béguine movement, when these sisterhoods were sinking under the influence of the Mendicant orders,—the confessor being a Dominican, and being invested with a power of dispensing from the observance of the rule itself, by counsel of the Prior of the Dominican convent. The rules were, moreover, the same as those of two other similar houses in the same city,—the " Offen-

burg" house and the "House at the Tower,"—
both, like the other, situate in the neighbourhood
of Dominican monasteries, by the monks of which
they were directed, and in the churches or chapels
of which the sisters attended divine worship :—

"In the name of the Father, of the Son, and of
the Holy Ghost, Amen. We, Mechtildis (Ma-
tilda) mistress, Adelheidis (Adelaide) sub-prioress,
and the other sisters assembled in the house called
of Innenheim in Strasburg, whose names are as
follows :—Gertrude, Elizabeth, Willeburgis, Anna,
Catherine, Ellekint, and her sister Gisela, to the
honour of our Lord J. C., wishing to flee all grounds
of a suspicious and painful dissolution, and to be
coerced to a commendable discipline, by counsel
and consent of our confessor, brother Frederic,
called of Ersthem, of the order of the Preacher-
brothers of Strasburg, do ordain these things
amongst us, and by plighted faith publicly avow
that we will inviolably observe them.

"We have ordained therefore, and by the plight-
ing of our corporal faith have promised to observe,
that whosoever shall come to us to take our habit,
and to remain with us, if in any year, changing
her design, she shall depart from us, she shall be
free to resume whatever, whether in movables or
immovables, she shall have brought in, yet so
that, in lieu of expenses or victuals, she do render
for every month sixty deniers ; and, moreover, that
if she have received anything in clothes or for her
other necessities from the sisters, she do refund it;
nor shall there be reckoned in diminution thereof

either services, if any were performed during her bearing the habit, nor her labour, nor the profit proceeding from what she brought in, nor that which might have resulted from it.

" But if she have been invested with the habit when little, at whatever time before the age of fourteen she may have departed, she may depart, as it is said above ; but if she die after coming to the sisters, and though she may not yet have been invested, whatever she may have brought, shall remain to the sisters.

" So, if after the age of fourteen, having pledged by faith of hand that she will obey, she shall afterwards recede from such her will, either for an honest cause, as, for instance, that she will remain in the seclusion of a prison (*in reclusorio carceris ?*) or otherwise, that she will pass to an honest society, of all the things brought in with her, whether immovable or movable, she shall not be able to carry anything out with her, except clothing and bed-gear, unless the benevolence of the sisters choose to do her larger favour. So if she will enter a cloister, she only receives five pounds of her goods brought in with her.

" *Item*, We will and ordain, and by giving of faith we guarantee (*vallamus*), that if any shall fall into a snare of the flesh, or shall be convicted of having introduced a man during the hours of night, or, during the hours of day, shall have been found with one in a secret and suspicious place, she alone with him alone, the other sisters being ignorant, or shall have some suspicious familiarity with men or women, which, on the third or fourth admonition she shall not have chosen to eschew, and shall have received letters from them, and hid them, or shall have failed to obey the command of the mistress, or shall have scorned to obey her, or shall have continually troubled her fellow-sisters of the same house, palliating her trespasses by the trespasses of others, reproaching others with their faults, or telling foul things to them, or shall have refused to bear the penalties enjoined for her trespasses, that for every such cause alone she be from our house ejected, expelled, and extruded, nor of the things brought in with her, whether movable or immovable, shall carry aught away, or cause aught to be carried away; so that, being excluded from all her goods, she carry nothing nor take aught away, not even her clothes which she had at the time; nor shall any pretext of the entreaties of relations and next of kin, nor of any friends or near ones, avail to commute aught herein, but so that those whom the fear of God recalls not from evil be at least coerced by bodily penalty.

" *Item*, We will and ordain, and by giving of faith do guarantee, that if anything of the premises be called in question by denial of the outgoer, sufficient proof shall be had by testimony of the mistress and sub-prioress, and of the more part of the sisters, and whatever they shall affirm concerning the things aforesaid shall be deemed a testimony efficacious and immutable.

" Moreover, we choose not that any be received so that she have not power to inherit by any title in goods paternal, maternal, or acquisitions by donation or purchase, save by our renouncement in any case.

"*Item*, We ordain, that if any one amongst us in the fellowship of sisters do depart this life, or not being rejected by us, shall leave of herself for any above-expressed cause, honest or not honest, that neither the party leaving shall demand any of the things brought in by her, nor any of her next of kin, heirs or friends, either in his own name or in that of the deceased; so that what is not lawful by one way, shall not be admitted fraudulently by another.

"Moreover, if in any event it shall happen that we should be separated, by reason of poverty or any other misfortune, we ordain that of all things which we then possess, whether movable or immovable, every one do receive her share by an equal division.

"*Item*, We ordain and promise, by pledge of faith, that in those things which shall be ordained and corrected concerning our state, we will obey our mistress and sub-prioress, and him who for the time being shall be assigned to us for confessor; and we do submit ourselves to them from this present ordinance so far as respects these things and all above mentioned and ordained, so even that our confessor, by consent of the Prior of the Preacher-brothers, may in any article of this schedule give us dispensation, if he shall see fit.

"Whosoever, therefore, being about to be received, after that the premises shall have been read and expounded to her, shall choose to keep the things promised and shall so promise, and by pledge of faith shall confirm the same so to be kept, let her be received for a sister of our congregation. But if she refuse to pledge her faith for the keeping of these things, let her never be received into our fellowship, neither for prayer or price, so long as she shall not promise to observe all and singular the same.

" We will also, in order to preclude any matter for future contention, that if any one, although not asked touching the aforesaid articles, whether she will keep them, shall have dwelt beyond the year (with us), that from and after the expiration of the first year she shall be held confessed and obliged to the hearing of all the aforesaid articles, and shall otherwise have no petition touching her goods, as if she had for her own trespass been excluded from our house and fellowship.

" But in order that all these things be held confirmed, we have made the present letters on our petition to be confirmed by the seals of our Lord the Judge in the Bishop's causes, and of our Lord Herman, the venerable Prior, and also Treasurer of Strasburg.

" We, the Judge of the Strasburg Court and the Treasurer of Strasburg, do publicly avow all the premises to have been ordained in our presence, and the present writing to have been, on the petition of the aforesaid ladies, confirmed by our seals. Done and given at Strasburg, A.D. 1276, Kal. May."

G.

" Deaconesses, or Protestant Sisterhoods," (see
p. 202.)[1]

[The following paper represents the last *author's*
" revise " of an article under the above title
which appeared in the *Edinburgh Review* for
April 1848. For the text as printed in the
Review I must henceforth disclaim all responsibility. I did indeed at the editor's suggestion forward a P.S. on the Training Institution
for Nurses, but the concluding paragraph of
the article on the subject represents neither
what I wrote nor what I thought in the matter.]

1. *Etablissement des Sœurs de Charité Protestantes
   en France.* Paris: Delay, 1841.
*Institution des Diaconesses des Eglises Evangéliques
   de France; Etats de Situation, 1842 to 1847.*
   Paris.
*An Appeal on behalf of the Institution of the Deacon-
   esses, established in Paris.* By the Rev. A.
   VERMEIL. London, 1846.
2. *Etablissement des Diaconesses de Strasbourg; Rap-
   ports Annuels, 1844–5.* Strasburg.
3. *Etablissement des Diaconesses d'Echallens; Rap-
   ports, 1843 to 1845, Echallens (Pays de Vaud).*
4. *Neunter Jahresbericht über die Diakonissen-Anstalt*

[1] Any notes on the present Appendix, marked with as-
terisks, belong to the original article. Notes marked with
numerals have been subsequently added.

zu Kaiserswerth am Rhein. Kaiserswerth, 1846.

5. *Report of the German Hospital, Dalston.* London, 1846.

At the eastern extremity of Paris, close to the Barrière de Charenton, which leads to the French "Bethlehem,"—on the outskirts of the Faubourg St Antoine, one of the great workshops of Parisian industry, — in a quarter which, though poorly peopled, is elevated, wide, and airy, and in one of the widest and airiest streets of that quarter, in the Rue de Reuilly, — is situate an institution which has attracted no small share of attention amongst the more earnest and philanthropic portion of French society, together with not a little envy and calumny, and which, as a necessary consequence, has awakened enthusiastic sympathy and support ; the Institute of Deaconesses, or Protestant Sisters of Charity. "The Institute of Deaconesses" (we quote from the 1st Article of its Statutes) "is a free association, having for its object the instructing and directing, in the practice of active charity, of such Protestant women as shall devote themselves within its bosom to the relief of bodily and spiritual misery, and particularly to the care of the sick, the young, and the poor."

Its existence dates now from the year 1841. Its foundation is owing to one of the most distinguished ministers of the Reformed (Calvinistic) French Church,—a child of the quick-minded, warm-hearted south,—the Rev. Antoine Vermeil,[1] who, after fulfilling for many years the arduous and conspicuous functions of the Protestant ministry at Bordeaux, at last, some years back, accepted functions still more arduous and conspicuous at Paris. Here it was that he was enabled to realise a long-cherished idea, and to do so in conjunction with a worthy minister of the Lutheran Church (one borrowed indeed, as it were, by her from her Calvinist sister), the Rev. M. Vallette. The institution has since grown up, under the joint and harmonious patronage of the two established Protestant churches of France (represented in its council, the one by a President, M. Vermeil; the other by a Vice-president, M. Vallette); swelling from a mere house to a vast establishment; from a Refuge for Female Penitents to a complete Normal School of Female Charity, which embraces at once the three great works of Education, Physical Relief, and Moral Reformation.

It was in the year 1844 that the Institute assumed its present development. Already was its then home,—its now adjunct,—a house in the neighbouring "Rue des Trois Sabres," too small for its inmates, and its council had been for two years on the look-out for larger premises, when those now occupied fell vacant. They had previously been used as a school for 200 children; the grounds covered a space of two French acres (of 100 square rods), and were surrounded by high walls. But how was it possible to acquire such a

---

[1] Dead, alas! within the last few months.

property, for which 100,000 fr. (£4000) were asked, with a yearly income not yet reaching the quarter of that sum?   A lease for a long term of years, with a right of purchase at a fixed price, was, however, proposed, and had been nearly accepted by the owner, when suddenly the news came that a Roman Catholic community, somewhat analogous in purpose, had agreed to the original terms, and that the purchase was to be concluded the very next day! By one of those happy temerities which are justified to vulgar eyes by the success which sometimes befalls them, to reflecting minds by the earnest faith which alone can inspire them, the President of the poor and struggling Protestant Institute hastened the very next morning to wait upon the owner, won back the once rejected bargain (assuming, moreover, on himself, the whole costs attending the transaction), and found himself the owner of a huge property, with a personal debt of 110,000 fr., of which 40,000 to be paid down immediately, and with scarcely a few hundred francs of ready money! In two days 75,000 fr. had been lent by a few Protestant friends (including the honoured names of the Andrés, the Delesserts, the Eynards, the Hottingers, the Mallets); other sums have since been lent from time to time; a sum of £6000 has been or will have to be expended on new buildings, fittings, and alterations; while the yearly income of the Institute has risen from about 21,000 fr. in 1842–3 to upwards of 80,000 fr. in 1846–7! Never did seeming madness prove greater wisdom.

The present buildings, we have said, are extensive ; a good frontage on the street, two long wings,
and a very large garden behind. To the façade
and wings correspond respectively, more or less
exactly, the three great divisions of the Institute—
the Hospital, the School, and the Penitentiary.
To the left stands the School, which, together with
the "Crèche" its adjunct, provides, in various departments, for the early care and education of
infants of both sexes, for the complete education
and training of girls until the age of eighteen.
The Crèche is small; the Infant School, on the
other hand, numbers 200 children of both sexes on
its lists, of whom from 90 to 120 are daily present ;
singularly plain-looking generally to an English
eye, but for the most part fat and happy. Next
comes the Upper School, for girls only, on the
monitorial system, comprising about 90 pupils, of
whom about 60 are day scholars, and the remaining 30 belong to the different branches of the
establishment.   Here not only the general principles of religion, but its distinctive dogmas begin
to be taught.   Nevertheless, many Roman Catholic
mothers have been so struck with the advantages
which their children have derived from the Infant
School, that they have solicited their admission to
the Upper School; making so many conversions
from Romanism, not by any proselytising spirit,
but by the mere influence of a good and holy
example.   No child, it may be added, is admitted
to either the Infant or the Upper School without

the written consent of the parents; if Roman Catholics, testifying that they are aware of the Protestant character of the Institute. And yet, of the infant pupils, upwards of three-fourths belong to Roman Catholic families.

Beyond the Upper School is the "Atelier d'Apprentissage" for girls only, who are trained up, from the age of thirteen to that of eighteen, either as servants or as workwomen; their intellectual and religious education keeping pace with their apprenticeship to labour. "One of the greatest moral dangers for young workwomen in Paris," says M. Vermeil ("Appeal," p. 6), "is to be found in those 'Ateliers d'Apprentissage,' where so many evil examples attend them, so many temptations, so many pernicious influences; and that particularly at the period when religious education is usually imparted." The same evils are deeply felt in London.

A link between the School and the Hospital is afforded by the Infirmary for scrofulous children. The effects produced in this department of the establishment by pure air, wholesome and abundant food, and kind attention, are perfectly marvellous. The education of the children is carried on, as far as practicable, at the Upper School.

Next comes a small Hospital, occupying the street-frontage of the establishment, containing separate wards for men, women, and children, and to which 115 patients were admitted in 1846-7, besides the dispensing of gratuitous advice to out-door patients, and the vaccination of children, all, of course, by competent medical officers.   So long as Protestant Sisters are excluded from those hospitals which Protestant money contributes to support, so long will this branch of the establishment (which is not, however, proposed to be much extended) be absolutely necessary, for the training of the " Diaconesses" to those functions which alone have sufficed to render famous the Roman Catholic " Sœurs de Charité," of hospital and family nurses. The Hospital is not entirely gratuitous, but the poor are admitted at reduced prices, descending as low as 1 fr. a day, although the average cost of each patient is 3 fr. a day.   An ingenious system has, however, been established, that of the patronage of beds; by which fifteen or twenty subscribers agree to give, if called upon, 2 fr. each a month; this, with the slight retribution almost invariably given by the patient himself, or by his special protector, is sufficient to make up the total expenditure.

Passing through a pleasant little chapel, where divine service is performed every Sunday, and a Sunday School is held, you enter the Penitentiary, if we may so call it, itself divided into three entirely distinct parts,—the Refuge, the Retreat, (*Retenue*), and the School of Discipline (*Disciplinaire*).   The former, containing twenty-five cells, is destined to penitent females of the Protestant persuasion on their dismissal from prison, or who wish of themselves to abandon the path of prostitution, and who are admitted on payment of a yearly sum of 300 fr. (£12). The last "Report" contains some interesting details as to the general results of this branch of the work of moralization. About one-third of those who have left the establishment have fallen away again into vice; about another third have kept aloof from outward shame; while the remainder may be confidently considered as restored to virtue. However, to give more certainty to their work of reformation, the committee have decided upon admitting penitents, not as heretofore for two years certain, but for an indefinite period. And as they are to be formed not for solitude, but for society, it has been thought proper to employ some of them, when practicable, in the laundry of the establishment; a hazardous, but necessary test of their sincerity.

The second branch is that of the "Retenue," destined originally to girls under age, convicted by a judicial sentence, or (by a peculiar provision of the French law*) confined judicially on their

* Code Civil, art. 375. "A father who shall have cause for very severe displeasure with respect to the conduct of his child, has the following means of correction :—

376. "If the child has not entered its sixteenth year, the father may have it confined during one month at most, for which purpose the President of the ' Tribunal d'Arrondissement' shall, on his demand, give the warrant of arrest.

377. "From the commencement of the sixteenth year till majority or emancipation, the father may only demand the confinement of his child during six months at most; he will have to apply to the President of the aforesaid tribunal, who, after having conferred with the ' Procureur du Roi,' will give or refuse the warrant of arrest, with power in the former

parents' demand.   But an asylum for the former class of minors having been opened at Ste Foy (a reformatory institution on the model of that of Mettray, for Protestants), it is intended from henceforth to confine the efforts of the Deaconesses to the latter class of girls, who were hitherto sent to the Roman Catholic establishment of St Michel.

The " Disciplinaire" again is intended to hold 25 girls of from 7 to 15 years of age, of vicious or stubborn dispositions.   No branch of the work of the " Diaconesses" is so toilsome and unattractive as this.   The poor children admitted to this department are mostly narrow-minded as well as evil-hearted ; and the Sisters observe that " the germs of sin are marvellously fostered by a certain want of intellectual development."   " Narrow-mindedness tends to wickedness," our own Arnold somewhere

case to abridge the time of confinement demanded by the father."

The same rule obtains, under arts. 380 and 382, where the father is married to a second wife, the child being the issue of a former marriage ; also where the child is possessed of private property, or is in the exercise of a calling ; and that, although in any of the above cases the child be under fifteen.

In case the child misconduct himself again after liberation, a further period of confinement may be ordered ; and so, we presume, *toties quoties* (art. 379).

The mother surviving and not having married again can only require her child to be confined with the consent of the two nearest of kin, and under the provisions of art. 327 (381).

Lastly, by art. 468, a guardian, with the consent of the " Conseil de Famille," exercises the same authority as the father in analogous cases.

observes, in a letter to his favourite pupil and since biographer.

In addition to their various household functions, of the multiplicity of which the foregoing pages will have given an idea, the Sisters, where they find time, pay charitable visits (to which their various schools afford superabundant opening); they distribute, in kind almost universally, 3000 fr. worth of relief, besides Bibles, tracts, and useful books. Already around them other Protestant establishments, charitable or otherwise, are springing up; a higher Protestant girls' school, a primary school for Protestant boys, a cheap lodging-house for the poor, a home for Protestant servants out of place. All these are unconnected except by sympathy with the Institute; but within its bosom are formed already a class of pupils, who, without seeking to become Deaconesses, come to study in the different fields of charitable activity which it opens to them, and a class of nurses for the sick, of a lower order than the actual Deaconesses.

It is almost incredible to state that the whole of these various functions are performed by a *personnel* of eighteen Sisters, of whom six are candidates, or "aspirantes." Nevertheless, the Institute has already been able to send forth Deaconesses from time to time, tó direct charitable institutions in the provinces; a Hospital, in particular, at Montpellier, a town which, since the good Sister's arrival, figures for a much higher sum in the subscription list, in full proof of the benefits derived from her stay.

But of course, with a central development so great, there are scarcely ever any Sisters to spare to applications which are constantly made to the Institute from the provinces.

The Sisters belong to all ranks of society; there are farm-servants and teachers, shepherdesses and ladies by birth. They come from various parts of France, though most of them from the south. Provence furnishes the admirable Directing Sister, one of the two master-minds of the establishment. One Sister already is an Englishwoman.

We have said that the Institution is supported by the two established Protestant churches of France, every minister of both of which at Paris (one only excepted)—sometimes after several years of opposition or reluctance—has at last acknowledged the usefulness of its aim, and the sincere piety of its direction.* Beyond the pale of French Protestantism, the clergymen of both Anglican congregations of Paris have expressed themselves, by subscription or otherwise, in its favour, as well as a worthy Wesleyan minister of Paris. From the municipal body of Paris it has obtained the highest testimony. In a Report of the Prefect to the Municipal Council, in 1846, that functionary says: —" I have inspected the establishment of Deaconesses in all its details, and observed everywhere that an intelligent directing spirit had presided over

* The lamented Frédéric Monod, a Protestant of the Protestants, was nursed by deaconesses on his death-bed (1863), and was deeply sensible of the value of their services.

its organisation—over the separation of its different works—over the excellent distribution of the various functions.   I saw that everything had been ordered after a thoughtful study of those improvements which have been introduced into other establishments, so as to facilitate the *surveillance* of any part of the institution, to spare time and trouble to servants, and to procure all possible economy; although nothing has been omitted for the material comfort of the different persons who are called to profit by the advantages of this important asylum. . . . The Institute of Deaconesses is so well ordered as to be worthy of serving as a model to other establishments of a similar nature, which might be founded upon a larger scale."

In concluding his report, the Prefect solicited from the body over which he presided, a first grant of 1000 fr. (£40.)   Some months afterwards, a committee named by the Municipal Council came unexpectedly to visit the Institute, and after a three hours' investigation, in their report proposed a grant of 1500 fr.   By the rarest of liberalities, the Municipal Council outbid its own committee, and by a unanimous vote, granted 3000 fr.

The general administration of the Institute is vested in a Directing Council, composed of two ministers of either church, of the Directing Sister, and of from four to six ladies, and superintended itself by a " *Comité de surveillance*," composed of from three to five lay members.   Beneath this central government, the three great branches of the institution form, as it were, so many federate states, each directed by a separate committee of ladies.

The Directing Sister constitutes, so to speak, the executive power as respects the other Sisters, towards whom she represents the association, and from whom obedience is due to her. The Sisters are admitted between the age of twenty-one and that of thirty-five years (subject to extraordinary exceptions), and only with the consent of their families ; unless they should be orphans, widows since a year at least, or morè than thirty years of age ; they must, in all cases, be free from special family duties. On their admission they are first received as candidates (*aspirantes*), then as assistants (*adjointes*), such period of trial lasting eighteen months. Every Sister must in turn go through all the various functions of the establishment, from the kitchen upwards ; but after her final reception as Deaconess, she devotes herself to that branch for which she feels the most decided vocation.

During the eighteen months of their noviciate, the Sisters have to pay a yearly sum of 400 fr., besides bringing in with them a " *trousseau;* " but, in exceptional cases, gratuitous or semi-gratuitous admissions may be granted (funds permitting) by the Directing Council. After her admission as Deaconess, every Sister is maintained in all points, in health and in sickness, during her years of labour and in her old age, by the association, to which she is reckoned to cost 300 fr. a year. All retribution for her labour and services belongs, in the meanwhile, to the association, which, nevertheless, leaves her the entire control of her capital. There are provisions for indemnifying Deaconesses who are dismissed by the Council, or withdraw from the association for reasons to be approved of by the Council (marriage being one of these), after four years' service at least. All are free to leave at any time, although a moral obligation of service for a definite period, or of otherwise indemnifying the association, is considered to lie on those who have received gratuitous or semi-gratuitous admission.

The total expenditure of the institution amounts to 87,000 fr., or somewhat more than its receipts ;—yet a small sum, surely, when we consider the magnitude of the establishment, with its three great divisions, its seven distinct yards or gardens, its 127 rooms, 148 beds, of which upwards of 100 are nightly occupied, and the 300 persons who are daily received beneath its roof for purposes of instruction or relief; and this, besides the occupation of another house—itself of large dimensions for any ordinary purpose—the original birthplace of the Institute, and still the private home, as it were, of the Sisters themselves. Add to this, however, a debt of about 250,000 fr. (£10,000), cost of the present establishment, of which 186,000 fr. owing on loan to various friends of the society, 25,000 fr. still due on the purchase-money, and 40,000 fr. for repairs and alterations.

We have been thus particular in describing the nature and arrangements of the Paris Institute of Deaconesses, both as offering the most accessible example, and at the same time, the most complete and systematically-organised of existing institutions of a similar nature. The question, indeed, arises, Why pursue so many objects at once? why join in one so many different branches of charity? There surely must be confusion, conflict of wants and interests, charitable bickerings and jealousies. It might be a sufficient answer, that nothing as yet appears of all this, after six years' trial, every year almost bringing with it a new foundation. But the very raising of the objection implies a misconception of the purposes for which the Institute exists. It is not a hospital, nor a school, nor a penitentiary; it is, we repeat it, a great Normal School of Female Charity. Neither the good education afforded within its bosom to the young, nor the care to the sick, nor the wise discipline to the vicious, can ever constitute its real end, its essential perfection; but the full development and wise training of all those impulses of the female mind, which may best serve to promote and fulfil those several aims. Considered in this light, variety of field is an indispensable condition of its existence. The same minds will recoil from the often loathsome duties of attendance on the sick, which will delight in the teaching of children; other women, again, patient watchers beside a sick-bed, are incapable of sympathising with the noisy exuberance of animal spirits in childhood. The duties of superintendence over the penitent female, over the perverted child, are different from either of the former ones, and different between themselves; whilst other characters again shew themselves most useful in the details of household administration. And yet the same spirit of humble, heavenward faith can inspire all alike, and bind them together by the golden link of heartfelt sisterhood. Thus the variety of human character can only be brought to bear its most efficient results, by supplying it with a variety of objects. How far the great axiom of Fourierist socialism, " Les attractions sont proportionnelles aux destinées," will ever be realised on a large scale in society, the future alone can shew. On a small scale, certainly, there is no surer index to success. " A man's inclination to a calling," says Dr Arnold, writing to a former pupil, "is a great presumption that he is or will be fit for it. . . . My advice to you would be to follow that line for which you seem to have the most evident calling; and surely the sign of God's calling, in such a case, is to be found in our own reasonable inclination, for the tastes and faculties which He gives us are the marks of our fitness for one thing rather than another."

As to the spiritual character of the Institute, the consideration of which would need far more space than we can here give to it, suffice it to say, that it is thoroughly Protestant. No vows, no poverty, no monastic obedience, no celibacy, no engagements, even temporary, no claustral seclusion, no vain practices, no domination over conscience, no tyranny over the will,—such are the "fundamental principles," which, with appropriate developments, stand at the head of its Statutes.[*]

The establishment of Deaconesses, founded by M. Vermeil, is not the only one in France. At Strasburg, that old focus of Protestantism, the Rev. M. Hærter stands at the head of a similar Institute, since October 1842. The germ of the Strasburg Institute arose amongst those young persons who had received their religious instruction from its founder; already in 1837 they had formed themselves into an association—which seems to have been but a stricter kind of visiting society—the members of which, without in anywise renouncing the ties of family or social life, devoted themselves to the relief of the poor. We have not the latest details on this establishment, but we see that in 1845 it already numbered twenty-four Sisters; one Superior Sister, three Conducting Sisters at the head of the different departments, eight Acting Sisters (*sœurs servantes*), two Affiliated Sisters (*sœurs agrégées*), and ten novices. It confines itself, as

* The above description of the Paris Institute is still substantially sufficient, except that the "atelier d'apprentissage" has been discontinued, whilst on the other hand there has been added a "Preparatory School for Deaconesses." There were in 1864 30 Sisters and 20 pupils, some 15 Sisters being employed outside of the "mother-house" in Paris, in the provinces, or at Geneva. The expenditure remains about the same (95,000 fr.), and keeps unfortunately still ahead of the receipts.

yet, to the two branches of education and physical relief, and devotes separate premises to each. The Hospital received in 1844–5 sixty patients, while the School, divided into the infant school for either sex, the lower and superior girls' school, numbered in its different divisions 80, 60, and 30 scholars respectively. Besides the Sisters in active employ at Strasburg itself, both within and without the Institute, there were five in charge of the Hospital at Mulhouse (which can receive as many as 200 sick), and two at Guebwiller, one as teacher in a parish girls' school, numbering 40 scholars, the other as administrator of a charitable foundation.

The growth of the Strasburg Institute has been proportionately as rapid as that of the Paris one. Its first location was in a small house, which, it was reckoned, would suffice for all purposes during three years. The year was not out, when removal to a larger establishment became indispensable. This, in turn, proved insufficient, and in September 1845 took place the dedication of a new house, for purposes of education only, the Hospital being confined to the former premises. The receipts of the Institute in 1844-5, which about balanced the expenditure, were somewhat above 30,000 fr. (£1240), the greater part, or about 23,500 fr., resulting from subscriptions.

The constitution of this Institute is somewhat less ecclesiastical than that of the Paris one, the founder, M. Hærter, exercising the cure of souls merely, whilst the whole administration is vested

in a committee of ladies, aided by a consulting
committee of gentlemen.   It is not to be considered
as having attained its full development, since, by
art. 2 of its Statutes, it has for its object "to offer
to those Christian women who wish to devote themselves to the Lord's service the means of qualifying
themselves, either to become teachers in infant
schools and lower girls' schools, or nurses for the
sick in hospitals, sanatoria, and private houses, or
again to exercise the functions of superintendents
in prisons, asylums, houses of refuge, and other
charitable establishments where their services may
be required."

Let us now proceed to Switzerland.   There are
several Deaconesses' Institutes in this country; at
Echallens* in the Pays de Vaud, one founded by
the Rev. M. Germond; at Boudry, in Neuchâtel,
one by the Rev. M. Bovet, and, we believe, others
besides.   Of the first-named alone have we any
details.   Its opening followed closely upon that of
the Strasburg Institute, as it dates from the 1st of
January 1843.   It is the smallest of the establishments which we shall have to consider in this article, and is confined strictly to the training of
nurses for the sick.   But we must say, that of the
various Reports before us, there are none that
breathe a more simple, earnest, unaffected faith, a
gentler and a larger-minded charity, than those of
M. Germond.   The third Report, in particular,
contains a painstaking and interesting account of

* Now St Loup.

the Deaconesses of the early Church; pointing out, at the same time, the difference between the original institution, as specially annexed to individual congregations, and its revival in the shape of distinct communities at the present day.

The field of labour of the Deaconesses of Echallens is thus set forth by its founder. First, the care of the sick at their own homes;—a department the importance of which would be specially felt in times of epidemic. For services of this kind, the demand constantly exceeds the supply; and although the Director of the establishment naturally prefers the affording in-door relief, where practicable, one Deaconess out of six, who are usually attached to the parent Institute, is set apart for out-door nursing. Secondly, the care of the sick in, or at the expense of, private charitable foundations, of which many appear to have been created in Switzerland of late years; five of these, besides one at Lyons for the Protestant sick, employ seven Sisters. "May we not hope," says M. Germond, " that as Christianity shall receive a more practical direction, similar establishments will become multiplied, till there shall be no more a single town in our land without its small infirmary, served by a Deaconess, and ready to receive those sick persons who could not without danger be transported to a greater distance." Thirdly, the care of the sick in public hospitals, which employs the remaining Sisters,—making in all fifteen Deaconesses received, and one who had completed her noviciate, and was already in active service, but without having been definitely admitted. Two Deaconesses of Echallens have, since November 1844, replaced, at the asylum of Abendberg, in Berne, for the care and education of "crétin" children, some Roman Catholic "sœurs grises" from Friburg, whom Dr Guggenbuhl had been compelled to admit, for want of qualified Protestant nurses. "If the number of Deaconesses were doubled or even trebled, employment could immediately be found for all." (Second Report, Echallens.)

Situated in a mixed commune, the Institute of Echallens rents of the Municipality a wing of the former Château of the place. The number of sick whom it received in 1844–5, was 159, of whom 134 gratuitously. Though placed in the midst of an agricultural population, far from any large town, and notwithstanding the vicinity, at no more than three leagues' distance, of a Cantonal Hospital, it is impossible for its Directors to comply with all the demands for admission that are addressed to them. Its receipts, in 1844–5, were under 12,000 fr. (£480), its expenditure under 7000 fr.,—the difference being owing to the endeavour to raise funds for purchasing a suitable house.

The Statutes of the Institute are similar to those of Paris and Strasburg. "The Deaconesses of Echallens are a free corporation, which devotes itself, for the Saviour's love, to the service of the unfortunate, and especially of the sick." There is, as yet, no internal hierarchy amongst the Sisters, who are placed under the authority of the worthy minister and his wife, as Directors. A superintending committee has been named to examine the accounts, and to provide for the maintenance of the establishment in the event of the founder's death.

We cannot forbear quoting from M. Germond's second report the account of the Deaconesses' day at Echallens. They rise at five in summer, six in winter; pray in private; pay the first attentions to the sick; do their own rooms; breakfast upon a " soupe," or upon coffee and bread; then assemble for family prayer. At seven or eight o'clock the doctor makes his rounds and gives his instructions; he is followed by Madame Germond. Medicines are given, and the Sisters read to such of the sick as wish for it, and finish the house work. Twelve is the dinner hour, the meal being composed of soup, meat, and vegetables, one dish of each. The Sisters are then free to choose their own occupations till two, when they meet to work at their needle. At four there is a " goûter,"—what with our own working classes would be tea,—here consisting of " café au lait," milk, or milk and water. Then the Director makes his rounds, celebrates divine service for the whole establishment, and pays pastoral visits to those sick who are detained in bed. The Sisters now take a walk for half an hour in summer, this short period of relaxing exercise being transferred in winter immediately after dinner-time.   At eight o'clock "soupe" is again served out; nine is bed-time.   Where watching is required, the Sisters take it by turns; one till midnight, one from that hour, whilst the men patients are watched over by a male nurse, or "infirmier." The food is the same for all inmates, unless the doctor should prescribe otherwise; the same table unites patients and nurses.   Few of the former remain untouched by the kindness with which they are treated, and, in general, as soon as they begin to recover their strength, they show themselves most anxious to make themselves useful.   Letters are frequently received from them after they have left, and some will go leagues out of their way to visit again " *les bonnes sœurs.*"   Observe, that these patients form a mixed assemblage of Swiss, French, Sardinians, and Germans ; the Roman Catholics being in the proportion of about one to six Protestants.

We now come to the oldest and most considerable of existing Deaconesses' Institutes, that of Kaiserswerth, on the Rhine, founded by the Rev. Th. Fliedner,* the ninth yearly report of which alone, for 1846, is unfortunately now before us. Like the Paris Institute, it commenced by a Refuge for females, comprising, apparently, those only who have undergone judicial sentence of conviction, and who are admitted on leaving prison. Although connected with the general foundation,

* Dead even whilst this work was passing through the press,—at only a few weeks' interval from M. Vermeil.

separate accounts are kept of the receipts and expenditure of the Refuge, and separate reports published. It was, in 1846, in the thirteenth year of its existence, and had received during the first twelve years 130 female criminals. Its results are so far satisfactory, that of that number fifteen had married, two had become teachers, and many more had regained at least outer respectability, although but few, perhaps, could be considered as having received a thorough moral reformation.

The Institute of Kaiserswerth numbers no less than 101 sisters, of whom sixty-seven are consecrated Deaconesses and thirty-four Candidate Sisters. The labours of these are distributed amongst public institutions, the service of particular communes, the care of the sick in private houses, and the various departments of the main establishment at Kaiserswerth. The first-mentioned class comprises forty-five Sisters, employed in various Hospitals, Lunatic Asylums, Poor-houses, and Orphan-houses at Berlin, Marsberg, Kirchheim, Elberfeld, Barmen, Kreuznach, Saarbrück, Worms, Wetzlar, Frankfort-on-the-Mayn, Cologne, and Soest, at the Deaconesses' Institute of Dresden, and at the Pastoral Aid Institute at Duisburg (a greatly analogous institution for the male sex). The second class, that of Commune-deaconesses (Gemeinde-diakonissen) numbered, in 1846, but five sisters, who were employed at Cleves, Neuwied, and Unterbarmen, but more were shortly to be sent out to Cologne, to Duisburg, &c. From fifteen to twenty Sisters were engaged out of doors as private nurses, while the remainder, or about one-third of the whole number, find ample employment in the Asylum, the Orphan-house, and Normal Schools, and the other branches of the parent institution, or " Mother-house" (*Mutterhaus*). A new hospital, on a large scale, has moreover been constituted at Berlin, to be placed under (we believe) the exclusive care of Deaconesses. The lady who has been designated to take charge of this establishment, herself the bearer of a name and title well known in history, and the early friend of the present Duchess of Orleans, was last year in London and Paris, carefully visiting the charitable foundations of either city, and spent a day with her foreign sisters at the Paris Institution.

The most interesting feature, perhaps, of the labours of the German Deaconesses is the recently-developed one of parochial activity (*gemeindepflege*). It is the exact reproduction of the functions of the early Christian Deaconesses, or Servants of the Church, of whom Phœbe of Cenchrea is, by name at least, the apostolical type. The Parish, or, rather, Commune deaconess, has to visit the poor and the sick at their homes, to procure for them, as far as possible, work and clothing, to work for them at her needle, instruct poor children in sewing and knitting, either singly, or in classes where practicable, giving a regular account of her labours to the clergyman, the diaconate, and the Ladies' Charitable Society, where such exists. But even

without being regularly attached to a particular
parish or congregation, Deaconesses are able,
from their experience in the care of the sick, and
in household management, to render the most important public services in times of epidemic.
Look, for instance, at the following picture :—

An epidemic nervous fever was raging in two
communes of the circle of Duisburg, Gartrop, and
Gahlen. Its first and most virulent outbreak took
place at Gartrop, a small, poor, secluded village of
scarcely 130 souls, without a doctor, without an
apothecary in the neighbourhood, while the clergyman was upon the point of leaving for another
parish, and his successor had not yet been appointed. Four Deaconesses, including the Superior
(*vorsteherinn*), Pastor Fliedner's wife, and a maid,
hastened to this scene of wretchedness, and found
from twenty to twenty-five fever patients in the
most alarming condition,—a mother and four children in one hovel, four other patients in another,
and so on,—all lying on foul straw, or on bed-
clothes that had not been washed for weeks, almost
without food, utterly without help. Many had died
already ; the healthy had fled ; the parish doctor
lived four German leagues off, and could not come
every day. The first care of the Sisters, who
would have found no lodging but for the then
vacancy of the parsonage, was to introduce cleanliness and ventilation into the narrow cabins of the
peasants ; they washed and cooked for the sick,
they watched every night by turns at their bedside,

and tended them with such success, that only four
died after their arrival, and the rest were left con-
valescent after four weeks' stay. The same epidemic having broken out in the neighbouring
commune of Gahlen, in two families, of whom
eight members lay ill at once, a single Deaconess
was able, in three weeks, to restore every patient
to health, and to prevent the further spread of the
disease. What would Dr Southwood Smith, or Mr
Chadwick, not give for a few dozen of such hard-
working, zealous, intelligent ministers in the field
of sanitary reform?

The Hospital at Kaiserswerth is, in itself, not of
inconsiderable magnitude, and received in 1845–6
568 patients (an increase of 147 on the preceding
year), for the most part men, and of all religious
persuasions, Protestants, Roman Catholics,—who
are attended by a Roman Catholic chaplain,—and
Jews ; nearly 200 of these were treated gratuitously. The mortality seems very small as compared with the whole number of patients—only
sixteen. The effects of care and a wholesome diet
upon scrofulous children are observed, as in the
Paris institution, to be most remarkable, both as
to bodily health and moral improvement. The
number of children patients is about 100 a year ;
a school is open for their instruction, and they resort to it with the greatest delight, those who are
able to attend being most zealous to communicate
the learning they acquire to those of their com-
panions whom their ailments keep away. In addi-

tion to their intellectual training, the children are employed as much as possible in industrial labours. The elder boys are taught to make baskets, lace, nets, rugs, slippers, various articles of pasteboard, &c. Each boy has also, where his health allows of it, some small department of household work to attend to, so as to help in keeping the children's wards and school-rooms in order and cleanliness. The very young children make lint, paper cuttings for pillows (!) &c., while the girls, again, sew and knit. Even older patients are provided as much as possible with employment, which is found to produce the most cheering effects on their disposition. Nay, moreover, when the renewal of the year draws nigh, "a great Christmas tree, with bright, glittering wax tapers," lights up the refectory for the sick, who crowd around it, young and old, "some borne aloft on others' arms, some leaning on crutches," and sing hymns to the child "Immanuel."

The Christmas tree seems, indeed, to be almost an article of faith with the good Deaconesses of Kaiserswerth, both within and without the "Motherhouse." "It was a subject of peculiar joy to us," says Pastor Fliedner, "to find that the prevailing endeavour of the Sisters in most of the institutions where they are employed was to confer pleasure on the sick and other objects of their care, and greater pleasure than they had ever yet enjoyed. Thus (quite without our suggestion) they have almost everywhere, of their own impulse, procured Christmas presents to be given for their charges, even where this had never taken place before; they have themselves collected in the town the money, clothes, and other gifts, set up the ' trees of Christ,' gladdened the sick; the poor, and the wretched with the bright glittering light, such as they had never seen before, with the pretty songs, with the presents of food, and drink, and clothes, so that they would often weep tears of joy in their surprise, and cry, ' No, never, in all our lives, did such a thing happen to us! Never yet had we such a pleasure! You are making us too happy! You are doing too much for us!'"*

Exquisitely German and childish this. Quære, though, whether, as a piece of political wisdom, it may not turn out better than forbidding p^lum-pudding in workhouses?†

After the Hospital comes the Normal School for female teachers, of whom upwards of fifty are sent out every year. Different in this from the other institutions which we have as yet examined, the Institute of Kaiserswerth has scarcely so wide a home field for practical teaching as might at first sight be expected from its general magnitude. Thus its Infant-school only numbers about forty children;

---

* Within the last few months, our London newspapers have duly recorded the Christmas tree of 1847, set up at the German Hospital of Dalston—an offshoot, as will presently be shewn, of the Kaiserswerth Institute—in the presence of H.R.H. the Duke of Cambridge.

† This alludes to a fact of recent occurrence before the publication of the above article, but probably impossible now.

its Hospital-school, we presume, contains but a comparatively small proportion of the hundred juvenile patients, and its Orphan-house, to which we shall presently advert, reckons about twenty inmates. The anomaly is explained, if we do not mistake some passages in the report, by the circumstance that the Sisters and pupils are admitted to the parochial schools of the town. Their theoretical education appears, also, to take a wider scope than in any other kindred establishments. The course of instruction lasts four months for Infant-school teachers (can this be enough?), and one year for teachers in Elementary Schools. Most of the pupils also attend the children's wards in the Hospital for a few weeks, to familiarise themselves with the management of children when sick.

The demand for teachers from the Institution, as from any other Deaconesses' Institute, greatly exceeds its capabilities of supply, and it is intended to give a great extension to the Normal Schools, by a sort of joint-stock company, or, rather, joint-stock loan (*actienplan*). May we venture to observe, however, that, in assuming the character of an ordinary normal school, the Institute impairs, to our mind, the completeness of the idea of a female Diaconate, by confining the functions of the latter to the care of the sick and the household management of charitable institutions? In the list of Deaconesses, we do not find one who is devoted to the work of education. Why is this to be left a mere secular calling, and

not hallowed by the bond of a religious fellowship?
The mission of the educator is, above all others,
the nearest to that of the minister of religion; and
if it be the highest to which a woman should aspire
in spiritual matters, this affords but a reason the
more for surrounding it with all practicable respect
and religious honour.   That a Deaconesses' Institute should contain within itself a Normal School
for female teachers, not Deaconesses, is most desirable; but we miss as yet from Kaiserswerth the
high ideal of the Christian Sister, devoted to education by her own free choice, without prospect of
earthly reward, and linked with a community of
other devoted women, not by mere gratitude for
the attention of a few months', or even a twelve-
months' stay, but by every tie of present and future
support, comfort, and fellowship.

It is true that this deficiency, if any such exist,
is in progress of being to some extent supplied by
the last branch of the Kaiserswerth Institute, the
Orphan-house, intended for the orphan daughters
of clergymen, teachers, and others of the educated
classes, or even for the daughters of missionaries
still living in foreign countries; these receive an
education which shall fit them for the middle ranks
of life, mingled, however, with a thorough training
to all household duties.   About twenty children
are here brought up, according to their dispositions, either to housekeeping, education, the care
of the sick, or that of the poor, and form, at once,
a seminary for the development of the various

modes of female activity, and especially one for the supply and maintenance of the Deaconesses' Institute itself. We fear, however, that even this will not wholly supply the want which we just now pointed out, of regular Deaconess teachers. If such were only to be admitted from among the pupils of the Orphan-house, it is to be feared that too great a sameness would be imparted to its educational system; that it would lose the advantages to be derived from a constant infusion of new blood, by the admission from without of grown-up members, earnest and zealous; that it would become stereotyped in spirit, like many a Roman Catholic educational convent, which is recruited but from among its own pupils.

We might here translate many interesting extracts from the accounts sent in by the Infant-school teachers who have been trained in the Institute. When, indeed, was there the report of an Infant-school which might not be made the most attractive and touching of tale-books? One teacher, who says, with great judgment, that she pays far less attention to the learning by rote than to exercises in narration and reflection, mentions that she is now telling histories out of the Old Testament, " which, however, the children do not seem to hear with such pleasure, nor yet to retain so well, as those out of the New. I often reproach myself for this (she says), as if it arose from my mode of narration, and redouble my efforts to do it well. But, in spite of all, when I think I have

told them ever so well the story of Joseph's brethren, or that of Moses, and ask again, of an afternoon, ' Children, what did I tell you of this morning?'   I always receive for answer, ' Of the Lord
Jesus!'   Two days back, I said to little Emma,
who has a peculiar feeling for these tales, ' Now,
tell me, how comes it that you behave now so ill,
and of an afternoon don't know any longer what I
told you of in the morning?'   ' I don't know,
aunty, but I am always thinking of the dear Lord
Jesus, and am so glad to be told of Him ; and so
I always think you have told us of Him this very
morning.'   A fortnight back, this child was to go
with her mother to Elberfeld.   When I asked her
whether she were glad to make the journey, she
said, ' Yes; but I would much rather go, some day,
to Bethlehem.   How far is it from here?   What a
pretty place it must be !   When you next go there,
you will take me with you, won't you?'   I don't
know how it happens, but the children have come
to think that I have been there often, and must be
well known there.   They even think that I must
often have spoken with the Lord Jesus, and stayed
with Him all His life through.   And they will not
be persuaded out of this idea.   I am, myself, as
happy as a child could be, to think that Advent is
coming, when I shall be able to begin again the
New Testament regularly."

Not a word of cavil over this little narrative,
most learned, most refined, most philosophical
reader !   This is the true spirit of the educator, to

be so absorbed in his work as to be " happy as a child could be" over the recurrence of some favourite lesson. In like manner did Arnold, in his own higher sphere, when asked "whether he did not find the repetition of the same lessons irksome to him?" answer, "No; there was a constant freshness in them; he found something new in them every time that he went over them." In like manner did he write on the kindred subject of private tuition :—" If you enter upon it heartily, as your life's business, as a man enters upon any other profession, you are not in danger of grudging every hour you give to it, ... but you take to it as a matter of course, making it your material occupation, and devote your time to it, and then you find that it is in itself full of interest, and keeps life's current fresh and wholesome, by bringing you in such perpetual contact with all the spring of youthful liveliness."

Another infant-school teacher from Kaiserswerth says, " A little girl of four years was ill, and taken with brain fever. She begged her mother that aunty might come to her. I found her lying quietly on her little bed; the pain had somewhat abated. But, above all, she was very patient in her sufferings, so that her mother had never yet heard her utter a cry of pain. I asked her, 'Caroline, my child, have you still a bad headache?' 'Yes,' said she, ' my head often hurts me very much; but I think that dear Lord Jesus had a much worse pain in His head than I have, when the wicked people put the crown of thorns on His head; and my head, too, does not bleed yet, like that of the Lord Jesus.'"

The material magnitude of the Kaiserswerth establishment is of course considerable. It has several gardens, an ice-cellar, a bakehouse, a laboratory, baths on the Rhine, two large bleaching-grounds, a dairy, with four cows, &c. It has to provide daily food for three hundred persons. Its income in 1845–6 was 17,303 ths. (under £2524), less by upward of 2000 ths. than its expenditure; whilst its debt amounts by this time, if the estimate of the Report before us be correct, to upwards of 6000 ths. (£875.)

Its influence has been most extensive. Not only have similar institutions, either offsets from it, or framed upon its pattern, sprung up in divers parts of Germany—at Dresden, at Berlin, and elsewhere—but it has sent Deaconesses to German Switzerland, to St Petersburg, to London; and in the course of next spring, its Director intends crossing the Atlantic, with several Sisters, to found a new Kaiserswerth among the German colonists of Pennsylvania.* Several Sisters are already in London, in charge of the German Hospital at Dalston, which a late unfortunate broil between its physician and

* See new *ante*, 206, 207. To quote one instance of the peculiar reproductive power of Kaiserswerth, the German Deaconesses' Home of Jerusalem now includes a hospital, orphan house, and schools. See Pressensé's "Pays de l'Evangile," (1854,) p. 156.

council has probably brought more prominently into notice than two previous years of silent usefulness. This institution, founded in 1845, occupies the former premises of the Infant Orphan Asylum, since removed to Wanstead; it is large and airy, and with a very extensive garden, and situate in the immediate neighbourhood of the class which furnishes it with the greatest number of patients—the sugar-bakers of Bethnal Green. There may be seen, in their especial sphere of activity, the Deaconesses of Kaiserswerth; cleanly, quiet, healthy-looking Germans, going about their work in the most orderly and noiseless manner; never haggling for higher wages, since they have none to receive; trained to obedience, and yet fully conversant with their duties; in fact at all points the very antipodes of a Mrs Gamp, that odious, and we fear often but too true type of the common nurse. The number of Deaconesses in the German Hospital of London was three at first; it is now five, of whom one has been appointed matron, and has the superintendence over the others.

And now the question arises,—Is an Institute of Deaconesses required; is it practicable in Protestant England? We must not here omit to state, that the foundation of one, confined, indeed, to the purpose of forming nurses for the sick, was already attempted in this country, more than eight years ago, by the late Mrs Fry, but we believe it has since been given up.* And yet it must be a

* A complete error. See *ante*, p. 202.

subject of comfort and thankfulness to those who
first projected such an institution amongst ourselves, to think that their then unsuccessful efforts
contributed not a little to the growth of the now
flourishing Institute of Paris. At the very opening page of M. Vermeil's first pamphlet of 1841,
(Etablissement des Sœurs de Charité Protestantes
en France), an account then recently given, in a
French Protestant newspaper, of Mrs Fry's foundation, is made use of in explanation of his own pro-
ject, and as an argument of its success. So true is it
that " one soweth and another reapeth," that the
seed which a man casts into the ground will
" spring and grow up, he knoweth not how."

But then, perhaps, the cuckoo cry will be raised:
The Church in danger !   The Papists are coming !
Because half-a-dozen single women will have agreed
to live in one house, put on one dress, and throw
their earnings and efforts into one fund for the relief of some acknowledged social evil, the whole
Apocalypse will be ransacked for the millionth
time, to prove that the mark 'of the beast is upon
them !   Grant that it were a new thing in Protestantism to form a female community; is that a
reason for condemning it ?   Bible societies, nor
Tract societies, nor Missionary societies, can trace
their pedigree to the Apostles, nor yet to the early
Reformers.   And what are they in themselves,
but the lower manifestations of that spirit of (to
use a much-abused word) socialism, of which religious communities are a higher manifestation;

that growing spirit of socialism which will be the most mighty worker of evil, if we make it not the most mighty instrument of good; the most ruthless of tyrants if not the most intelligent of ministers for every wise and holy purpose? If it be lawful for half-a-dozen people to meet together year after year, and week after week, on the committee of an hospital, why should it be unlawful for the same number of persons to spend their lives together as nurses in that hospital, for the same purpose of glory to God and good will towards men? Does uniformity of dress offend you? Who does not know that wherever economy is sought after, such uniformity is a necessary means towards realising that end? Is it not still more necessary, where the question is how to associate "in one and the same work, under the same direction, for the same purposes, with the same rights, persons of different classes?" "We have to receive Sisters of all ranks," continues M. Vermeil (6th Report, p. 18.), "from the humble farm-servant in *sabots*, to the young lady clad in silk and velvet." And least of all surely can such an argument be urged in a country like this, where uniformity of costume is enforced more than in any other; where the workhouse has its livery like the prison, and the college or school like the footman's hall; where bishops are perennially cumbered with the apron, and barristers with the wig; where the cleaning of the hideous cauliflower of a marquis's coachman can be the subject of a judicial action, and charity (whose left hand should not know what her right hand doeth) takes pleasure in dressing out her scholars as the most ungraceful of merryandrews throughout every parish in the kingdom.

But the great objection to a deaconesses' institute is, no doubt, not formal, but radical. "We would not mind the community of life, nor the costume, nor the charitable purpose, if Romanism had not given the example of such Sisterhoods. It is an imitation of Romanism." Let M. Germond of Echallens answer. "An imitation of Roman Catholicism? God forbid! but of a work which should have borne fair fruit in the bosom of Catholicism? why not? where would be the sin? Does not the Holy Scripture command us to 'prove all things,' to 'hold fast that is good?' You will say, perhaps, that the Church of Rome holds no more anything worth holding fast. Ah! we repel with all our strength those blind prejudices of party spirit, which estrange hearts from one another, chain down all progress; we are persuaded that there is, on the contrary, no section of Christianity which is utterly deprived of God's graces; we should feel happy to hasten by our example, as we do by our wishes, that blessed time when the various Churches, divesting themselves at last of their mutual jealousies, shall come to exchange freely with one another all that each has of really good, and pure, and lovely, and Christian!"

It is incorrect, however, to say that an order of

Deaconesses is but a copy of Romanism; it is not so even in outward form. It would be easy to shew that in that particular branch which it has shot forth as yet in Germany alone, the Parish-deaconess, it exactly reproduces, as we have already stated, the Deaconess or "servant of the church," (Διακόνισσα, ἡ Διάκονος, diaconissa, diacona), of the earliest times, an institution which seems to have subsisted in the Eastern Church at least till the eleventh century. Whereas, in its more general form, of an association of females for all purposes of charity, it is not only not Roman Catholic, but historically Protestant in its origin,* since eighty years before the institution of the " Filles," or "Sœurs de Charité," by St Vincent de Paule, a Protestant prince, Henry Robert de la Marck, sovereign prince of Sédan, "in 1560, instituted in his dominions a society of 'Demoiselles de Charité,' for assisting at their own homes the poor, the aged, and infirm, and supplied it with the needful funds for rendering it permanently efficient. The mission of these new servants of the Church was one wholly of free-will; they pronounced no vows, and were chosen from among those persons who were free from the marriage-tie, and the duties which it entails. The only engagement which they took was that of devoting themselves to works of mercy." In our own country, indeed, it may be said that an

---

* This is quite wrong. I was writing at this time with too slight acquaintance with the subject of Romish Monachism. See *ante*, p. 161.

institute of Deaconesses will only be, as it were, the crystallised precipitate of those numberless ladies' charitable societies, amongst which all its elements float already dissolved and shapeless.

But let us not, however, haggle about these miserable questions of outward form, of historical precedence. Look to the spirit of the continental Deaconesses. No vows, no poverty, no monastic obedience, says the founder of the Paris Institute. "We took as the ground of our efforts, not the pretence of salvation by works, but the duty of witnessing by works our love to Him who came down from heaven to save us." And such is the testimony of every one of his fellow-labourers. If you want further proofs, look to the hatred of Romanism for the institution, wherever it has sprung up. What calumnies have not been lavished on the Deaconesses of Paris by the Romanist papers of that capital! Ask M. Germond of Echallens, whose establishment receives so many Roman Catholic patients, how many donations he has received from the Roman Catholics of Switzerland! Ask the founders of the German Hospital in London how the idea of introducing Sisters from Kaiserswerth was at first received by the German Roman Catholics of our own metropolis!

To prove their utter want of connexion with Romanism and Romanising feelings, the friends of Protestant Deaconesses' Institutes have indeed sometimes assumed, to our taste, almost too militant a position. Thus, we regret to see the most complete and original in its constitution of existing Institutes, and certainly not the least liberal and charitable in its spirit, in its appeal to the English public, address itself especially, through its title at least, to the anti-popery of Exeter Hall : " An appeal on behalf of the Institution of the Deaconesses, established in Paris, for the purpose of supporting and extending French Protestantism against the efforts of the Papists." Protestantism has other means of conversion,—were it only its yearly millions of Bibles,—than through its present or future Deaconesses ; nor have we the slightest wish to see our Protestant Sisters, like their Roman Catholic namesakes, become an engine of religious propagandism, instead of confining themselves to their cardinal object, that of practically setting forth that faith which is " shewn by works," which " worketh by love."   Let them convert by example, that is enough.

It would take us too long in this place to shew, as we think we could, that in England as elsewhere the Sisters, and not the priests, are the main agents in those conversions to the Roman Catholic Church which, we are sorry to say, do take place amongst our lower classes ; and that against their stealthy advances the surest, perhaps the only, barrier is the creation of similar orders in our own churches. God forbid, indeed, that disclaiming the fundamental principle of Protestantism, the fallibility of human reason, and its inevitable consequence, the right

T

of private judgment,* we should seek for a moment to deny to others that freedom which we claim for ourselves. Let the last fragment of the penal laws be swept to the winds! Let Roman Catholicism not be furnished by persecution with the cloak of darkness, but, by the conferment of equal civil and political rights, be dragged forth into the searching light of publicity! Wherever we can see it plainly, we fear it not. Convinced as we are that the greatness of England is the greatness of Protestantism, we ask in good English phrase, but for "a fair field and no favour." But so long as through prejudice, through indolence masked in the garb of religious conservatism, through cunning indifference joined in chorus with every shape of blindest zeal, we allow Romanism to usurp one Christian virtue, to monopolise one useful institution, to do one good work which we leave unattempted, so long is the field unfair, are the weapons unequal. Rome wields no more powerful weapon than that of her religious Sisterhoods. Can we not wrest it from her? When Lutheran Germany and Calvinist France agree in saying Yes, shall England say No, —or say nothing?

One word more. Years have elasped since one, whose memory is now surrounded with more of

* The above passage represents a stage of thought which is far from being my present one. I did not then see that Protestantism is essentially relative, and implies a Catholic truth and faith, against all, or at least some, deviations from which it " protests."

personal respect and love,—even from those who knew him not, or misknew him when living,—than perhaps any other contemporary name; one whose thoughts have frequently recurred to us (far oftener than we have cared to recall them to our readers) whilst writing these pages,—wrote as follows in the introduction to his " Christian Life, its Cause, its Hindrances, and its Helps" :—" The true Church of Christ would offer to every faculty of our nature its proper exercise, and would entirely meet all our wants. No wise man doubts that the Reformation was imperfect, or that in the Romish system there were many good institutions, and practices, and feelings, which it would be most desirable to restore amongst ourselves. Daily church services, frequent communions, memorials of our Christian calling, continually presented to our notice in crosses and wayside oratories; commemorations of holy men of all times and countries ; the doctrine of the communion of saints practically taught, *religious orders, especially of women, of different kinds, and under different rules, delivered only from the snare and sin of perpetual vows ;*—all these, most of which are of some efficacy for good even in a corrupt church, belong no less to the true Church, and would there be purely beneficial."

Such were the words of one whose life was spent in warfare with Romanising tendencies, who, to use one of his most characteristic expressions, would have rejoiced " in fighting out the Judaisers, as it were in a saw-pit !"   And yet of that long catalogue of " institutions, practices, and feelings," which would be "purely beneficial to the true Church," not one has yet been realised, or generally adopted by his own.   And ourselves, in presenting this sketch of a few continental religious orders of Protestant women, delivered "from the snare and sin of perpetual vows ;" and in urging their introduction into this country, we feel that we have been but working out one passing hint given by that great and good man, Dr Arnold.

[The above article having been republished a year or two later in a French translation (which I have not seen) in the *Revue Britannique* of Paris, exception was taken to that passage of it which recorded the fact of the Paris Deaconesses' Institute having been approved of by every single minister of both the Established Protestant churches of Paris, one only excepted,—*i.e.*, M. Coquerel— by Count M. Agénor de Gasparin, in a long letter addressed to the Editor, and which was forwarded on to me by the latter.   Hence a note, substantially by myself, which will be found at the close of the number of the *Edinburgh Review* for January 1851, pointing out the literal correctness of the statement, but also that since the date of the article had taken place the disruption of the French Reformed Church, resulting in the formation of the French "Eglise Libre," the members of which were then (although many of them have long ceased to be) in open opposition to the Institute. It should be observed that not only was M. Agénor de Gasparin the real leader of the French disruption, but that his wife, Madame de Gasparin, the now celebrated authoress, has written a book against such institutions, the very title of which implies a libel on them (" Des Corporations Monastiques au Sein du Protestantisme," Paris, 1855).]

H.

Miss Sellon's Sisterhood of Mercy, (see p. 203.)

The Devonport Sisterhood is prudently pretermitted by Dr Howson in his work. This is hardly fair as respects an institution which has been the first boldly to introduce the idea of sisterhood practically amongst us, and which for years gave, as it were, a very battlefield to opposing parties in the Church.

At the time when this work was first prepared, I had carefully read up the whole (as far as I had been able to procure them) of the publications issued on the subject. Since then, I have only read Miss Goodman's work on " Sisterhoods in the Church of England" (London, 1863), which, however, was sufficient to shew me that the character of the institution was substantially the same as when I first judged it. I shall, therefore, simply reproduce here in an abridged form what I wrote in 1852 :—

Let us hear from Miss Sellon's own lips how her institution arose. In 1848, she tells us, she was in—she had well-nigh written happy ignorance— of the state of the lower classes in large towns; when one evening, accidentally glancing over a newspaper, her eye fell upon a letter of the Bishop of Exeter's, setting forth the spiritual destitution and utterly demoralised condition of the towns of Devonport and Plymouth, and appealing for help. She *could* not forget the picture, and in about a fortnight's time she was in Devonport, with the one hope that she might be permitted by God to help in alleviating some part of its misery. About four months afterwards she was joined by another lady, and the two soon arrived at the conclusion, " that the work before them could only be effectually done, if at all, by entire devotion to it;" that "it was not only the children who were neglected, and who had to be gathered into schools, but their parents had to be taught, to be raised step by step, as they would bear it, out of the deep moral degradation and spiritual darkness in which they were living;" that "nothing less than the great principles of civilisation and Christianity had to be taught and worked out amongst them, and that nothing less than this would effectually serve them."

The " Sisterhood of Mercy" had now come into existence. Miss Sellon, as its Superior, went to the Bishop, and asked him for the blessing of the Church upon herself and the work which she then contemplated. She returned home for a few days, to bid her friends farewell ; and then, with the other sister, returned to lodgings in Devonport. They had then three schools, and visited the poor only in Morice Town and Devonport. A short time after, being joined by two or three more young women, who afterwards entered into the Sisterhood, they left their lodgings for a little house in Mitre Place. Here the adoption of a common dress, the use of the cross, some womanly fondness for flowers in religious services, first drew upon them the suspicion of Romanism.

In 1849 the cholera came, and the Sisters were occupied unceasingly in tending the sick in or out of the Hospitals, and were indeed the means of first staying the scourge. It left them unthinned in numbers, but much weakened in bodily strength, three of them falling seriously ill for a length of time. During the autumn an Industrial School was founded. The court-yard, and part of the garden, were covered in for children's school-rooms ; a large barn was got to provide for the still increasing number of little scholars ; houses were taken for parents, and let out as lodgings, schools being opened in them for the children, and reading-rooms for the men, and a moral and religious discipline being introduced ; a good sized meeting-house was turned into the Industrial School for the young women who were without proper protection and employment; two houses were converted into a college for boys who were homeless in the streets, in order to educate them for the sea; a large building in Devonport became a kitchen, where a hundred poor could have their dinners, and have their cases inquired into; besides a small room in Plymouth partly for the same purpose. In the space of four years, the Sisterhood could reckon "among our own people" about a thousand souls, including children as well as men and women; and the Superior could write (Jan. 14, 1852) that "the experiment had proved that the poor could be reformed, that old as well as young could be educated, that their moral character could be greatly raised, and that they would submit, as a body, to rules of moral and religious government."

Of this number of a thousand, there were twenty-seven orphan girls, of whom the greater number had lost both parents, in training for servants. The little college had room for twenty-six sailor boys, though there was not that number yet. The lodging-houses for families, or Houses of Hope, were eight in number, the applicants on the list for admission always exceeding the number of rooms, and contained in all 152 inhabitants. They included also reading-rooms, and two schools for elder girls and infants, into which were admitted children from the poor of the district visited by the Sisters,—

fifty-six girls in all, and fifty-three infants. The elder girls of the school were allowed, as a reward, to join the little evening working-school in these houses, where they received small wages, and were employed in making clothing, which was sold afterwards to the inhabitants and others at a moderate price, which they were permitted to pay by instalments. The families in these houses could of course be helped with clothing and food, and relieved in time of sickness, far more effectually than the poor outside. To the reading-rooms strangers of respectable character were also admitted on paying a small subscription, and being balloted for by the members. At the soup-kitchen in Devonport from eighty to a hundred persons were daily fed with soup and bread, eaten in the kitchen; hot puddings being moreover given " to families we know, who are church-goers, every Sunday,"—a little unconscious trait of the Lady Bountiful, at which we can well afford a smile. Fifty or sixty persons received relief in the same way in Plymouth. The House for Destitute Children, not necessarily orphans, contained nine of these; the House of Peace for elder girls, fourteen; the Industrial School numbering eighty-five in all. Finally, there were three old men maintained, and the wife of one of them; thus completing the " motley company," which the Sister supplying these details thus particularises,—" orphan girls, little and big, from three years old to fifteen; sailor boys, old men, little destitute children, and young women of various ages, from twelve to twenty-five years." There were also " very little offshoots at Bristol and Portsmouth, too young to deserve notice." *

Such was the rise of the famous Sisterhood of Mercy of Devonport or Plymouth, an institution of which it is impossible to consider the history without the most painfully mingled feelings. On the one hand, I cannot mistake the spirit of deep, earnest, ardent piety, which gave rise to the institution, and bore fruit in an abundant crop of noble charities. " It has been my lot in life," wrote Mr Hetling, a medical man who had taken orders in the Church of England, to the Bishop of Exeter, "for one quarter of a century, to have seen and borne an active part in very much of suffering, pain, and death ;—formerly, in medical practice, I have seen the whole course of cholera in London, Paris, and. Bristol, and lastly here in my office of deacon, I have beheld many acts of self-devotion to its sufferers and victims, *yet never have I witnessed anything that surpassed, or even equalled, the self-abandonment and self-sacrifice of these lowly Sisters.*" But, on the other hand, whilst most fully crediting Miss Sellon's attachment to the Church of England, and her desire to make her Sisterhood a very bulwark against Rome, I am bound to say that the attentive consideration of her statements, and of those which have been put forward in her favour, impresses me

---

* See a letter of Miss Sellon's to the Rev. Edward Coleridge, not published ; also, " A Letter to Miss Sellon," by Henry, Lord Bishop of Exeter : John Murray, 1852.

with the conviction, that the spirit and tendency of her institution are essentially Romish, and if not diverted into quite different channels, will inevitably, sooner or later, land the Sisterhood in actual and professed Romanism. I am not going to discuss such trifles as flowers and rosaries, crossings and canonical hours. I feel on these points, I own, as Luther did of old; who, when told in full Reformation, as a very awful piece of Popery, that a minister had preached in a surplice, answered simply,—Let him put on two, if he pleases. But I address myself, I repeat it, to the spirit of the institution, and what do I find in it? That it is the Romish spirit of depreciating God's natural order of the family, and exalting some spiritual one, resting upon practical, if not yet avowed celibacy. What else means this title of Mother, taken by the Superior? What does the gospel know of such a title? "Call no man your father upon earth, for one is your Father which is in heaven." Does not this forbid titular and nominal motherhood, as well as fatherhood? just as the words almost immediately preceding, "Ye are all brethren," afford, on the contrary, the scriptural consecration of religious sisterhoods as well as brotherhoods. It is this title, this dangerous, deadly title of a spiritual mother, which enables Miss Sellon, nay, which compels her,—to exact that conventual obedience which bids the Sisters,—grown women, individually responsible to God,—not only fulfil the commands of the spiritual mother, but "banish from their mind any question as to the wisdom of the command given them,"—neither ask for nor receive anything without permission,—read such books and editions only as are approved of by the spiritual mother,—speak to no one out of the society, except with her permission,—give no messages nor commissions, receive no letters nor send replies, without direction or permission. It is this title which has cheated her into the fancy that there was no dishonesty of the heart in telling a daughter that " she did not think it would be at all wrong for her to see her (Miss Sellon) without her mother's knowledge, unless she had absolutely forbidden her," and that " she did not think it needful to ask." It is this title which has seemed to justify her in reminding a Sister who had separated from her, that " the ties which are spiritual and not natural are eternal," as if the God-given ties of nature, the blessed relations of parent and child, brother and sister, husband and wife, the sole perfect types of the Fatherhood of the Almighty Father, of the Brotherhood of the Elder Brother, of the Marriage of the Lamb with His Holy Bride, were unspiritual and temporal ! It is this title, finally, which has led her into a breach of all church order and tradition so glaring, that I cannot express my wonder at the slight insistance which has been placed upon it, in those admission services and others, in which the Mother Superior is made to fulfil actual presbyteral functions of exhortation, and to perform certain acts which look very like ordination; and above all in that benediction which she is stated to give to the Sisters,—an act expressly forbidden by the early Church to the ordained deaconess.

I have thus plainly expressed my sense of the dangerous tendency of Miss Sellon's Institution. I have now to state as plainly what I conceive to be the cause of evil. I deem it to be this mainly, that there is no man in the institution. I believe that for Sisterhoods of Mercy or Deaconesses' Institutes to be really honest and healthy, to preserve their due relation to the family order of the Church, to strengthen instead of weakening it, it is absolutely necessary that they should be under the direction of a man, and that one who is, or at least has been, a husband. Left to the direction of an unmarried woman, it seems absolutely impossible that they should not gradually merge into ascetic celibacy,—Romish celibacy,—that celibacy which is an insult to marriage, to motherhood, and which sooner or later only sustains itself by the polygamous figment of a special union of the individual Sister with Christ. I can see the germ of this feeling already in those words of one of Miss Sellon's letters, in which she uses the expression, "Called to a close union with the Beloved, the chief among ten thousand, you may not adorn yourself for other eyes." The one thing that has been wanting to make the Devonport Sisterhood of Mercy a true normal school for all English female charity, from whence Christian women should issue forth to all quarters of our country to battle with all the evils of our social state, has been that the proud and noble spirit of its founder should have owed obedience to an earthly husband—through the joys and woes and trials of real motherhood, should have learned the hollowness and the blasphemy of a so-called spiritual one.*

* Miss Goodman's evidence, after making full allowance for the personal bitterness which visibly tinges her statements, abundantly confirms the conclusions which I had come to on this subject twelve years ago.   Perhaps the most remarkable fact which she mentions, is the superior freedom and cheerfulness of the genuine Romish Sisterhoods to what is found in these wrong-headed Anglican ones.

INDEX.

A

ADRIAN I., Pope, 69.
Age of ordination for Deaconesses, 51, 53, 57, 61, 62, 260.
—— of admission of Widows, 8.
—— do. of Béguines, 119.
Agnes, Daughters of St, 180.
Aix la Chapelle, Council of, 113.
Alexander VII., Pope, 169, 175.
Alexians, 144 and foll., 150.
America, see "Spanish," "United States," "Canada," "Guatemala."
Amprucla the deaconess, 33, 34.
Amsterdam, Former béguinage of, 141.
——, Deaconesses at, 198-9.
Andrew, see St Andrew.
Angela of Brescia, 156.
Angelicals, 155.
Aniane, Benedict of, 103, 115, n.
Apostolical Constitutions, see Constitutions.
Arles, Council of, 101.
——, Nunnery of St Cesarius at, 107.
Arnold, Dr, referred 263, 280-1, 290-1.

Arras, Daughters of St Agnes at, 180.
——, Sisters of charity at, 184.
Asceteries and *ascetriæ*, 54, 55, 60, 238-9.
Athanasius referred to, 78-9, 234-6.
Attaliotes, Michael, referred to, 61, n.
Augusti referred to, 62.
Augustin referred to, 27, 86, 88-9, 235.
Augustinians, 124-6, 135-6, 158-9, 172.
—— their Tertiarians, 135, 172.
Autun, Council of, 113.

B

BAILLET referred to, 85.
Balsamon referred to, 61, 224.
Baptism, Functions of deaconesses in, 16, 32, 47, 59, 62, 222.
Baronius referred to, 26, n., 51, 70, 89.
Bartholomew, see St Bartholomew.
Basil referred to, 28, 60, 83, 84, 89, 91.
—— and Chrysostom, Liturgy of, 17, n.
——, Monks of St, in Gaul, 66.

Basil, Rule of St, 97-8, 100-1.
——, Nuns of, 106.
Beaune, Hospitallers of, 240-2.
Beauvais, Grey Sisters of, resist claustration, 146.
Bede referred to, 107.
Beggar synonymous with béghard, 137.
Begging, treated as a religious privilege, 138.
Béghards, 117, 122, 136-7, 149, 194.
Béguinages, 118, 119, 141, 195, 201.
Béguines, 117 and foll. 215-16.
—— their struggle with female monachism 134, and foll.
—— condemned by Councils and Popes, 137-9.
—— adopted into monastic system, 140-1.
—— merge partly into Alexians, 144-5.
—— or Gerardins, 149-50.
—— excepted from suppression by Joseph II., 182, n.
—— at the Reformation, 194-5.
——, A rule of, translated, 242 and foll.
Benedict, and Benedictines, rule of St, 100-1 ; reformed, 103, 115-16, n.
——, Order of, 104, 115.
——, Nuns of, 106-7, 160, 185.
Bernard, St, 116, n., 123.
Bernardines, 116.
——, Benedictine, 160, n.
Bethlehemites of Guatemala, 172.
Bigot from Begutta, 137.
Bingham referred to, 18, 70, 71, n., 77, 224, 234.

Black Sisters, 147.
Blastar, Matthew, referred to, 62.
Blind Sisters of St Paul, 189.
Blosset, Mlle., 180.
Boniface IX., 140, n., 144.
Bordeaux, Ursulines of, 157.
——, Order of "Our Lady" of, 160.
Boudry, Deaconesses' Institute of, 266.
Bouquet, Mother Geneviève, 173.
Bovet, Pasteur, 266.
Bradford, Governor, his dialogue, 198-9.
Bremer, Miss, referred to, 189.
Brera, Monastery of Umiliati at, 123.
Brotherhood, The principle of, 93-4, 191-2.
Bruges, Béguinage of, 141.
Burgundy, Ursulines of, 157.
——, Hospitallers of, 240-2.
Bussage, Sisterhood of, 206.

C

CAEN, House of Refuge of Our Lady of Charity at, 175.
Calvin referred to, 4.
Canada, Sisterhoods in, 169, 177.
Canonesses, College of, at Genoa, 148.
——, Lutheran and Zwinglian, 195-6.
—— in Justinian's Code, 239.
Canons, see Councils, Basil, rule of the, 102-3.
Capitularies regulating Monachism, 103.

Capucines, see "Clarissans."
Carmelites, 116.
—— their Tertiarians, 135.
Carthage, Fourth council of, 26, 224-6.
—— nuns of, 27, n.
Carthusians, 116.
Cartwright and Travers, "Conclusions," 197.
Catherine, St, Hospitallers of, 143.
Celestins, 135.
Celibacy, the vow of, 74-5, 77 and foll., 214.
—— do., consistent with female monachism, 95.
—— enforced on the clergy, 104.
—— Béguines not bound to, 119.
—— nor Tertiarians, 133.
—— female diaconate must be free from vow of, 208.
Cellites, see "Alexians."
Cesarius, St, nunnery of, 106, 115.
Chalcedon, Council of, 52, 53.
Châlons-sur-Saône, Hospitallers of, 241-2.
Charitable Sisterhoods, see "Béguines," "Tertiarians," &c.
—— the later, 161 and foll.
Charity, Damsels of, 161.
—— Sisters of, 162 and foll., 183-6.
—— of our Lady, order of the, see "Our Lady."
Charlemagne, 69, 100, 102-3.
Choir of the Perpetual Virgins, 29-30, 48, n.
—— of the Widows, 48, n.
Christ, marriage of the soul with, 79 and foll., 227 and foll.

Christmas-tree, German deaconesses and the, 275-6.
Chrodegand, bishop of Metz, 102.
Chrysostom, on the New Testament deaconesses, 5.
—— his relations with various deaconesses, 32-46.
—— reforms the Church widows, 47-50.
—— reforms the "Sister-women, 50, n.
—— his praise of virginity, 83.
—— his letter to Gothic monks, 87.
—— on the nuns, 88.
—— and see 235.
Church, progress of monachism in the, 96 and foll., 126 and foll., 151 and foll.
—— Virgins of the, (see "Virgins,") institute of, 77 and foll., 234 and foll.
—— compared with early nuns, 85 and foll.
—— in the Code, 96, 236-9.
—— Widows of the, in the New Testament, 7-10.
—— in the Greek Apostolical Constitutions, 19.
—— in the Coptic do., 219 and foll.
—— in Basil's Canons, 28, n.
—— in the Council of Carthage, 225-6.
—— in Chrysostom's days, 47-49, 235.
—— in the Codes, 52, 54.
—— in Jerome, 64.
—— Hooker confounds them with deaconesses, 198-0.
Clara, St, and Clarissans, 130, 148, 159.
Clement of Alexandria referred to, 24.

Clement V., Pope, 136, n., 140.

Clergy, the deaconess part of, 59.

—— the monks incorporated in the, 101-2.

—— Celibacy enforced on, 104.

—— Béguines not part of, 120.

Clerks of the Common Life, 148-50.

Clewer, House of Mercy of, 203, 206.

Code, Civil, 255-6; the Theodosian, 51, 52.

—— of Justinian, 53-55, 96, 236-7.

Collective Female Diaconate, 96, 183.

Collestines, 147.

Cologne, Béguines at, 117.

Combé, Madame de, 174.

Common Life, Clerks of the, 148-50.

Communism, Monastic, 91-2.

Confréries de Charité, 163.

Congregations affiliated to orders, 129, 134.

—— the Ursuline, 157-8.

—— of St Joseph, 168-170.

—— and see 171, 172, 178, &c.

Consorte, Brotherhood of the, 133.

Constance, Council of, 140, n., 150.

Constantinople, the deaconesses at, 55.

—— Synod of, in Trullo, 60-61.

—— deaconesses' porch at, 61, n.

Constitutions, the (Greek) Apostolical, 14 and foll.

Constitutions, the Coptic, 22, 23, 219 and foll.

—— the Jesuit, 151, n.

Convocation considers the question of Woman's Work in the Church, 206.

Copenhagen, Protestant nuns of, 196.

Coptic Apostolical Constitutions, 22-3, 219 and foll.

Coquerel, M., opposed to Paris deaconesses, 292.

Cotelerius referred to, 31, n, 61-2.

Councils of Nicea and Laodicea, 26.

—— of Carthage, 26, 27.

—— of Chalcedon, 52-3.

—— of Worms, 69.

—— of Arles, 101.

Councils of Autun, 113; Aix-la-Chapelle, *ibid.*; Paris, *ibid.*

—— Provincial, of Mentz, 137.

—— of Constance, 140, n., 150.

—— and see Synods.

Crimean war, its bearing on the diaconal work of women, 203-4.

Croce, the Santa, Community of, 176.

Croix, Marie Elizabeth de la, 173.

—— Filles de la, 176.

Crusades, the, develop sisterhoods, 114-7.

Cyprian referred to, 27, 77, 83, n.

D

DAMSELS of Charity of Sédan, 161.

Deaconesses or female deacons, mentioned in the New Testament, 1-6; not the same as widows, 9, 10, 19, 20, 47-49, 54, 60, 61.
—— in the (Greek) Apostolical Constitutions, 15-19.
—— ordination of, 17, 18.
—— in Hermas, the pseudo-Ignatian Epistles, Clement, Origen, 23, 24.
—— in Pliny junior, 24.
—— in Tertullian, 26.
—— in the Nicene and other Councils, 26, 223-6.
—— in the Fathers of the 4th and 5th centuries, 28 and foll.
—— in the history of Chrysostom, 32, and foll.
Deaconesses, their condition in the 5th century, 46 and foll.
—— in the Theodosian Code, 51-2.
—— in Justinian's Code, 53-55, 60, 236-8.
—— in the Novels, 55-60, 237-8.
—— their condition in the 6th century, 58-60.
—— in the 7th, 60, 61.
—— Last Greek notices of, 61-3.
—— in the later Latin Church, 63-70.
—— of early Protestantism, 196-200.
—— Institutes, 200 and foll.
—— or "Protestant Sisterhoods" (article on), 248 and foll.
Deacons in Apostolical Constitutions, 15 and foll.
—— Male, take precedence of deaconesses, 19.

Deacons, female, see "Deaconesses."
Denmark, Lutheran nuns in, 196.
Devonport, Miss Sellon's Sisterhood of Mercy at, 293 and foll.
Devonshire House, Nursing Sisters of, 202, 206.
Diaconate, the female (see "Deaconesses"); why it died out, 72 and foll.
—— revived at the Reformation, 196 and foll.
Diacones, the form, 27, n.
Dijon, Ursulines of, 156, n.
—— and Langres, Hospitallers of, 171.
Dominic and Dominicans, 126-8, 141, 150.
—— their Tertiarians, 135.
—— Lutheran nuns of St, 196.
Douay, Community of the Holy Family of, 180.
—— Sisters of Charity at, 185.
Dramas, sacred, of Hrotsvitha, 108-13.

E

EARCONBERTII, King of Kent, 107.
Echallens, see "St Loup."
Edinburgh Review, article in, referred to, 202; reproduced, 248 and foll.
Educational communities, early, 147 and foll.
—— Orders, Female, 155 and foll.
—— *Magazine*, the, 71, n., 121, n., 201.

Elizabeth, St, of Hungary, 142.
Elizabethan Sisters, 182, n.
Epaône, Synod of, 65.
Epidemics, services of German deaconesses in, 272-3.
—— of Miss Sellon's sisters in, 294 and foll.
Epiphanius, referred to, 28, 31, 63-4.
Erasmus, educated by Gerardins, 149.
Eudes, Father, 175.
Eugenius IV., Pope, 144-5.
Eulogies, the, 21, n., 222.
Exorcists not ordained, 20.

F

Fara, Abbess, 107.
Faustin, St, Monastery of, 66.
Female Diaconate, see "Deaconesses," "Diaconate."
—— Monachism, see "Monachism."
Ferrar, Nicholas, 196, n.
Fliedner, Dr, referred to, 199, 201, 270 and foll.
Fortunatus, Venantius, referred to, 67, 107-8.
Foundling · Hospital, V. de Paule's, 166, 185.
France, Béghards in, 117.
—— Béguines in, 119 and foll., 141.
—— the heart of Romanism, 182, n.
—— Monachism in modern, 184 and foll.
Francis, St, 127-31.
Franciscans, 126-9, 141, 185, 186.

Franciscans, Tertiarian, 130, and foll.
François de Sales, see Sales.
Fraunberg, Abbey of, partly Lutheran, 195.
Fry, Mrs, 202, 203, 283.

G

Gandesheim, nunnery of, 108.
—— Lutheran canonesses of, 195.
Gasparin, M. and Mme. A. de, 292-3.
Gaul, female diaconate in, 65-9.
—— Early monasteries of, 66, 98-9.
Geneviève, Daughters of St, 179-80.
—— Community of St, 180.
Genoa, Canonesses of, 148.
Gerardins, 148-50.
German Hospital, 276, 282-3.
Germany, Béguines in, 117 and foll.
Germond, Pasteur, referred to, 266 and foll., 285.
Gerson, defends Gerardins, 150.
Gervais, St, Hospitallers of, 143.
Ghent, Béguinage of, 141, 201.
Gibbon, referred to, 50, n.
Good Shepherd, Daughters of the, 174-5, 187.
—— Asylum of the, 183.
—— in America, 189.
Goodman, Miss, referred to, 293, 301, n.
Gothic Monks, 87.
Governo, Rosa, 181, n.

Grabon, Matthias, denounces Gerardius, 150.

Greek Church, deaconesses more needed in, 25.

—— the female diaconate in the, 28-63.

—— Sisterhoods of mercy in, 192, n.

Gregory of Nyssa, referred to, 28, 30, n., 31, n.

—— VII., Pope, 71, 104.

Grey Sisters, 145-7, 183.

Groot, Gerard, 148.

"Grilles, A Glance Beyond the," referred to, 184 and foll.

Guatemala, Bethlehemites of, 172.

Guérin, Curé, 176-7.

Guizot, referred to, 96, 99, 101, 107.

H

HÆRTER, Pasteur, 264-5.

Hélyot, Father, referred to, 107, n, 122, 125, 130, 133, 141, 143, 145-8, 154-60, 163-81, 195-6, 241.

Hermas, referred to, 23.

Hermits, the early, 85-7.

Hetling, Rev. Mr, his testimony in favour of Miss Sellon's sisters, 297.

Hildebrand, see Gregory VII.

Hippolytus, Bunsen's, referred to, 22.

Holy Family, Community of the, 185.

—— Sacrament, Daughters of the, 160.

Hooker, referred to, 197-8.

Hospital, head - nurses in, called sisters, 203, n.

Hospital, and see "German."

Hospitallers of St John of Jerusalem, 124-5.

—— Tertiarian, 142.

—— nuns, various convents of, 143, 146, 173.

—— of St Joseph, 169-70.

—— of Toulouse, 170.

—— of Dijon and Langres, 171.

—— reform of the Paris, 172-3.

—— of St Martha, 240-2.

"Hospitals and Sisterhoods," referred to, 176, n., 183, n., 187, n., 190, n., 204.

Hôtel-Dieu, 125, 164-5, 173.

—— de Ste. Catherine, 143; de St Gervais, *ibid.*

Howson, Dr, referred to, 62, n., 71, n., 192, n., 199, 204, 205, 207, 293.

Hrotsvitha, the nun, 108-31.

Hugo, Victor, referred to, 160, n.

I

IGNATIUS, the epistles attributed to, on the deaconesses, 23.

—— Loyola, 151, 155.

Infant Jesus, Daughters of the, 158-9.

Innenheim, Rule of Béguines of, 242, and foll.

Innocent, X., Pope, 157; XI., *ibid.*

Italic version, 24, n.

J

JACOBITE Deaconesses, 62, n.

Jameson, Mrs, referred to,

156, n., 181, n., 182, n.,
204, 241, n.
Jerome, referred to, 64-5, 88,
91.
Jerusalem, Hospitallers of St
John of, 124.
—— German deaconesses at,
282.
Jesuitesses, 155.
Jesuits, 151-5, 158.
John XXII., Pope, 137-8,
140, n.
—— Bishop of Strasburg,
140, n.; and see "St John."
Joseph II., exempts Béguines
and Elizabethan Sisters
from suppression, 182, n.
—— of the created Trinity,
Congregation of St, 159.
—— Sisters of, 168-9, 183.
—— Hospitallers of, 169-70.
Julian the Apostate, 29, 30.
Justinian, see "Code,"
"Novels."

K

KAISERSWERTH, referred to,
201-3, 205-7, 270 and foll.
Krishna, worship of, 233.

L

LAMPADIA, Deaconess, 30, n.
L'Amy, Madeleine, 175.
Laodicea, Council of, 26, 224.
Latin Church, Deaconesess
in the, 24, 25, 63 and foll.
—— its language, 22, 24,
27.
Laura, the, 92, 97.
Lazarists, 162-3, 166, 185.
Legras, Mlle., 163-7.

Leo Ostiarius, referred to, 70
—— III., Pope, 70.
Libanius, 226.
Limon, the, of John Mos-
chus, 61.
Little Sisters of the Poor,
185, 187.
Loches, Hospitallers of, 172.
Lombardy, Umiliati of, 122-3.
—— Béguines in, 140, n.
Loup, see "St Loup."
Loyola, 151, 155.
Lubeck, Béguinages of, 195, n.
Lucian, 226.
Lupus, see "Wolf."
Luther, quoted, 194.
Lutheran Abbeys, 195-6.
—— Deaconesses, see Kais-
erswerth.
Lyons, Ursulines of, 157.

M

MALINES, former béguinage
of, 141.
Marforium, the, 62.
Mariolatry, 82-3.
Mark, Henry Robert de la,
161, 287.
Marriage of the deaconess,
when forbidden, 56, 60, 66.
—— of the church-widow,
28, n.
—— of the church-virgin,
77-8.
—— dissolved by ordination
of deaconess, 68.
—— of the soul with Christ,
unscriptural, 79 and foll.,
227 and foll.
—— of monks, 84.
—— not forbidden to Bé-
guine, 119.
—— nor to Tertiarian, 133.

Martha, St, Hospitallers of, 240-2.
—— and Mary, 220.
Martin V., Pope, 150.
Mathurins, 116.
Maurice, Mr, referred to, 11, n.
Médard, St, 67-8.
Melun, Mlle. de, 169.
Mendicant orders, the, 126 and foll.
Mentz, Provincial Council of, 137.
Mercy, Miss Sellon's Sisterhood of, 203, 292.
Metropolitan District-Visiting Society, 200.
Middlesborough institution, 206.
Ministra, the term, 24, n.
Miramion, Madame de, and Miramiones, 179-80.
Missionary Priests, see " Lazarists."
Missouri, Convents in, 189-90.
Molême, Robert de, 116, n.
Monachism, early female, 85 and foll.
—— the social principle of, 90 and foll.
—— female, as a collective diaconate, 96.
—— sketch of history of, till 11th century, 96 and foll.
—— history of female, till 11th century, 106 and foll.
—— missionary, 127-9.
—— Jesuitism, the last term of, 151 and foll.
—— and the Reformation, 193 and foll.
—— female contemporary, 182 and foll.
Monasteries, early, in southern France, 66, 98-9.

Monks, the early, 86-7, 91.
Monod, Pasteur Frédéric, 258, n.
Moreri, referred to, 62, 69, 71.
Moschus, John, referred to, 61.
Mosheim, his work on the Béghards and Béguines, 117, 149, &c., 194, 242 and foll.
—— his Ecclesiastical History, referred to, 149.
Motherhood, spiritual, unchristian, 299.

N

NANCY, Grey Sisters of, resist claustration, 146.
Neal's " History of the Puritans" referred to, 197.
Neander, referred to, 25.
Nectaria, deaconess, 29.
Nestorian Deaconesses, 17, n.
Newman, Professor, F. W., referred to, 232-3.
Nicæa, the Council of, 26, 223-4.
Nicarete, deaconess, 30, n., 32, 33.
Nightingale, Florence, 203.
—— her pamphlet referred to, 196, 203.
Nilus, St, 70.
Nonna, the word, 88.
Normal school of female charity, the Deaconesses' Institute a, 208, 262.
North London Deaconess' Institution, 204.
Novels, the, 55 and foll., 223, n., 237-9.
Noviciate, long, essential to diaconal orders, 95, 126, 158, 173.

Nuns, the African, 27, 87,
224-6.
—— spoken of by Jerome,
Chrysostom, and Augus-
tus, 88-9.
—— of St Cesarius at Arles,
106.
—— of Brie, 107, of Tours,
ibid.
—— of Gandesheim, 108.
—— of St Augustin, 124-6.
—— Tertiarian and Hospi-
taller, 142-3.
—— less efficient than sisters,
171.
—— Protestant, 195-6.
—— and see Monachism.
Nurses, Training Institution
for, see "St John's House,"
and see "Deaconesses,"
"Sisterhoods," &c.
Nursing Sisters, Institution for,
see "Devonshire House."
Nyssa, see "Gregory."

O

Odo, Abbot, of Cluny, 103,
115, n.
Olympias the Deaconess, 37
and foll.
Orange, Synod of, 65.
Order, the monastic, 103-4.
—— and see "Benedict,"
"Francis," "Dominic,"
&c.
Ordinal, the Roman, 17 n., 69.
Ordination of Deaconesses,
17, 26, 38, 51, 53, 56, 57,
59, 62, 64, 68-70.
—— forbidden, 65.
—— of Queen Radegund, 68,
—— none, of widows, vir-
gins, confessors, exorcists,
19, 20, 221.

Origen, referred to, 24, 63,
99, n.
Orleans, Synod of, 65.
Orsini, Nicolas, founds college of canonesses, 148.
Our Lady, Order of, 160.
—— Order of the Visitation
of, 171.
—— Hospitallers of the,
Charity of, 172.
—— of the Refuge, order
of, 173-4.
—— of Charity, order of, 175.

P

Palladius, referred to, 33, 38,
n., 39, 43, n., 50, n.
Paris, Council of, 113.
—— Ursulines of, 157.
—— Hospitallers of, 125-6;
reformed, 173.
—— Romish Sisterhoods in,
at the present day, 185-
6.
—— Deaconesses' Institute
of, 202-3.
—— account of do. in 1848,
249 and foll.
—— Matthew, referred to,
117-8.
Parish-deaconess, the, 75, 217,
272 and foll.
Parma and Foligno, Ursulines
of, 156.
Parthenon of church-virgins,
234-5.
Past, how to be used, 210-2.
—— how it bears fruit, 213.
Paul, St, see St Paul.
—— V., Pope, 157.
Paule, Vincent de, 162-6.
—— Sisterhoods of St V. de,
see "Charity."

Paulianist Deaconesses, 26, 223-4.
Pelagia, 30.
Pentadia, Deaconess, 34-38.
Perpetual Virgins, see "Church-Virgins."
Peter, see St Peter.
Philippines, 160.
Phœbe the deacon, 1, 3, 9, 16, 24, 46.
Pius V., Pope, 123.
Pliny junior, tortures two deaconesses, 24.
Polaillon, Madame, 177-8.
Poland, Sisters of Charity in, 166.
—— Nuns of the Visitation in, 171-2.
Pontoise, Hospitallers of, 143.
Popes; Soter, 26, n.; Adrian I., 69; Leo III., 70; Gregory VII., 71, 104; Pius V., 123; Clement V., 136, n.; John XXII., 137-8, 140, n.; Boniface IX., 140, n., 144; Eugenius IV., 144-5; Martin V., 150; Urban VIII., 155; Paul V., Innocents X. and XI., 157; Alexander VII., 169, 175.
Porch, the Deaconesses', at Constantinople, 61, n.
Port Royal, 160.
Præposita, the, 89.
"Praying and Working," referred to, 205-6.
Presbyters, Female, none in the New Testament, 6, n.
—— forbidden by Council of Laodicea, 26, 224.
—— their existence denied by Epiphanius, 31.
—— in the 8th century, 69.
Presbyteral functions forbidden to women, 113.

Pressensé, M. de, referred to, 282, n.
Procla, deaconess, 34, 38.
Profession, the church-virgins', 84.
Protestant nuns, 195-6.
—— Deaconesses' Institute, its special characteristics, 207 and foll.
—— Sisters of Charity (pamphlet,) referred to, 201.
Providence of God, Daughters of the, 177.
Publia, deaconess, 29, 30.
Puritans, their views of the female diaconate, 197 and foll.

Q

Quarterly Review referred to, 205.
Quedlinburg, Lutheran canonesses of, 195-6.

R

RACINE, referred to, 160.
Radegund, St, story of, 67-9.
—— her nunnery, 107-8.
Readers, 20, 22, 219, 221-2.
Reform of the Benedictines, 103, 115-6.
—— of the Paris Ursulines, 157.
—— of the Paris Hospitallers, 173.
Reformation, the, 150.
—— and female monachism, 194-6.
—— revives the female diaconate, 196-9.

Reformatory sisterhoods, 173 and foll.

Reformed (C a l v i n i s t i c) Church, sanctions deaconesses' institutes, 258.

Refuge, Order of our Lady of the, 173-4.

Religion and religious, monastic sense of these terms, 101, 171-2.

Richard, referred to, 71.

Rimini, Synod of, 28.

Rochelle, Augustinians of La, 159.

Romana, deaconess, 30, 31.

Rome, Synod or Council of, 69.

—— deaconesses at, 70.

—— Ursulines and Augustinians of, 158.

—— Capucines of, 159.

—— the Santa Croce community of, 176.

——, Church of, her early sisterhoods, 124 and foll. ; her educational orders, 151 and foll. ; her later charitable sisterhoods and reformatory orders, 161 and foll. ; her diaconal sisterhoods at the present day, 181 and foll.

Rosines, 181, n.

Rule, the, of St Basil, 97.

—— of St Benedict, 100.

—— of the Canons, 102-3.

—— of the Clarissans, 130, n.

—— Third, of St Francis, 130 and foll.

—— Béguine, translated, 242 and foll.

S

Sabiniana, deaconess, 33.

Sacré Cœur, Convents of the, 161, n.

Salvia or Silvia, 43, n.

Sanctimoniales, the, 27, 59, 87-89, 224-5, 236 and foll.

St Andrew, in Coptic Apostolical Constitutions, 220.

—— Bartholomew, Greek Constitution attributed to, 17.

—— James, in Coptic Apostolical Constitutions, 221.

—— John, in Coptic Apostolical Constitutions,

—— John's House, 202, 206.

—— Louis (Missouri), convents at, 189-90.

—— Loup, (Echallens,) Deaconesses' Institute of, 202, 226 and foll.

—— Paul, mentions deaconesses, 1, 3.

—— on widows, 8.

—— on virgins, 10, 11, 227.

—— no authority for marriage of soul with Christ, 227 and foll.

—— Blind Sisters of, 189.

—— Peter, in Coptic Apostolical Constitutions, 219-20.

St Stephen of Strasburg, see " Strasburg."

Ste. Beuve, Madame de, 157.

Saintonge, Françoise de, 156, n.

Sales, François de, 171.

Salvia or Silvia, the model of Olympias, 43, n.

Santa Croce, Community of the, 176.

—— Rufina and Santa Seconda, Ursulines of, 158.

Sédan, Damsels of Charity of, 161-2.

Seelen-weiber, title given to Béguines, 195.

Sellon, Miss, her sisterhood, referred to, 203, 205, n., 206.

—— account of rise of, 293 and foll.

Serapion, 87.

Servants of the poor, 163 and foll.

Sisterhoods, the principle of, 93-4, 299 ; disentangled from monachism, 167; and see 212, 285 and foll.

—— the béguine, 117 and foll.

—— early Romish charitable, 131 and foll.

—— later do., 161 and foll.

—— modern do., 181 and foll.

—— of the daughters of the Infant Jesus, 154.

—— of Charity, 165-8.

—— of St Joseph, 168-9.

—— of Mercy, Miss Sellon's, 203, 205, n., 206, 293 and foll.

Sisters more efficient than nuns, 171-2.

—— in London hospitals, 203, n.

—— parochial, 209, n.

Sister-women or συνείσακτοι, 13, 50, n., 57.

Social principle, the mainstay of monachism, 90 and foll.

—— its progress in monachism, 104-6, 129-30, 151-2.

Sophia, Deaconesses of St, 55.

Soter, Pope, 26, n.

Soul, Marriage of the, 79 and foll., 227 and foll.

Southey's Colloquies, 201.

Sozomen, referred to, 28, 30, n., 32, 38, 39.

Spain, deaconesses in, 69.

—— convents in, 155-6.

Stanley, Miss, see " Hospitals and Sisterhoods."

Stevenson, Rev. W. F., see " Praying and Working."

Strangers' Friend Society, 200.

Strasburg, Zwinglian canonesses of, 195.

—— rule of Béguines of, 242 and foll.

—— Deaconesses' Institute of, 202, 264-6.

Sub-deacons, 18, 20, 221-2.

Suicer, referred to, 48, n., 71, n.

Syncletica, 85-6, 90.

Synods of Rimini, 28.

—— of Constantinople, in Trullo, 60, 61.

—— of Orange, Epaône, Orleans, 65.

—— of Rome, 69.

—— of Wesel, 196-7.

—— and see " Councils."

T

TATTAM, Archdeacon, his edition of the Coptic Apostolical Constitutions, 22, 219 and foll.

Terence, studied by nuns, 108-9.

Tertiarians of St Francis, 130-4.

Tertiarians of St Dominic, &c., 155.

—— (nuns,) 142, and foll.

Tertullian, referred to, 25, 26.

Theodoret, referred to, 28, 29, 48, n., 234.
Theodosian Code, 51, 52.
Theophylact, referred to, 61.
Thierry, Augustin, referred to, 67-9, 107.
Third Rule of St Francis, see " Tertiarians."
Thomas de Villanueva, Hospitallers of St, 172, 186-7.
Tillemont, referred to, 48, n.
Toulouse, Ursulines of, 157.
—— Hospitallers of, 170-1.
Tours, Radegund's nunnery at, 107.
Trappists, 116.
Trullo, see "Constantinople."
Tulle, Ursulines of, 157.
Tulloch, Principal, referred to, 23.
Turin, Rosines of, 181, n.
Tuscany, Béguines in, 140, n.

U

Umiliati, the, 122-3, 130.
Union Chrétienne, Community of the, 178.
United States, Convents in, 189-90.
—— Protestant deaconesses in the, 282.
Urban VIII., Pope, 155.
Ursulines, 156-8, 184.

V

Vermeil, Pasteur, founds Paris Deaconesses' Institute, 250 and foll.
Villanueva, Order of St Thomas of, 172, 186-7.
Villeneuve, Madame de, 176-7.

Vilmar, referred to, 136, n.
Virgil, studied by nuns, 108.
Virgins in the New Testament, 10-12.
—— in the (Greek) Apostolical Constitutions, 19, 20.
—— in the pseudo-Ignatian epistles, 23.
—— ruled by deaconesses, 30.
—— in the early Church generally, 234 and foll.
—— in Justinian's code and Novels, 54, 55, 236-8.
—— in the Coptic Apostolical Constitutions, 221.
—— in the Council of Carthage, 224-5.
Virginity praised by the Fathers, 78-9, 83, 236.
—— the Profession of, 84.
Visitation of our Lady, Order of the, 171.
Vitry, Cardinal Jacques de, 125.
Vows of perpetual celibacy, 84.
—— solemn, the three, 101.
—— simple, 129, 158, 167.
—— of the Hospitallers of Pontoise, 143.
—— of the Ursulines, 157-8.
—— Luther on, 194.
—— incompatible with Protestant Deaconesses' Institute, 287, 291-2.
Vulgate, referred to, 5, 24, n.

W

Wantage, Sisterhood of, 203, 206.
Warsaw, Sisters of Charity at, 166.
Wesel, Synod of, 196.

Wesel, Protestant deaconesses at, 199-200.
Widow, see "Church."
Wine-song, German, referred to, 136, n.
Wolf, Christian, referred to, 70, 71, n., 75, n.
Woman, as to ordination of, 18, 20.
—— relation of, to man, 73 and foll.
—— do., to Christ, 230.
—— her natural ministering functions, 208.
—— her work in the Church, conclusions as to, 214 and foll.
Wordsworth, Dr, referred to, 202.

Wycliffe, referred to, 5.

X

XENODOCHIA, 239.
Ximenes, Cardinal, 155.

Y

YOUNG's "Chronicles of the Pilgrim Fathers," referred to, 198-9.

Z

ZONARAS, referred to, 224.
Zwinglian canonesses, 195.

Ballantyne and Company, Printers, Edinburgh.

THE BOOK-LIST

OF

ALEXANDER STRAHAN.

𝕭ooks 𝕵ust 𝕻ublished.

HENRY HOLBEACH: STUDENT IN LIFE AND PHILOSOPHY.

A NARRATIVE AND A DISCUSSION.

With Letters to Mr. Matthew Arnold, Mr. Alexander Bain, Mr. Thomas Carlyle, Mr. Arthur Helps, Mr. G. H. Lewes, Rev. H. L. Mansel, Rev. F. D. Maurice, Mr. John Stuart Mill, Rev. Dr. J. H. Newman.

Two vols. post 8vo. 14s.

THE

POETICAL WORKS OF HENRY ALFORD,

Dean of Canterbury.

A New and Enlarged Edition.   Small 8vo.

IDYLS AND LEGENDS OF INVERBURN.

By ROBERT BUCHANAN,
Author of "Undertones."

Small 8vo, 5s.

UNDERTONES.
By ROBERT BUCHANAN.
Second Edition.   Revised and Enlarged.   Small 8vo, 5s.

ESSAYS ON WOMAN'S WORK.

By BESSIE RAYNER PARKES.

Small 8vo, 4*s*.

THE REGULAR SWISS ROUND, IN THREE TRIPS.

By the Rev. HARRY JONES,

Incumbent of St. Luke's, Berwick Street, Soho, London.

With Illustrations.   Small 8vo. 5*s*.

HEADS AND HANDS IN THE WORLD OF LABOUR.

By W. G. BLAIKIE, D.D., F.R.S.E.,

Author of "Better Days for Working People."

Crown 8vo. 3*s*. 6*d*.

THE COLLECTED WRITINGS OF EDWARD IRVING.

Edited by his Nephew, the Rev. G. CARLYLE, M.A.

Vols. I. to V., demy 8vo, 12*s*. each.

OUTLINES OF THEOLOGY.

By ALEXANDER VINET.

Post 8vo, 8*s*.

OUTLINES OF PHILOSOPHY AND LITERATURE.

By ALEXANDER VINET.

Post 8vo, 8*s*.

CHRIST AND HIS SALVATION.

By HORACE BUSHNELL, D.D.,
Author of "Nature and the Supernatural."

Second Edition.   Crown 8vo, 6s.

CHRISTIAN COMPANIONSHIP FOR RETIRED HOURS.

Small 8vo, gilt, 3s. 6d.

LETTERS FROM ABROAD IN 1864.

By HENRY ALFORD, D.D.,
Dean of Canterbury.

Second Edition, Crown 8vo, 7s. 6d.

PLAIN WORDS ON CHRISTIAN LIVING.

By C. J. VAUGHAN, D.D., Vicar of Doncaster.

Small 8vo, 4s. 6d.

WOMAN'S WORK IN THE CHURCH.

BEING HISTORICAL NOTES ON DEACONESSES AND SISTERHOODS.

By JOHN MALCOLM LUDLOW.

Small 8vo, 5s.

PERSONAL NAMES IN THE BIBLE.

By the Rev. W. F. WILKINSON, M.A.,
Vicar of St. Werburgh's, Derby, and Joint-Editor of "Webster and Wilkinson's Greek Testament."

Small 8vo, 6s.

CONVERSION:
ILLUSTRATED FROM EXAMPLES RECORDED IN THE BIBLE.
By the Rev. ADOLPH SAPHIR.

New and Cheaper Edition.   Small 8vo, 3*s*. 6*d*.

A YEAR AT THE SHORE.
By PHILIP HENRY GOSSE, F.R.S.

With Thirty-six Illustrations by the Author, printed in Colours
by LEIGHTON BROTHERS.

Crown 8vo, 9*s*.

LAZARUS, AND OTHER POEMS.
By E. H. PLUMPTRE, M.A.,
Professor of Theology, King's College, London.

Second Edition.   Small 8vo, 5*s*.

STUDIES FOR STORIES, FROM GIRLS' LIVES.

Cheap Edition.   Crown 8vo, 6*s*.

DE PROFUNDIS: A TALE OF THE SOCIAL DEPOSITS.
By WILLIAM GILBERT,
Author of "Shirley Hall Asylum," &c.

2 vols. crown 8vo, 12*s*.

LILLIPUT LEVEE.
With Illustrations by J. E. MILLAIS and G. J. PINWELL.

Square 8vo, gilt, 5*s*.

DUCHESS AGNES, Etc.

By ISA CRAIG.

Second Edition.   Small 8vo, cloth, 5*s.*

A PLEA FOR THE QUEEN'S ENGLISH.

By HENRY ALFORD, D.D.,
Dean of Canterbury.

Second Edition, Tenth Thousand.   Small 8vo, 5*s.*

TANGLED TALK: An Essayist's Holiday.

Second Edition.   Post 8vo, 7*s.* 6*d.*

OUR INHERITANCE IN THE GREAT PYRAMID.

By Professor C. PIAZZI SMYTH, F.R.SS.L. and E.,
Astronomer Royal for Scotland.

With Photograph and Plates.   Square 8vo, 12*s.*

MEMOIRS OF THE LIFE AND PHILANTHROPIC LABOURS OF
ANDREW REED, D.D.,

Prepared from Autobiographic Sources, by his Sons,

ANDREW REED, B.A., and CHARLES REED, F.S.A.

With Portrait and Woodcuts.   Second Edition.   Demy 8vo, 12*s.*

THE FOUNDATIONS OF OUR FAITH:
Ten Papers recently read before a Mixed Audience.

By Professors AUBERLEN, GESS, and Others.

Second Thousand.   Crown 8vo, 6*s.*

STORY OF THE LIVES OF CAREY MARSHMAN, AND WARD.

(A Popular Edition of the large Two-volume Work.)

By JOHN C. MARSHMAN.

Sixth Thousand. Crown 8vo, 3s. 6d.

HUMAN SADNESS.

By the COUNTESS DE GASPARIN,
Author of "The Near and the Heavenly Horizons."

Fourth Thousand. Small 8vo, 5s.

The TWENTY-FOURTH THOUSAND is now ready of

THE RECREATIONS OF A COUNTRY PARSON.

First Series. Popular Edition.

Crown 8vo, 3s. 6d.

The THIRTY-SECOND THOUSAND is now ready of

THE GRAVER THOUGHTS OF A COUNTRY PARSON.

By the Author of "Recreations of a Country Parson."

Crown 8vo, 3s. 6d.

The FIFTEENTH THOUSAND is now ready of

COUNSEL AND COMFORT, SPOKEN FROM A CITY PULPIT.

By the Author of "Recreations of a Country Parson."

Crown 8vo, 3s. 6d.

The NINTH THOUSAND is now ready of

PAPERS FOR THOUGHTFUL GIRLS.

WITH SKETCHES OF SOME GIRLS' LIVES.

By SARAH TYTLER.

With Illustrations by MILLAIS.   Crown 8vo, cloth, extra gilt, 5s.

The THIRTY-EIGHTH THOUSAND is now ready of

SPEAKING TO THE HEART.

By THOMAS GUTHRIE, D.D.

Handsomely printed and bound in crown 8vo, 3s. 6d.
POCKET EDITION, small 8vo, 2s.

The SIXTH THOUSAND is now ready of

MY MINISTERIAL EXPERIENCES.

By the Rev. Dr. BÜCHSEL, Berlin.

Crown 8vo, 3s. 6d.

The SECOND THOUSAND is now ready of

THE LIFE OF OUR LORD UPON THE EARTH,

CONSIDERED IN ITS HISTORICAL, GEOGRAPHICAL, AND GENEALOGICAL RELATIONS.

By the Rev. SAMUEL J. ANDREWS.

Crown 8vo, cloth, 6s. 6d.

The SIXTH THOUSAND is now ready of

DREAMTHORP;

A BOOK OF ESSAYS WRITTEN IN THE COUNTRY.

By ALEXANDER SMITH,

Author of "A Life Drama," &c.

Crown 8vo, 3s. 6d.

The SIXTEENTH THOUSAND is now ready of

THE EARNEST STUDENT;

BEING MEMORIALS OF JOHN MACKINTOSH.

By NORMAN MACLEOD, D.D.,
One of Her Majesty's Chaplains.

New Edition, considerably enlarged.

Crown 8vo, 3s. 6d.

The TENTH THOUSAND is now ready of

THE OLD LIEUTENANT AND HIS SON.

By NORMAN MACLEOD, D.D.

Crown 8vo, 3s. 6d.

The TENTH THOUSAND is now ready of

PARISH PAPERS.

By NORMAN MACLEOD, D.D.

Crown 8vo, 3s. 6d.

The TENTH THOUSAND is now ready of

THE GOLD THREAD; A STORY FOR THE YOUNG.

By NORMAN MACLEOD, D.D.

Illustrated by J. D. WATSON, GOURLAY STEEL, and J. MACWHIRTER.

Fine Edition, cloth gilt, 3s. 6d. Cheaper Edition, 2s. 6d.

The THIRTY-FIFTH THOUSAND is now ready of

WEE DAVIE.

By NORMAN MACLEOD, D.D.

Crown 8vo, 6d.

The THIRD THOUSAND is now ready of

WORDSWORTH'S POEMS FOR THE YOUNG.

Illustrated by MACWHIRTER and PETTIE, with a Vignette by MILLAIS.
Elegantly bound, in square crown 8vo, cloth gilt, 6*s.*

The SEVENTIETH THOUSAND is now ready of

BETTER DAYS FOR WORKING PEOPLE.

By WILLIAM G. BLAIKIE, D.D., F.R.S.E.

Crown 8vo, boards, 1*s.* 6*d.*

The FIFTEENTH THOUSAND is now ready of

PRAYING AND WORKING.

By Rev. W. FLEMING STEVENSON.

Crown 8vo, 3*s.* 6*d.*

The SIXTH THOUSAND is now ready of

FORTY YEARS' EXPERIENCE OF SUNDAY SCHOOLS.

By STEPHEN H. TYNG, D.D.

Foolscap 8vo, 1*s.* 6*d.*

The EIGHTH THOUSAND is now ready of

BEGINNING LIFE:

CHAPTERS FOR YOUNG MEN ON RELIGION, STUDY, AND BUSINESS.

By JOHN TULLOCH, D.D.
Principal of St. Mary's College, St. Andrews.

Crown 8vo, 3*s.* 6*d.*

The SECOND THOUSAND is now ready of

GOD'S GLORY IN THE HEAVENS.

By WILLIAM LEITCH, D.D.,

Late Principal of Queen's College, Canada.

With Illustrations. Crown 8vo, cloth extra, 6*s.*

The TWENTY-FIFTH THOUSAND is now ready of

PLAIN WORDS ON HEALTH.

By JOHN BROWN, M.D.,

Author of "Rab and his Friends," &c.

Small 8vo, 6*d.*

The TENTH THOUSAND is now ready of

THE THRONE OF GRACE.

By the Author of "The Pathway of Promise."

Foolscap 8vo, cloth antique, 2*s.* 6*d.*

The TWENTY-FOURTH THOUSAND is now ready of

ABLE TO SAVE;

Or, ENCOURAGEMENT TO PATIENT WAITING.

By the Author of "The Pathway of Promise."

Fcap. 8vo, cloth antique, 2*s.* 6*d.*

The NINETIETH THOUSAND is now ready of

THE PATHWAY OF PROMISE.

Neat cloth antique, 1*s.* 6*d.*

The TWENTY-SEVENTH THOUSAND is now ready of

THE NEAR AND THE HEAVENLY HORIZONS.

By the COUNTESS DE GASPARIN.

Crown 8vo, gilt cloth, antique, 3*s.* 6*d.*

The FOURTH THOUSAND is now ready of

NATURE AND THE SUPERNATURAL,

AS TOGETHER CONSTITUTING THE ONE SYSTEM OF GOD.

By HORACE BUSHNELL, D.D.

Crown 8vo, 3s. 6d.

The SEVENTEENTH THOUSAND is now ready of

THE NEW LIFE.

By HORACE BUSHNELL, D.D.

Crown 8vo, 4s. 6d.; Cheap Edition, 1s. 6d.

The FIFTH THOUSAND is now ready of

CHRISTIAN NURTURE;

OR, THE GODLY UPBRINGING OF CHILDREN.

By HORACE BUSHNELL, D.D.

Crown 8vo, 1s. 6d.

The TWENTIETH THOUSAND is now ready of

THE CHARACTER OF JESUS.

By HORACE BUSHNELL, D.D.

Cheap Edition, 6d.

The FOURTH THOUSAND is now ready of

WORK AND PLAY.

A BOOK OF ESSAYS.

By HORACE BUSHNELL, D.D.

Crown 8vo, 3s. 6d.

The SECOND THOUSAND is now ready of

CHRISTIAN BELIEVING AND LIVING.

By F. D. HUNTINGDON, D.D.

Crown 8vo, cloth, 3s. 6d.

CHRISTINA, AND OTHER POEMS.

By DORA GREENWELL.

Small 8vo, 6s.

The THIRD EDITION is now ready of

THE PATIENCE OF HOPE.

By DORA GREENWELL.

Small 8vo, 2s. 6d.

The THIRD EDITION is now ready of

A PRESENT HEAVEN.

By DORA GREENWELL.

Small 8vo, 2s. 6d.

TWO FRIENDS.

By DORA GREENWELL.

Small 8vo, 3s. 6d.

The SIXTH THOUSAND is now ready of

THE WORDS OF THE ANGELS:

Or, THEIR VISITS TO THE EARTH AND THE MESSAGES
THEY DELIVERED.

By RUDOLPH STIER, D.D.,

Author of "The Words of the Risen Saviour."

Crown 8vo, 2s. 6d.

The FOURTEENTH THOUSAND is now ready of

PERSONAL PIETY:

A HELP TO CHRISTIANS TO WALK WORTHY OF THEIR
CALLING.

Cloth antique, 1s. 6d.

The TENTH THOUSAND is now ready of
AIDS TO PRAYER.
Cloth antique, 1s. 6d.

The TENTH THOUSAND is now ready of
THE SUNDAY-EVENING BOOK
OF PAPERS FOR FAMILY READING, BY

JAMES HAMILTON, D.D.	Rev. W. M. PUNSHON.
DEAN STANLEY.	JOHN EADIE, D.D., LL.D.
Rev. THOMAS BINNEY.	J. R. MACDUFF, D.D.

Cloth antique, 1s. 6d.

The SIXTH THOUSAND is now ready of
THE POSTMAN'S BAG;
A STORY-BOOK FOR BOYS AND GIRLS.

By the Rev. J. DE LIEFDE, London.
Author of the " Pastor of Gegenburg."

With Sixteen full-page Illustrations.   Square 8vo, cloth gilt, 3s. 6d.

THE RESTORATION OF THE JEWS:
THE HISTORY, PRINCIPLES, AND BEARINGS OF THE QUESTION.

By DAVID BROWN, D.D.
Professor of Theology, Aberdeen, Author of "The Second Advent.'

Crown 8vo, 5s.

The TWENTY-SECOND THOUSAND is now ready of
THE HIGHER CHRISTIAN LIFE.
By the Rev. W. E. BOARDMAN.

Foolscap 8vo, 1s. 6d.

The FORTIETH THOUSAND is now ready of
LIFE THOUGHTS.
By HENRY WARD BEECHER.
Cloth antique, 2*s*. 6*d*.

The SIXTH THOUSAND is now ready of
ROYAL TRUTHS.
By HENRY WARD BEECHER.
Crown 8vo, 3*s*. 6*d*.

The THIRD THOUSAND is now ready of
EYES AND EARS.
By HENRY WARD BEECHER.
Crown 8vo, 3*s*. 6*d*.

The THIRD THOUSAND is now ready of
ROMANISM AND RATIONALISM
AS OPPOSED TO PURE CHRISTIANITY.
By JOHN CAIRNS, D.D.
Crown 8vo, 1*s*.

The TWENTIETH THOUSAND is now ready of
THE STILL HOUR.
By AUSTIN PHELPS.
Cheap Edition. 4*d*.

The THIRTY-SECOND THOUSAND is now ready of
BLIND BARTIMEUS AND HIS GREAT PHYSICIAN.
By the Rev. W. J. HOGE.
In neat cloth, 1*s*.

𝔉orthcoming 𝔅ooks.

A SUMMER IN SKYE.

By ALEXANDER SMITH,
Author of "A Life Drama," "City Poems," &c.

Two vols. post 8vo.

MILLAIS'S ILLUSTRATIONS;

BEING A COLLECTION OF HIS DRAWINGS ON WOOD.

By JOHN E. MILLAIS, R.A.

Royal 4to.

SIX MONTHS AMONG THE CHARITIES OF EUROPE.

By the Rev. JOHN DE LIEFDE, London.

With Illustrations.   Two vols. post 8vo.

DAYS OF YORE.

By SARAH TYTLER,
Author of "Papers for Thoughtful Girls," &c.

Two vols. square 8vo.

JUDAS ISCARIOT:

A DRAMATIC POEM.

Small 8vo.

TRAVELS IN THE SLAVONIC PROVINCES OF TURKEY IN EUROPE.

PART I.
From the Ægean to the Adriatic, through Bulgaria and Old Serbia.

PART II.
From the Danube to the Adriatic, through Bosnia and the Herzegovina.

By G. MUIR MACKENZIE and A. P. IRBY.

With numerous Illustrations.   Demy 8vo.

THE AUTOCRAT OF THE BREAKFAST TABLE.

By OLIVER WENDELL HOLMES.

Small 8vo.

THE HYMNS AND HYMN WRITERS OF GERMANY.

By the Rev. W. FLEMING STEVENSON,
Author of "Praying and Working."

With New Translations of the Hymns by GEORGE MAC DONALD
DORA GREENWELL, and L. C. SMITH.

Two vols. post 8vo.

FAMILY PRAYERS FOR THE CHRISTIAN YEAR.

By HENRY ALFORD, D.D., Dean of Canterbury.

Small 8vo.